FORTUNE:

PIRATES OF CRUXES

BY KELLI COOK

FORTUNE: THE PIRATES OF CRUXES
Copyright ©2025 Line By Lion Publications
www.pixelandpen.studio
ISBN 978-1-948807-94-4
Cover Design by Thomas Lamkin Jr. .
Editing by Dani J. Caile

For more information, email www.linebylionpublications.com

Still for you, Dakota. Eleven years and counting.

Table of Contents

Prologue

THE roar of the cannons drowned out his thoughts and left his ears ringing. The air, usually salty and crisp, was thick with smoke and the acrid scent of gunpowder. It crawled its way down his throat and into his lungs with every breath. There was a searing ache in his shoulder, where a lead bullet had buried itself a few minutes ago, but he hardly paid it any attention. His focus was on the four-masted galleon just forty yards off his brigantine's bow. She was riding low in the water, and he was filled with greedy longing for the cargo that must have been weighing her down.

"Captain Stonecraft!" His quartermaster's voice somehow reached him over the sound of firing cannons, pistols, and wind rushing past him. Stonecraft tore his gaze from the prize – just thirty-five yards away now – to search deck of the *Pelican* for Archie Benton. He picked him out among the throng of pirates scrambling in every direction as they fired the deck cannons over off the bow and hurried to ready themselves to board the galleon. Benton had a pistol in one hand and a sword in the other, and not for the first time, Edward Stonecraft was glad that this man was on his side.

"She's going to turn!" Benton called to him above the chaos, and Stonecraft had known him far too long to doubt his intuition. The galleon had put up an admirable fight to stay ahead of them, but now that the pirate ship was closing in, her crew would have no choice but to fight for their lives. The fancy, printed letters across her stern were easy to read from this distance: *Weeping Cherub*. Stonecraft had never heard of her, but she was almost within his grasp.

As if Benton's words had made it happen, the *Cherub's* bow began to swing leftward. All twenty of the cannon ports on that side of her hull were open, and Stonecraft knew that each one would be manned by sailors desperate to sink his brigantine. He cupped his hands around his mouth and called out over the fray to his helmsman. The bow of the *Pelican* shifted starboard, aiming to slip behind the turning galleon. She may have been twice the *Pelican's* length and had more than double the cannons, but the *Pelican* was much more agile, and her crew knew how to use that.

"Port cannons!" Stonecraft heard Benton bellow. The pirates scrambled to respond. Stonecraft hurried to the port side of the deck, his blood racing just as hotly as it always did when victory was just ahead and death was on his heels. As the *Pelican* drew closer to his prize, he saw the faces of dozens of sailors peering back at him in terror from the deck of the *Cherub*. They were all clad in the red coats of the royal navy, and Stonecraft's heart leapt. Whatever prizes were weighing down the ship, they belonged to the king of Chaumont. The haul of a lifetime was just within reach.

The *Pelican's* port cannons came to life with a chorus of thunderous explosions, and splinters of broken wood flew as the cannonballs crashed into the stern of the *Cherub*. Stonecraft's crew let out a cheer. As the cannons were reloaded down below, the pirates on the deck lobbed bullets from their pistols toward the galleon's deck, shouting and cawing with the fervor of it all.

Around and around they went, with the *Cherub* trying desperately to shake her, but the *Pelican* was too agile and swift. Her cannons were merciless, but for a while, it seemed like the *Cherub* would withstand whatever was thrown at her. In the eight years he'd spent as a pirate on the seas, however, Stonecraft had never relented, and he wasn't going to start now. He ordered his crew of cutthroats to angle the deck cannons up high, and their cannonballs wreaked havoc on the *Cherub's* masts and sails. The salty water between the two ships churned, and the ocean spray mingled with the cannons' pungent smoke.

Finally, one of the four tall, heavy masts gave way, and with a loud creak of tortured wood, it fell across the starboard side of the *Cherub*. The ropes held, and as the huge, square sail dipped deep into the water, the ship suffered a massive shudder. The bow was forced toward starboard against the helmsman's will. Stonecraft leapt up onto the bow of his own ship, raised his hands above his head, and loosed a shout to all of his men.

"Board the bastards!"

The pirates used planks and grappling hooks to cross the short distance over churning waters between the two ships. The sailors aboard the *Cherub* met them on the deck, and they clashed together in a struggle for murder. Stonecraft personally led the charge, and he soon lost count of the number of men his cutlass and pistols fell. One by one, they tried to kill him, and one by one, he cut them down.

The fight on the deck may have lasted only a few minutes, or it may have been an hour; Stonecraft lost all sense of time. Finally, a call went out among the tattered remnants of the *Cherub's* crew to lay down their arms and surrendered. The pirates cheered once more, and Stonecraft allowed himself a victorious grin. The *Weeping Cherub* was his.

*   *   *

BENTON marched the *Cherub's* captain down the length of the deck. Stonecraft waited for them beside the splintered stump of the broken mast and couldn't help but gloat. The man in the red captain's jacket scowled as he made his way past the jeering pirates who lined up to watch. When they reached Stonecraft, Benton set a heavy hand on the man's shoulder, and he came to a stop obediently. Stonecraft had expected him to look like any of the other officers of the royal navy that he'd had the pleasure of killing over the years, but he was surprised to find that he didn't exactly match the mold. He couldn't have been any older than nineteen or twenty. His cheeks hadn't seen a razor in more than a month, by the looks of his scraggily beard, and his sweat-slicked hair hung down over his eyebrows. He was the most unkempt naval captain Stonecraft had ever seen.

He asked the man, "What's your name?"

The man spat at him. Benton cupped the back of his neck with one hand and set the blade of his cutlass against his ribs, growling, "Think long and hard before you do that again, boy."

"Morris," the man said past gritted teeth. "Reginald Morris."

"The ship's log says the captain's name is Sennet," Benton warned.

Morris stood a little taller, raised his chin a bit higher and said, "George Sennet is dead. I killed him a month ago."

Stonecraft gaped at him for a moment, certain that he was lying, but when Morris didn't seem ready to take it back, Stonecraft let out an unrestrained laugh. "A mutiny?" he asked, and although Morris didn't answer, the look in his eyes told him he was right. Stonecraft laughed again and clapped the younger man on the shoulder. "Bad luck, my friend."

"I'll split it with you," he offered, and despite how high his chin was still raised, the first trace of fear showed itself in the quiver in his voice. "You and your crew can take half of everything on board…"

"I didn't come here to bargain," Stonecraft said firmly. He nodded to Benton, who gave Morris a merciless shove toward the banister that ran along the edge of the deck. The pirates who had gathered to watch the exchange began to jeer loudly once again. Morris began to plead with Benton, but Stonecraft paid none of this any attention. Instead, he started for the nearest hatchway that would take him to the cargo hold. Behind him, Morris let out a shrill shriek, which was followed by a splash as he met the water over the side of the ship. The pirates whistled and cheered.

The ruckus on the deck faded behind him as Stonecraft made his way into the belly of the massive ship. When he reached the main cargo hold, he found only a single oil lamp burning in its place on a metal hook on the wall. He took it down and held the lamp out before him, his eager eyes straining to penetrate the darkness with the aid of the little flame.

He'd hoped for a load of precious ores that he could ransom back to Chaumont, or perhaps even a haul of the finest pistols and rifles the kingdom's navy had to offer. What he found as the lantern's meager light splashed over the barrels and crates before him, however, made his breath catch in his throat. For a moment, he was certain that he was seeing things, or that he was sleeping, and this dream would surely vanish in an unfortunate whisp of wakefulness.

Gold, diamonds, and silver sparkled in the warm glow of the lantern. There must have been hundreds of large, wooden crates brimming with the stuff. Several bars of gold had spilled from a nearby barrel and were currently resting in a pile at his feet. Paintings and stone statues were nestled securely between stacks of treasure-laden casks, many of which were so full of heavy riches that there were sparkling gaps between their wooden staves. Beyond the light cast by the lantern, hulking shapes in the darkness promised more of the same. In all his years of pirating, Stonecraft had never dared to dream of such a haul. Looking at the riches packed into the hold before him, he doubted anyone had ever possessed such an imagination.

In the dim glow of a stolen lantern on a ship laden with more riches than he would ever know what to do with, Stonecraft heard a deep, dumbfounded laugh begin to echo off of the barrels and crates. It took him a few seconds to realize that the sound was coming from himself.

Chapter One

THE light rain drifting down from the gray, dreary sky wasn't enough to dampen Journey Travert's spirits. He stepped off the gangway and onto the smooth, wooden boards of the dock. The dockworkers greeted him politely as they finished tying off his little sloop, called *Lady Swift*. She was so new that the first coat of green paint on her banisters hadn't yet started to flake. She had cost a bit more than he'd wanted to spend, but the last three years since retiring from piracy had been profitable ones, and the Travert family could certainly afford it. In fact, Journey had just returned from the Twin Islands, where he'd seen with his own eyes that the sugarcane crops there were some of the best the islands had ever produced. Harvesttime was just around the corner, and if all went well, this would be a record year.

He made his way down the dock and onto the dry, rocky land that he called home. Stonewell Island was abuzz with workers hurrying about their daily tasks, and Journey weaved between them as he made his way up the sloping, gravel road that climbed toward the top of the hill. His hair and clothes were damp from the rain, but he hardly noticed. After three days spent on Nymph's Rest and Green Plot, he was glad to be home.

The mansion loomed over him, dominating the tallest point of the island and overlooking the various warehouses and offices that kept the business running. He reached its front door – ornately carved with images of sailing ships like the one he'd just stepped off of – and let himself into the foyer. Everything was just how it always was: elegant, red drapes covered the windows, expensive rugs graced the floor, and beautiful artwork hung on the walls. Journey ignored all of this, however; his attention was stolen by the two-year-old child near the foot of the staircase just before him. She was clad in a yellow dress that revealed scraped knees, doubtlessly from time spent playing in the garden yesterday. Her hair was the same shade as Journey's. In fact, almost everything about Mirelle Travert spoke of her father, from her hazel eyes to the spattering of freckles across her shoulders.

She was currently being held in the arms of Hannah Gladwin, who was a kindhearted twenty-something who had been her caretaker for over a year now. As soon as Mirelle caught sight of Journey, however, she squirmed to be put down, squealing, "Daddy!"

Hannah set her on the floor, and she hurried across it with as much speed as her small legs could muster. Journey caught her as she hurled herself into his arms, and he hoisted her onto his hip with an exaggerated groan. Mirelle laughed and placed a hearty kiss on his cheek. He asked her, "Have you been good while I was away?"

Mirelle gave an enthusiastic nod, even as Hannah shook her own head behind her. She reported, "Mrs. Travert is resting, and it's well past naptime for this one."

"I'll take her off your hands, Hannah," Journey told her, and the young woman made no effort to hide her relief. He left her there in the foyer and headed for his study, Mirelle still on his hip. She informed him of her day's activities in the joyful gibberish that made up most of her vocabulary. She was learning new words every day, but still relied on meaningless noises when she just wanted to fill a silence. Journey let her talk. He wouldn't have stopped her for anything in the Realm.

When they reached his study, he set Mirelle down on the floor, and she immediately toddled over to the bookshelf near his desk. The bottom shelf was dedicated to storybooks, and she plucked one from its place after a moment of careful consideration. Then she hurried back to Journey and offered it up to him with big, pleading eyes. Despite how tired he was from his trip, he couldn't say no. Instead, he sat down on the floor in the middle of his study and took the young girl into his lap. The story was about a mermaid, and it was one that he'd read to her a hundred times. As he recited the tale once more, Mirelle placed her hands on the page to hide the words, giggling. Journey played along and moved her hands out of the way so that he could continue reading. The fourth time she did it, he set the book aside on the floor and began tickling her sides. The girl shrieked with laughter, squirming to escape him, but Journey got her on her back on the floor and continued to tickle her. The entire wing of the house was filled with the warm sound of her mirth – something that was common these days.

Abigay Laval entered the study after a polite knock on the open door, and she smiled at the sight of them on the floor. Abigay was in her mid-forties now, but still didn't look it. Except for the two years while Journey had been at sea, she had served the Travert family her entire adult life. Mirelle called her "Auntie Abby," just as Journey had done as a child, and Abigay loved the girl like she was her own. Now, as she squirmed in her father's clutches, she called toward the door, "Help!"

Abigay pretended to scowl at Journey, but there was too much love in the look for it to be threatening. "The whole island will hear her squeals. Mrs. Travert is trying to get some rest."

He stopped tickling the girl, but she didn't move from the floor, panting heavily as her giggles finally tapered out. He placed a finger against his lips in a shushing gesture and told her, "Mummy's sleeping. We shouldn't wake her."

The drapes in the room were still closed in an attempt to shut out the dreariness of the rain outside, but the clouds were clearing off now, and warm sunshine was making its way through. Abigay began opening all of the drapes to let it into the room, humming a happy tune as she went. Mirelle asked her from where she was still laying on the floor, "Garden?"

"Soon, love," she answered, pulling back another drape. "It looks like the weather's going to turn for the better."

"Let's hope so," Journey said as he stood. He stretched to get rid of the ache in his back from sitting on the hard floor. He promised Mirelle, "If the rain clears, I'll take you down to the docks to see the ships."

She squealed in delight over the very idea. There was another knock on the open door, and a butler named Samuel Brown stepped into the study and gave a light bow. "Sir, a ship is requesting to dock."

Journey cast a doubtful glance out of one of the windows Abigay had just uncovered. "If it's the *Sovereign Hope*, she's a day late. Captain Fielding is going to have to hurry if he wants her loaded before dark."

"No, sir," Samuel replied. "It's the *Jubilee*."

Journey brightened at that. Dallion had made good on his claim that he was going to use Stonewell as a safe port, and he'd made occasional visits to do so more than a dozen times over the three years since Journey's resignation from his crew. Journey had made him agree not to cause any trouble for the nearest islands, with which he and Saige had good relationships. Besides, if any of the companies caught wind that a private island owner was providing safe harbor for a pirate ship, it would spell trouble for all involved.

Abigay had paused in what she was doing, and out of the corner of his eye, Journey saw her watching him. The fact that she'd helped raise him from infancy often gave her the boldness (and the right, he supposed) to be blunt with him, and she'd expressed her disapproval concerning the pirate's permitted presence here more than once before. To her continued dismay, Journey told Samuel, "The *Jubilee* is welcome to dock anytime. Once she has, invite Captain Romilly up to the house."

Samuel gave another bow and left to carry his message down the hill outside. Before she could say anything, Journey turned to Abigay and said, "I know, Abby. It'll be fine."

She muttered something about playing with fire and went back to uncovering the windows. Mirelle had gotten herself into a sitting position on the floor, and she was now watching her father with curious eyes. Journey sat down in a nearby chair and patted his knee with one hand. The girl's small face broke into a precious smile, and she hefted the book from the floor to bring it to him.

Chapter Two

JOURNEY was still reading to Mirelle when Dallion stepped into the study a little while later. By then, Abigay was gone. When Mirelle saw Dallion, she let out a gasp, and her hazel eyes lit up at the sight of him.

"Dally!" she cried, using her best attempt at his name that she'd been capable of, so far. Journey let her go and watched as she hurried across the room. Dallion scooped her up without hesitation and tossed her into the air, making her squeal with delight. Then he set her on his hip, opposite the one his gun was currently strapped to. Mirelle set a loving hand on his cheek, which was scruffy and in need of a shave.

"What have they been feeding you?" the pirate asked her, pretending to struggle with her weight. "Have you been eating bricks?"

"No!" she laughed, and then put her arms around his neck in the tightest hug she could manage. Dallion squeezed her tightly. Journey smiled at the sight. He'd last seen the Dallion three months ago, and at the time, Dallion had been depressed about the death of several members of his crew that had occurred during an especially messy attack on a ship owned by an up-and-coming company called Dover Trading. Old Rube had been one of the casualties, and Journey had hated receiving that news. Old

Rube had been a good friend and an even finer supplies officer. According to Dallion, he'd taken a bullet to the heart during the skirmish and had died quickly. It was as good a way as men in that line of work could hope for.

Now, however, Dallion seemed to be his usual bright and cheery self again. He was wearing a teal shirt and black pants that appeared to be relatively new. There were a few more rings on his fingers than he'd worn last time he was here, and there was now an earring in his right ear. There were so many in his left that he'd run out of room for new holes.

Dallion set Mirelle on her feet on the floor and squatted before her, reaching into a pocket in his pants and bringing something out for her. Her eyes widened at the sight of the small, wooden doll in his hand. The hair on its head was fine, white horsehair, and its dress was real silk. She snatched it from him with an excited, "Thank you, Dally!"

"Spoiling angels is what Dally's best at," he told her, and watched her toddle off with the doll, babbling to it in that baby gibberish that only she could understand.

Journey left his chair and went to Dallion to hug him. Dallion hugged him back, and when he stepped away again, Journey asked, "Shouldn't you be out near Port Kelsey this time of year?"

Dallion shrugged, but there was something written on his face that told Journey he had something up his sleeve. He said simply, "You know winter's the slow season. I got bored."

Winter was actually a busy time for piracy in the west, but Journey didn't tell him he knew better. Instead, he said, "Have dinner with us tonight. You should invite Lucien and a few others up, too."

"After dinner, we need to talk about something. Just you and me."

Journey didn't dare ask him what the discussion would be about. Whatever it was, Dallion was clearly excited and anxious about it. Journey decided to wait until after dinner, and then he'd likely have to turn him down. He was a married man with a daughter and another child on the way. His time for pirate antics was over.

He nodded toward Mirelle, who was play walking her new doll across the arm of Journey's desk chair. "Keep an eye on the little hellion, and I'll go wake up Saige. She'll kill me if she knows I let her sleep through your visit."

"Hear that, hellion?" Dallion asked, dropping his voice into a gravelly growl. He crouched down onto his hands and knees and began to crawl across the floor toward Mirelle. The girl saw the imitated monster coming and let out a joyful scream, then hurried around the other side of the chair in a futile attempt to hide. Dallion kept crawling toward her, growling that he would eat her up, and received a fresh batch of giggles in response. Journey left them there to go fetch Saige, the sound of his daughter's laughter following him down the hall.

Journey reached the room he shared with his wife and let himself inside. Everything in it spoke of Saige's tastes. The canopied bed was draped in white linens that matched the curtains on the windows. The dressers were made of dark hardwood, and the small table that sat in the middle of the room was graced with beautiful seashells. They were pink and gray in color, matching the pillows on the bed. Saige's long hair was spread out across one of them, and as Journey sat beside her, he gently brushed one of her curls off her cheek. She stirred at his touch, and he whispered, "If you want to keep sleeping, I can go."

"No," she said, turning onto her side to face him. "I don't want to sleep the day away."

"Good, because Dallion's here."

"Tell me you didn't leave him with Mirelle. The last time you did that, he taught her to curse."

"I threatened to kill him if he ever does it again."

"You won't have to," she assured him, sitting up in the soft bed. "I will."

Chapter Three

DALLLION lived to see another day, as Journey returned to find him still chasing Mirelle around the study. When Saige arrived, he noticed the swell of her belly immediately, and he threw his arms around both of his friends in congratulations and true joy. They spent the rest of that morning and early afternoon catching up with one another. Journey and Saige shared the business' latest achievements, which included the hiring of a dozen new workers and the purchase of an old schooner that they planned to see repaired and readied to ferry sugarcane shipments to and from islands outside their current range of trade. Mirelle recounted a story about her new doll, at least as well as her limited vocabulary would allow. Dallion told a few new tales of his own: the successful attack he'd levied against a port town farther south, a man they'd found marooned on a tiny island and had taken on as part of their crew, and a few other stories that he undoubtedly embellished a great deal. He mentioned a new frigate that had set sail a year ago, under the flag of The Whitefish Trading Company. She was called the *Huntress*, and that was an apt name for her, from the sound of it. She was tasked with hunting down as many pirate ships as possible, and in the past six months, she was rumored to have sunk one nearly every week. The pirates aboard were given no quarter, and no would-be survivors were pulled from the water, but were left to drown.

Journey found it hard to believe that the *Huntress* had really been responsible for the doom of that many ships…but the hint of fear in Dallion's eyes as he talked about her said that he believed every word of it. His voice dropped a little when he told them that the crew of the *Jubilee* had seen her once. It had been from a distance, but she could be recognized by her purple sails.

"We got out of there as fast as we could," he said, giving a laugh that didn't fool Journey. "She's rumored to have more than thirty cannons. And she's fast. Do you remember the *Cruel Mistress*? She was Garrett's boat."

Journey nodded. The *Mistress* was a sloop that had been custom-rigged by her captain, a man named Joseph Garrett. He'd often boasted to other pirates that he could coax an unfathomable fifteen knots from her, if the wind was right. Journey had been invited aboard one time in Port Kelsey, where Garrett had showed her off to him, personally. He was known in pirate circles as Captain Speed Devil.

"The *Huntress* chased her down," Dallion told him. There was a grin on his lips, but it was thin and lacked any sort of joy or humor. "It happened somewhere north of Runes. Ran her down and sent her to the bottom, even after Garrett tried to surrender. The captain's name is Fleury. Rumor has it that he used to be a pirate, and he caused Whitefish so much trouble that they offered him a salary and command of a fancy ship if he changed sides."

Saige had left them alone for a few minutes as she put Mirelle down for a nap. When she returned, Dallion changed the subject, and when Journey tried to shift it back to this mysterious warship, Dallion wouldn't take the bait. Journey didn't think he'd ever known the man to be so afraid of something.

*   *   *

THEY hosted Dallion, Lucien, Pigeon, and Brain for dinner. Saige introduced them all to her adopted father, Francis, who lived here with her and his son-in-law. Francis didn't seem all that happy to be in the company of men whom he knew to be pirates, but he kept quiet about it, and no one objected when he excused himself from dinner early. The kitchen servants kept the wine coming per Journey's request, though he didn't drink much. He noted that Dallion was pacing himself, as well, and that was an oddity. The others grew steadily drunker and louder as the evening wore on, until most of the conversations around the table were comprised of old jokes and laughter. Thankfully, the mansion was large enough that Mirelle slept soundly through the ruckus two floors below.

Eventually, Brain sat down at the piano in the corner of the dining room and began to play. Journey was surprised to find that he was rather good, though he had no idea where he'd learned to play. Pigeon asked Saige to dance with him, and she obliged, allowing him to spin her in wild circles across the floor before the table. Journey watched her graceful twirls, and the sound of her laughter more beautiful to him than any combination of chords played on a piano could ever be. Her fiery curls bobbed around her shoulders as she danced. Journey doubted that she would ever lose the ability to take his breath away, and he marveled at his luck of having won her heart.

Dallion slipped away from the others and came to Journey's side, where he said quietly enough so that only he could hear, "Let's talk."

Journey's response was to leave the chair he'd been sitting in and head for the door without a word. They left the others and headed down the hall and into a parlor. A large fireplace dominated one wall, and thoughtful servants had left the fire burning in case the dinner party chose to venture in here. Two couches and a few chairs were set up in a semicircle to allow visitors to converse, and Journey took a seat in one of the chairs. Dallion closed the door behind him, and Brain's upbeat piano melody was muffled, at last. Journey watched in silence as Dallion wandered across the room, admiring the paintings on the walls and the occasional knickknack sitting on small tables and shelves. He came to a stop before the fireplace to study a portrait hanging above it. Jubilee Travert peered down at him from within its frame, clad in a regal-looking gown of blue silk. There was a kindness in her eyes that added to her beauty.

"Saige looks a lot like her," Dallion marveled without turning. "I don't know what that says about your relationship with the woman you thought was your mother, though."

Journey frowned, but decided not to give him any more of a reaction than that. Instead, he asked, "What did you want to talk about, Dal?"

Dallion took his gaze from the portrait and turned to him. In the warm light of the fire, the man looked older and wiser than Journey knew him to be. Dallion asked, "Are you sober?"

He was – he hadn't even finished his second glass of wine – and he nodded. Dallion seemed pleased. He came to a nearby couch and perched himself on the arm of it, bringing one of his boot-clad feet up to rest it on the cushion. It was something that Saige would have scolded him for, if she'd seen it.

"I've been thinking," he said.

Journey shook his head immediately. "No."

"You don't even know what I was going to say."

"Whatever it is, the answer is no."

He scowled. "You're too good to hear me out now? Is that it, Prince? You've gone back to being pampered and coddled around here, and now you're too good to listen when the best friend you've ever had has something to say…"

Journey groaned, waving one hand to stop him. "Fine. You can tell me, but the answer is still going to be no."

Dallion must not have believed that, for a slight grin crossed his lips. "That's more like it. Now, what do you know about the *Weeping Cherub*?"

He knew a little about it, mostly from old stories he'd heard from other pirates during his time at sea with this man. He replied, "I know it's a myth that sailors like to argue about when they're drunk."

Dallion made a *tsk tsk* noise with his tongue. "I never thought I'd see the day when I had to educate you about something, Teach. The *Weeping Cherub* was a galleon that belonged to King Antoine de Chaumont, back when there were still kings out west. She's rumored to have been a four-masted beast of a ship. She was famous in her time for transporting precious cargo for the royal family. Her last voyage was to the neighboring kingdom of Darcey, where Antoine had finally won a decade-long war against his biggest rival. According to the stories, the *Cherub*'s cargo holds were packed to the brim with all the best spoils of war: gold, silver, jewels, precious metals, artwork, statues, you name it. All the gold in the national treasury was melted down into bars and put on board. When the *Cherub* set sail to head back to Chaumont, she was literally carrying the entire wealth of a nation."

The way he was telling the story told Journey that he'd rehearsed it many times, and likely for this moment. He said doubtfully, "Even if those stories are true…"

"Let me finish," Dallion pressed. "The *Cherub* never made it back home to Chaumont. You see, her captain was a loyal servant to the throne, a man named Sennett. But his crew didn't exactly share his loyalties. They mutinied not long after leaving Darcey so that they could keep the treasure for themselves. They headed east, probably wanting to get to the Whaleskin Islands, or maybe even come all the way out to Cape Kelsey. Even back then, Kelsey was a haven for pirates, and that's what they were, by then."

Journey didn't believe a word of the tale he was spinning, but he'd been taken in by the plot, anyway. He asked, "What happened?"

Dallion chuckled. "The pirates were out-pirated. At some point, a captain by the name of Stonecraft attacked, and he almost had to sink the *Cherub* when her crew refused to surrender. Finally, they gave up, and he marooned them all. Only a few of them survived and managed to make their way back to Chaumont, where they were punished for the mutiny by being put in prison for the rest of their lives. Anyway, Stonecraft probably shit himself when he opened up the cargo holds and realized what kind of haul he'd just taken. But he had to act fast, because Darcey's last few ships and half of Antoine's fleet from Chaumont were out looking for the *Cherub*. He had to hide her, and I mean quick."

Journey gave him a few seconds to continue, and when he didn't, he urged, "And?"

Dallion shrugged. "No one's sure what happened after that. Stonecraft managed to stay out of everyone's grasp. Some people say that he took what treasure he could fit onto his own ship and then scuttled the *Cherub*. But I don't think that's what happened. Stonecraft is said to have been sailing a brig, and not a very big one. I don't care how scared of getting caught with the ship he might have been; he wouldn't have been able to fit even half of that treasure horde on his own boat, and there's no way any man in his right mind would willingly send the rest of it to the bottom. Not a chance."

Journey sat back in his chair with a sigh, but decided to take the bait and asked, "Alright, then what do you think he did, instead?"

Dallion beamed at the chance to impress him, and he took something out of his pocket. He offered it to Journey, who took it after only a moment's hesitation. It was a folded piece of fine leather, from the look and feel of it. He unfolded it and spread it out on the small table beside his chair. In the orange glow from the fireplace, he saw a few dark blobs of ink on it, but that was all. One of the misshapen blobs was circled. The ink was old and faded.

Dallion explained, "It's a map."

"No, it's a scrap of leather that someone kept under the inkwell on their desk."

"Nice try, but you're wrong. This is a copy of an older version that burned up in a fire. Look at the bottom corner. Can you see the writing?"

The ink was faded the worst there, but Journey could make out a few shadowy letters. He may have been able to see more in the daylight. Dallion said, "It's in the old writing ways, and I can't read that. Some of the letters are the same, but the pronunciations are weird."

"You're a fool for believing any part of that old myth."

"Look, if we can put names to the islands on that map, we can find…"

"No," Journey said firmly, and tossed the piece of leather at him. Dallion caught it so tenderly that it may have been as fragile as an egg or piece of glass. Journey crossed his arms at his chest and told him, "You're on your own. If you want to chase fairytales, go ahead. But leave me out of this."

"Journey…"

"I can't," he said, his tone softening into something less stern and more apologetic. "It's not like it was before, Dal. I have a family to look out for now. Saige is expecting. I have responsibilities that have to come first. I can't go chasing adventure with you."

Dallion's face took on a look of sadness so deep that it was as if he'd received news that someone he loved had died. Even with the shadow caused by having his back turned to the fire, Journey could see the desperation on his face.

"Don't you think I know that?" he asked him. "Don't you think that Lucien told me you'd say that? Again and again and again, he wouldn't shut up. But I need your help with this. You're the smartest person I've ever known, except for maybe Brain, in some ways. This is just a puzzle, and who would be better at figuring it out than you?"

"I can't…"

"Please," he said, and Journey hated the despair in his friend's voice. "Look, maybe I didn't make it sound all that serious before, but this stuff with the *Huntress* is no joke. The whole crew is scared out of their minds about it, and I'd be lying if I said that I wasn't scared, too. And now there are rumors that some of the other companies are commissioning their own pirate-hunting ships. This map couldn't have come to me at a better time. If we find the treasure that was aboard the *Cherub* and it's even half as big as the stories say, the whole crew and I can retire and live out the rest of our days comfortably, without having to always look over our shoulders for purple sails on the horizon." He paused, then added, "We're not all as lucky as you are, Prince. We don't have mansions waiting for us anywhere."

Journey was tempted to agree to go with him, and if Saige had been the only one depending on him here, he might have done so. She was an able and intelligent woman who could take care of herself while he was away…but he had Mirelle and the coming baby to think about, too, and when he had promised his bride on their wedding night that he was finished with pirating, he'd meant it.

Dallion saw this conviction in his face, and his shoulders drooped in disappointment. Before Journey could tell him no again, he said with forced casualness, "Don't worry about it. I get it. You've got babies and the business and a bunch of other things. I shouldn't have even asked."

"You're welcome to stay here as long as you want," Journey said quietly. "If you need some money to get the search underway, Saige and I can help you with that."

"I don't want your money," he muttered. "Don't worry about it. Lucien was right: everything you've got here is too good to risk. I don't blame you."

His tone said otherwise, but Journey wasn't about to argue with him about it. As Dallion started for the door into the hall, he said, "I need to get back to the ship. We'll be out of your hair around sunrise tomorrow. Take care of yourself, Journey."

He didn't ask him to stop or offer the use of the guestrooms for the night. He knew Dallion well enough to be sure that it would only make him angrier. Once he was gone and Journey had the parlor to himself, he fetched a bottle of liquor from the cabinet in the corner and poured himself a glass. He needed a drink.

When he collapsed into bed a half an hour later, Saige was already there. She was still awake, but only barely. She stirred as he got beneath the blankets beside her, and she moved to rest her head on his chest. He held her close and stared up into the darkness of their bedroom. Downstairs, a pair of servants were nearly finished cleaning up after the guests they'd hosted. Dallion and the others had returned to the *Jubilee* to sleep before heading out in the morning. Soon, everything would be back to normal, although Journey didn't think it would feel that way for a while.

Saige drew him back from his thoughts with, "What's wrong?"

He considered telling her that it was nothing, but he didn't like lying to her, even if it was over something as small as this. Besides, Saige had an uncanny knack for knowing when he was just trying to appease her. Instead, he confessed, "It's Dallion."

"I noticed you two snuck off to chat about something, and as soon as Dallion came back, he was ready to leave. Did you argue?"

"He wants me to go with him on some fool's errand out west. He doesn't understand that I have responsibilities here. He's never had a family of his own, or even a reason to stick around somewhere for longer than a week or two."

She was silent for a moment, but then she admitted, "Lucien told me about the *Weeping Cherub*. Not long after you two left the dining room, he took me aside and told me that's why they were here. I think he was trying to warn me that you might want to take Dallion up on it."

He kissed the top of her head, squeezing her tight. "You don't have to worry about that. I'm not going anywhere."

"I think you should go."

For a moment, he was certain that he'd heard her wrong. With no candles or lamps lit, it was too dark for him to look for any expression on her face that might indicate that she was joking. When he didn't respond, she said, "At first, I was annoyed that Dallion would ask you to go do this with him. But now I've had some time to think about it, and I know that this might be his best chance at getting out of pirating. How long has he been doing this? It's a dangerous lifestyle, and almost no one stays with it for as long as he has, already. They either retire or get killed, and I don't want to see Dallion get killed. I know that you don't, either."

"He can stop pirating at any time. No one has gun to his head to force him to keep going."

"What else would he do for a living?"

As much as he hated to admit it, she had a point. Dallion was a talented pirate and possessed more knowledge about sailing than anyone else Journey had ever met, but he had little in the way of other skills. He had no experience farming, and the conditions for workers on most islands were bad enough that Journey wouldn't want that for him, anyway. He was known to the companies in the region as a criminal, so he wouldn't be able to sign up for a legitimate sailor's position…not that he would be any good at taking orders from some potbellied lieutenant, anyway. He could read, but his penmanship was atrocious. He had no culinary skills, no experience as a potter, tailor, carpenter, or tanner. No, if Dallion was going to get out of the pirating business, he was going to need to be able to retire wholly on whatever he could steal, first. It was that simple.

He thought of Dallion telling him that he and the rest of the crew didn't have mansions waiting for them anywhere, and was that guilt following quickly on the heels of that memory? Journey hadn't been entitled to anything he now had. Without Saige, he would have had about as many options as Dallion currently did.

"Besides," Saige said, as if to verify the thoughts in his head, "it was Dallion's idea to find me and take me to settle my inheritance with Commercial Horizon. Without him, neither of us would be here right now. We owe him everything we have."

Journey took a long time to think this over, but it was pointless. He knew that she was right. Saige planted a kiss on his bare chest and then rested her head on it once again, saying, "Sleep on it, love. See how you feel about it in the morning." With that, she closed her eyes to sleep. Journey doubted that sleep would come easily tonight, with all of the thoughts currently running through his head.

He was right.

Chapter Four

WHEN he woke the following morning, Saige's side of the bed was empty. The flowery scent of her perfume still lingered on her pillow. Journey laced his hands behind his head and stared up at the bottom of the bed's canopy. Early sunlight was drifting lazily through the room's windows. He wondered if the *Jubilee* had left yet, and supposed that Dallion would wait for a good hour after sunrise in the hopes that he might change his mind, but not much longer than that. Why did he have to be so exasperating?

He dressed and went downstairs, where he found Saige eating breakfast in the dining room. Francis most often joined her, but he was nowhere to be seen this morning. Journey's place at the table was set, but as he sat down in the chair, he made no move to fill his plate from the half a dozen dishes on the table. Saige was devouring a small mound of bacon with the ravenousness that so many pregnant women throughout time have known. Neither of them spoke for a while, even as one of the housemaids came into the dining room to see if they needed more to drink. Once she was gone, there was silence between them again. Journey supposed she was waiting for him to give her his final decision about Dallion, but he still didn't know what it was. He toyed with the edge of the napkin on the table before him for a while, and eventually, he told her, "I don't want to leave you here on your own while you're with child, Saige. That seems like an irresponsible and uncaring thing for a man to do."

"On my own?" she asked, setting the last bit of bacon aside on her plate. "I have my father here, and I have Abigay, and a dozen servants to take care of things. And even if I didn't have all those people around, I would still be alright. You didn't marry some helpless, coddled girl, Journey. You know that."

He did, and he wondered if he was just trying to talk himself out of going. Still, he argued, "The baby is due soon…"

"Not for another four months or so." She smiled at him from across the table, and one look at that smile reminded him that he was at her command. She asked him, "When do you leave?"

He didn't answer that. Instead, he stood and came around to that side of the table. She stood as he reached her, and he put his arms around her to pull her close. She hugged him back and assured him, "I'll take care of everything here. Don't worry about anything: me, Mirelle, the workers, the crops. Just be back in time to see your new son or daughter come into the world, alright?"

"I promise," he whispered, and placed a kiss on the lobe of her ear. "I'll be back within three months, whether we find Dallion's damn treasure or not. I won't keep you waiting any longer than that. I love you, Saige."

"I love you, too," she said, stepping back. "You should get going. You still need to pack."

"If they haven't already left," he agreed, starting for the door into the hall at a jog.

Saige smiled after him, knowing that they hadn't. After all, she'd sent Abigay down to the docks over an hour ago to tell them to wait for him.

*   *   *

DALLION was waiting atop the gangway when Journey arrived. He made no effort to hide his satisfaction, and Journey knew it wouldn't have been any use if he had. Stepping onto the main deck of the *Jubilee* felt like coming home, and in a sense, he supposed it was. Pirates were hurrying in every direction as they prepared to set sail. One glance around told him that very little had changed – the graceful banisters, smooth boards, and straight masts were exactly how they'd been the last time he'd been here. The *Jubilee* was a thing of beauty, and it was clear that Dallion and his crew had been putting everything they had into her care.

Dallion threw his arms around him, still beaming, and Journey hugged him back. When they stepped back, Dallion said, "You're not going to regret this."

"I doubt that," he replied, but couldn't help but return Dallion's grin. Lucien joined them near the banister, and he offered Journey his hand, which he shook warmly.

"You're crazy for coming along with us," he assured him, and Journey didn't even try to argue that. He realized that a number of crewmen had paused their chores and were gathering around them. Some were faces he recognized, but he'd never met others. Dallion pointed them out, one by one.

"That's Catfish. He took over as the supplies officer after Old Rube died. That tall guy is Jimmy Two-Tales. He's the deck officer. You remember Horus and Wee Bit. And this," he said as he clapped another man on the shoulder, "is Lil Gabe. He's Lucien's son."

Journey had no idea why the eighteen-year-old before him was called "Lil" anything, as he had inherited his father's height. He shook Journey's hand and clarified, "Gabriel Dumas. I've heard good things about you, Mr. Travert."

"Mr. Travert!" Dallion laughed. "If we're so formal now, why don't you get back to work, Mr. Dumas? That mainsail isn't going to set itself."

Lil Gabe hurried off to do so, and most of the others scattered with him. Dallion motioned for Journey to follow him, and he shouldered the pack he'd brought with him – clothes, money, and the gun that had once belonged to Landon Travert – and started off across the deck. Dallion led him to a man who was coiling a bit of rope near the bow. He was a thin and frail-looking man in his late twenties, with a tangled nest of blond hair on his head. He stopped what he'd been doing as Dallion and Journey reached him, and Dallion said, "This is Laurence Watts. We picked him up on a tiny scrap of land a few weeks ago. He's behind this whole trip."

"Call me Watty," the man muttered, and when Journey offered his hand, he hesitated for a few seconds before shaking it. His eyes shifted from side to side, but wouldn't quite meet Journey's gaze, and he let go of his hand almost as soon as he took it.

Dallion gave Watts an amiable slap on the back and told Journey, "He's not great with people, but he's alright. He's going to help us figure out what happened to the *Weeping Cherub*."

Before Journey could ask how he intended to that, Lucien's voice called out over the deck in a flurry of orders, and the pirates who weren't already scrambling to get the ship underway hurried to do so now. Watts abandoned the coil of rope and scurried to help Lil Gabe and Jimmy Two-Tales as they wrestled with one of the masts. Journey unshouldered his pack and handed it to Dallion. Then he seized the nearest ratline and started climbing up it. The feel of the ropes in his hands and the breeze on his face was as familiar as his own thoughts or his wife's voice. It was good to be back.

Chapter Five

THEY made good time that day, although Pigeon only had vague orders to head west. Dallion invited Journey, Lucien, Pigeon, and Horus to his cabin for dinner that evening. The other furniture in the room was moved aside to make way for a long, wooden table and its chairs. Saige had sent food supplies down to the dock for them before they'd left, and Catfish had prepared a hearty meal for them from it. He wasn't quite as good as Old Rube had been, but he was close. He sent a couple of men to set the table with chicken, guava, potatoes, boiled eggs, mangos, cheese, and soft, fresh bread. As they men ate their fill, washing it all down with ample amounts of rum and ale, Journey caught up on the *Jubilee*'s latest exploits. They had been busy, and Horus bragged with pride that Dallion now had a bounty of over ten thousand marks on his head, offered by The Whitefish Trading Company. Dallion pretended not to care, but Journey wasn't fooled. He'd been trying for years to make a formidable name for himself, and with a bounty that size, he'd finally succeeded.

As they finished eating and settled back in their chairs to continue drinking, Dallion said from his place at the head of the table, "Let's get down to business. We're going to keep heading west for a little while. I'm making Journey my first mate again. He's still signed on from before."

"And what about the *Cherub*?" Horus asked from Journey's left. "What's the plan to find her?"

Dallion poured himself another cup of ale and took a drink before saying, "We don't need to find the *Cherub*. We just need to find the fortune that Stonecraft unloaded off of her."

"I wonder what happened to him," Pigeon mused. "I mean, obviously he didn't get to spend any of the money. Otherwise, his great-grandkids would still be rolling in it."

"More reason to believe she was scuttled," Lucien supplied. "If she's any more than a few fathoms deep, there's no way to reach her."

"She didn't go under," Dallion said with a confidence he hadn't earned. "At least, not before the treasure was offloaded. Besides, the map proves that he hid it somewhere." He took the folded piece of leather out of his pocket and laid it out on the table between a few of the empty dishes. Pigeon and Horus both stood to come to that end of the table to study it.

Journey asked, "Where did you get the map?"

Dallion grinned. "Maybe it was providence. Remember how I told you that we found Watty marooned on an empty island? He had the map on him. He offered it to me in trade for rescuing him and taking him on as part of the crew."

"And where did he get it?"

"He bought it off a man on Courier Island who said that it had been passed down to him from his father. So Watty took it back to his captain, a guy named Marne, and they decided to go looking for the island that's circled on the map. Only they didn't find it, and after four months, the rest of the crew got sick of looking and accused Watty of making it all up. They marooned him as payback for wasting their time, and he was stuck there for almost a week before we came across him."

Journey merely stared at him, wondering if Dallion was crazy. He must have understood the look on his face for what it was, because he shrugged. "Sometimes, good things just fall into your lap in life. That's what happened when you walked into the Hoary Witch in Port Kelsey and found me, isn't it?"

"Do we really trust this guy?" Journey asked anyone at the table who was willing to answer.

Lucien was the only one willing to meet his gaze at that, and he replied with a shrug, "I don't, but I've been outvoted about it. The general idea is that he hasn't given us any reason not to trust him, yet."

Journey shot Dallion a look that told him exactly what he thought about that, but Dallion pretended not to see this. Instead, he said, "Look, we've already voted and decided to do this. We aren't here to decide that again. We're supposed to be figuring out where to start looking."

Journey struggled to set aside his doubts and the half a dozen arguments that he wanted to make. He was already here, after all. He asked, "Has Brain had a look at the map?"

Lucien nodded. "Dallion and I asked him if he recognized the shapes on it as real-life chain of islands. He said he didn't."

"But that doesn't mean they don't exist," Dallion clarified quickly. "It just means he hasn't seen a map with them on it and we've never visited any of them. That's not surprising."

He was reaching, and they all knew it...but as Journey looked around the table, he saw men who were too afraid of the alternative to give up on what they saw as their saving grace. He dared to ask, "Do we have any idea where the *Huntress* is right now?"

They all shared glances at that. Pigeon offered, "Two weeks ago, there were rumors in Port Kelsey that she was somewhere near the Isle of Runes. But she could be anywhere now."

"The *Jubilee* is too quick for her," Dallion said dismissively, but they all knew that was a lie. Before Journey could call him out on it, there was a knock on the door, and Dallion called for the person to come in.

Watts opened the door and stuck his head inside the cabin. "You wanted to see me, Captain?"

Dallion motioned for him to sit down at the table, and he took the last remaining chair to sit between Lucien and Pigeon. Journey studied the man from across the table and tried hard to see the promise in him that Dallion claimed to have found. Dallion went to a cabinet against the far wall to fetch a map, and the others moved dishes and bowls out of the way so that he could lay it out over the center of the table. He asked Watts to show them where his previous ship, the *Sporting Gale*, had already searched for the islands. He pointed out areas of vast, empty ocean on the map, and Pigeon fetched a quill and some ink to cross the areas off, one after another. When Watts was finished, there was still a great deal of the map left unmarked. Everyone drew close to hover over it, but it was anyone's guess as to where they should start looking.

Watts pointed to an area near the corner, where there was nothing drawn or written. "We'd heard from a few fishermen that there were unnamed islands somewhere around here, and that's where we were going to head next, but the rest of the crew…" He shrugged. "They decided to give up instead."

"We'll run a grid pattern out there and see what we can find," Dallion decided, and he ignored Journey's look of disappointment. If the first area didn't pan out, and neither did the next, or the next…this search could take months and months. Journey didn't have that kind of time.

Lucien must have noticed the look on his face, for he grinned at him, revealing all four of the remaining teeth he had. "Still glad you agreed to come along, Teach?"

"It was worth it just to see your smiling face again, Lucien," he assured him, but deep down, he was beginning to wonder if he should have told Saige she was crazy for suggesting this.

Chapter Six

CRAZY or not, Journey slipped easily back into his old role as first mate. For the next few days, he relayed orders from Lucien and pitched in with chores that needed to be done. As the sun rose on his eighth day out at sea, he found himself hauling a mop and a bucket out onto the main deck to swab it. He let his thoughts roam as he ran the mop back and forth across the deck's smooth, wooden planks. Swabbing was a task usually left to inexperienced crewmen, but Journey had made it a point the last time he'd been a part of this crew to never see any of the daily tasks as being beneath him, and he was determined to do the same thing, this time.

The day was already a hot one, and he paused after working awhile to wipe the sweat from his brow. The sound of two men chuckling reached his ears, and he scanned the busy deck to find Horus and Wee Bit farther astern, detangling a small mound of ropes that had become jumbled. When they saw that he'd noticed them, they allowed themselves to laugh a little louder, and Horus asked him, "What's wrong, Teach? Got a little too used to life on your island?"

As much as he wanted to, he couldn't tell him he was wrong. He'd caught himself panting and out of breath several times while doing chores, and his arms and back had been aching the entire time. He merely shook his head, and his lack of a rebuttal made Horus and Wee Bit laugh harder. Wee Bit told him, "If that bucket's too heavy, I can move it across the deck for you."

Journey had known both men long enough to recognize that their teasing was all in good fun. He considered slinging some of the salty water on his mop at them, much in the same vein, but before he could do so, a crewman he only vaguely recognized lowered himself from the ratline he'd just climbed, and as he set his feet on the deck, he announced, "I don't know what a well-off islander is doing out here, anyway. I know you're chummy with the captain, but that doesn't mean you belong here."

Wee Bit and Horus stopped laughing. Just as Journey had understood that they'd been joking, he understood that this man certainly wasn't, and there was something in his eyes that challenged someone to respond. From his pile of ropes, Horus said sharply, "Settle down, Boar. It's not like that."

"It's alright," Journey soothed, and Boar blinked, surprised by his calmness. "We haven't met, yet…"

"I know you're the captain's pet, and I know that doesn't matter. You should've stayed on your island, where you understand how things work."

It had been a long time since Journey had let his anger get the better of him; these days, he was hardly apt to scold Mirelle for misbehaving, let alone a stranger for being rude. Perhaps it was being out on the sea again, or maybe it was being in a place that he thought of as home, but something allowed a vehement flame to spark in his heart, and he growled, "I chose the type of wood for the deck planks you're standing on now. I spent weeks with a shipbuilder, pouring over the plans for this ship. I was there for every stage of her construction. I named her the *Jubilee*. I know everything there is to know about her, including why it's a bad idea to be an asshole to her first mate."

Boar looked very close to panicking, and that set Wee Bit and Horus off again. They roared with laughter, and Boar's face reddened with embarrassment. He muttered something about not being serious, but Journey couldn't hear him well enough over the sound of the others laughing at his chastisement. He turned on his heels and marched hastily away, headed anywhere that wasn't here. Wee Bit called after him to suggest he think twice before opening his mouth again. Journey watched him go, but felt little satisfaction. He wasn't out here to make enemies.

"Starboard bow!" a voice rang out from somewhere near the top of the ratlines, and Journey's attention was immediately pulled away from Boar's retreat to focus on whatever the lookout had spotted. Just before the place where the sea kissed the sky at the horizon, a small, brown speck was bobbing on the waves. It was hard to see from here, but he thought it may have been a small sloop of some sort. He heard Dallion's voice call out for him and Lucien to join him at the bow, and he abandoned his mop and bucket to do so.

Dallion was peering through a spyglass when he arrived at the front of the ship, and he offered it to Journey as he came to stand beside him. Journey held it to his eye and found the little ship amidst a canvas of blue water. It was a sloop – he'd been right – that couldn't have been more than thirty feet long. Her triangular sails were flapping loosely in the wind, as if their rigging had come loose, and although the spyglass didn't make it clear enough to be certain, he could have sworn her single mast was standing at an odd angle.

"What do you think?" he asked Dallion.

"I think someone's having a shitty day. I'm pretty sure I saw smoke when I first looked at them."

As he said it, Journey spotted a whisp of the same drifting up from the little ship. Whatever had happened out here, Dallion was correct: the crew of the sloop was having a very shitty day. Lucien joined them, at last, and Journey offered the spyglass to him. As he peered through it, Dallion decided, "We'll head over there and see what's going on."

"And offer to help?" Journey asked.

Dallion shrugged his shoulders, grinning, and Journey supposed he shouldn't have been surprised. All the same, he reminded him, "I agreed to come out here to look for your fabled treasure, Dal. I never said I wanted to help you rob damaged ships."

"True, but I think you forgot one important thing: once a pirate, always a pirate."

"Stop bickering," Lucien grumbled, still peering through the spyglass. "I've got a bad feeling about this. Something isn't right. Whoever smashed up their ship might still be around to try to do the same to us."

Dallion swept an arm around at the vacant sea around them. "I don't see anybody else out here. Do you? It's going to be fine. We'll just stop and have a chat. Maybe see if they've got anything we'd like to have."

Journey started to object, but just as he'd told Boar that he knew everything there was to know about the *Jubilee,* he also knew as much about her captain. Dallion's mind was made up, and that was all there was to it. As if to prove him right, Dallion called toward the helm that he wanted to shift course toward the sloop. Journey braced himself for whatever was to come. During the years he'd spent pirating with Dallion, he'd never been squeamish about this sort of thing before…but Lucien had said it best: something about this just didn't seem right.

Dallion tasked some of the crew to ready the cannons, just in case, but as the *Jubilee* drew closer to the damaged sloop, it became clear that it wasn't necessary. A handful of her crewmembers were gathered at her stern, and they were waving a makeshift flag they'd made out of what appeared to be a white sheet. Lucien kept a watchful eye all around as Pigeon brought the *Jubilee* up close, and once they were within shouting distance, they heard a man's voice call out, "Ahoy! We need help!"

Journey thought that was an understatement. They were close enough now that he could see that the little ship had suffered some serious damage. Her mast had suffered a catastrophic split up the center, and she was leaning dangerously toward port. Much of her rigging had been blasted loose by cannonballs, and a few of them had also left long, splintery grooves along her deck and hull. Six men were huddled near the bow, and they all sported bloodied bandages and the bewildered look of a man who was struggling to judge how close to death he was. The four men at her stern appeared uninjured, but as they hurried to the side of their ship that the *Jubilee* was coming alongside, he saw that their faces showed the same, disoriented look.

"I'll take the longboat over for a chat," Dallion announced to his gathered crew. "I'll take Journey, Horus, Roach, Jimmy Two-Tales, Venom, and Lil Gabe with me. Get the boat ready. We're going to go make some new friends."

Journey had no interest in doing whatever Dallion actually meant by that, but that feeling of something being wrong – dangerous, even – wouldn't leave him, and he wasn't about to let Dallion go without him. He climbed into the longboat along with the others, and as they set off across the short gap between the two ships, he checked to make sure his pistol was loaded and hoped he wouldn't need it.

The able-bodied men left aboard the sloop hauled them aboard with lengths of rope, and once they were all standing on her scarred and battered deck, one of the crewmen stepped forward. He was void of any company's uniform, just as the rest of his crew seemed to be, and although they could have passed for merchants who were down on their luck, Journey had lived their kind of life long enough to recognize them as fellow pirates. The man who had stepped forward offered his hand to Dallion, and as they shook, he told him, "Welcome aboard the *Tyrant*, or what's left of her. I'm Captain Borly."

"Captain Romilly," Dallion replied. "It looks like you boys have seen better days."

"You could say that. We were run down before we knew what was happening. They blasted us all to hell. I think we can keep her afloat long enough to get somewhere safe, but we're going to need as much help as you're willing to give us. I can pay you. We need to hurry, though."

"Why?" Dallion asked, glancing around the deck, likely for any sign of valuables to pilfer. "Do you think they might come back?"

Borly nodded. "We were sailing for Old Bank with another ship, the *Golden Tide*. The next thing we know, this frigate is bearing down on us out of nowhere. She flew a Whitefish flag, and I swear on my name that her sails were the darkest hue of purple you've ever seen."

Journey felt that anxious feeling in his stomach solidify into cold, hard fear. A chill ran up his spine as he felt his blood run cold. He glanced at Dallion and saw the last traces of color run from his face. He asked in a voice that wavered, "A frigate with purple sails?"

Borly nodded. "They wrecked our mast and made sure we weren't going anywhere, then chased after the *Golden Tide*. We lost sight of them about an hour ago. We put out the fire on our deck, but we couldn't do much else. We're low on supplies. If you could spare some wood and line, we could probably rig something up to brace our mast. If we can just get out of the area, we might be alright…"

"We'll send a few things over," Dallion assured him, but he was no longer looking at Borly; his eyes were darting out over the sea. "Which way did the frigate go?"

"North," Borley answered, pointing. "The *Tide* is a quick ship, and her captain's been on the sea for longer than you've probably been alive. He might even be able to outrun her, if he's lucky."

"He's not going to outrun this ship," Dallion muttered. He instructed the men he'd brought over, "Get back in the longboat. We'll send over some supplies, and then we're getting out of here."

"I can pay you whatever you think is fair…" Borly said, but Dallion had already started ushering his men back down into the longboat.

Journey was the last one over the side of the *Tyrant*, and he paused long enough to tell her captain, "The sooner you can get out of here, the better. Don't underestimate that frigate."

"What do you know about her?" he asked, and for that moment, the hardened seaman looked more like a terrified child who had just discovered a monster beneath his bed.

Journey said, "She's called the *Huntress*. If you value your life, you won't be here when she gets back."

Borly said nothing, but the fear that had overtaken him said enough. Dallion called Journey's name from the longboat, and he hurried over the side of the sloop to join him and the others there. They rowed back to the *Jubilee* with all their might.

*   *   *

JOURNEY took Lucien's offered hand and pulled himself up over the banister of the *Jubilee*. Dallion had climbed up before him, and he now told Lucien, "Throw some wood and a barrel full of tools and rope over the side. The tide is right to take it to them. We need to get out of here."

Lucien started to ask him something, but Dallion barked, "Now!"

That sent the surrounding crew scurrying, and Lucien howled orders to each of them. Journey helped Lil Gabe and Venom up onto the deck, then cast his gaze back toward the wounded *Tyrant*. Her men were waiting on her deck, looking back at him. He didn't envy their predicament. Even if they were able to rig something up to strengthen their mast, their odds of escaping the *Huntress'* wrath were shrinking with each passing minute.

"Get to the helm, Pigeon!" Dallion called. "As soon as those supplies are in the water, I want us moving southwest. I want eleven knots. No questions. Just go."

Lucien heaved a barrel full of ropes over the side of the ship, and it splashed down into the water below. Then he leaned in close to Journey to say into his ear, "What are we running from?"

"Purple sails," Journey murmured. "Purple sails and death."

Chapter Seven

THOSE sails never showed up on the horizon, and Lucien and the rest of the crew managed to coax enough speed out of the *Jubilee* to keep it that way. Dallion was on edge for two full days, but he finally seemed to relax after that. Journey wondered about the men on the *Tyrant*. He knew what their fate had most likely been, but he didn't want to admit it, even to himself. The ominous ship that Dallion had spoke of in a lowered voice on Stonewell finally seemed real to him. The farther they could stay from the *Huntress*, the better. For now, Journey busied himself with daily tasks and tried not to think about it.

Three weeks passed in a blur of chores, shanties, and rations. Journey was helping Catfish repair a busted barrel on the foredeck one day when Lucien's booming voice called his name from near the bow. He left Catfish to finish up and headed that way, and he arrived to find Dallion and Lucien standing together, looking out toward the horizon ahead. His heart felt like it had dropped into his stomach, and he expected them to point out a cluster of purple sails on the horizon. He raised a hand to shield his eyes from the afternoon sun, and he followed Dallion's pointed finger to spot a lonely speck of green in an otherwise empty sea, instead. As he looked, Pigeon hurried up beside him, and he held out a map full of creases and markings for the other three men to see.

"It's not on this one or any of the others I've checked. I don't have any other land marked until White Crest."

Journey let out his breath in audible relief. It wasn't a ship, but an island. The fact that it wasn't on a map wasn't unheard of; the oceans were vast, and ships often stumbled upon small, unnamed islands during their voyages. Dallion was gripping the top of the ship's banister in excitement, however, and he held his spyglass up to his eye to get a better look. He mused, "It's right where Watty thought it might be."

"The map shows a chain of four islands," Lucien reminded him. "I only see one."

"There might be more. We'll know when we get closer."

The *Jubilee* did get closer, with Pigeon maneuvering her around dangerous shallows that Wee Bit had spotted from atop one of the masts. By the time they were close enough to see that the small island was covered in tall, leafy trees and thick brush, it was clear that there were no other islands within site. By then, Brain had joined the others at the bow, and he gave Dallion a sympathetic pat on the shoulder. "I'm sorry about your islands."

Dallion moped for a moment longer before declaring, "We'll keep up the search. It's out here somewhere."

"I wish we knew someone local," Lucien said, and that must have given Dallion an idea, for he ordered Pigeon to turn the ship south. Lucien asked him, "What's south?"

"Espoir. The port there doesn't care if you aren't flying company colors, if you know what I mean. It's not far from Calico Island, where I grew up."

"And what are we going to do in Espoir?" Lucien pressed.

Dallion shrugged his shoulders. "We'll find ourselves a local."

*　　　*　　　*

A week later, the *Jubilee* put in at Espoir. The seedy town was a smaller, tamer version of Port Kelsey, and as Dallion stepped off the gangway and onto the docks, there was a bounce in his step. Surely, someone here would know more about uncharted islands in the region. If they were lucky, they might even find someone who would recognize the chain of islands they were looking for. If so, he was prepared to pay a pretty price to guide them there.

Lucien and Catfish set to work replenishing the ship's supplies, while Dallion took Journey and Horus with him to find the nearest tavern. They ended up in a dingy, stone building called Maurice's. For such a small town, it was an exceptionally busy place, with all manner of sailing men accounted for. Dallion marched past most of them to head directly to the bar to order a few drinks, first. There were priorities, after all.

Dallion perched himself on a barstool and took a long draw from a glass of rum that an attractive, young bartender poured him. He watched her backside as she walked away to serve someone else farther down the bar and reminded himself not to get distracted from his current goal. Journey was beside him, and as he sipped his own drink, he asked, "What's our next move if we don't get anything new here?"

Dallion frowned. "You weren't always this negative. I remember a time when you would have been just as excited about all of this as I am."

"I'm trying, Dal," Journey replied, but his dismissive tone said otherwise. Dallion's frown didn't go anywhere. From

Journey's left, Horus said something, and the two embarked on a conversation that Dallion couldn't make out over the noisiness that came with having so many people packed into one room. He turned his attention away from them, anyway, and let himself brood over Journey's current attitude. He hadn't expected everything to be the same as it had been three years ago, before Journey had ditched the crew – at Dallion's own urging, admittedly – to take up a life on land. But he also hadn't expected Journey to have changed so drastically. It was as if he'd forgotten how to set aside any semblance of responsibility and simply embrace the moment. Dallion had no doubts that Journey would have his back, if necessary, but he wished that he'd learn to lighten up again, in the meantime.

The bartender walked past him again, and he watched her make her way to the next customer. He was trying to decide whether he should try his luck and flirt with her when the man she was currently serving grabbed his attention, instead. He was tall – almost as tall as Lucien, he thought, although it was hard to be certain while the man was sitting on a stool a short distance down the bar. He was wearing a Dover Trading uniform. As the bartender said something to him, he turned his face so that Dallion could see most of it. He looked familiar, though he couldn't quite place him. He couldn't think of anyone he knew who sailed for Dover, aside from the men he met briefly while raiding their ships. He was going to dismiss the man, but something in him urged him to take another look.

He looked to be just a little older than Dallion was, somewhere in his early thirties. He was clean-shaven, doubtlessly because of some company policy that said he had to be. Dallion watched him as he tossed a few marks on the bar for the drink that the bartender had just poured him. There was something about his movements, his posture, and his very demeanor that spoke of Dallion's past, and when it finally came to him, he almost couldn't believe it.

"Bo," Dallion said aloud, the name startled out of him. He hadn't seen this man in years, since Bo had left Calico to seek a position with Western Straights. He did the math in his head to figure out when that had been. Dallion, himself, had left Calico on the stolen *Ocean Sprite* eight years ago, and Bo had left six years before that. Dallion had been no more than a kid when they'd last spoken, and he was surprised he'd recognized him after all that time.

There was another man in a Dover uniform sitting to Bo's right, but as Dallion watched, he left some money on the bar, clapped Bo on the shoulder, and headed for the door. Bo remained, sipping on whatever he'd ordered a few moments ago. Dallion cast a glance to his left, but Journey and Horus were still conversing about something, and neither of them were paying him any attention. Dallion grabbed his drink and left his stool to saunter down the bar. Bo looked up as Dallion sat down on the stool beside his, but there was no hint of recognition on his part.

"Hurry up and drink that," Dallion said, nodding toward his cup, "so I can buy your next one."

Bo raised an eyebrow. "Generous of you. What brought this on?"

"You don't recognize me?"

Bo studied his face, and after a moment, the first traces of familiarity crossed his. He couldn't quite grasp it, however, so Dallion hinted, "We were kids on Calico together."

"Dallion Romilly!" Bo cried, at last, and Dallion was glad that he was happy to see him. Bo gave his hand a warm shake and marveled, "It's been fourteen years, hasn't it?"

"About that," he agreed. "What are you doing out here? When you left, you said you'd never get close to these islands again."

"Life doesn't always take us where we expect it to," Bo chuckled. "I worked for Western for about five years, but then I switched over to Unique Investments. A few months ago, I started with Dover Trading, instead. I go where the money is, and right now, Dover's offering the most." He noticed for the first time how Dallion was dressed, and the grin on his face faltered. "What about you?"

"I work for a private island owner," he lied. "I have my own ship. It's a good gig."

He seemed convinced. His grin returned as he said, "I'm not that surprised, Dallion. I knew you wouldn't stay on Calico forever. I'm glad you're doing well for yourself."

There was a commotion toward the far end of the bar, where two men were bickering about something. Dallion stood, motioning for Bo to follow him, and led him to a vacant table in the corner of the room. There was less light over here, where the shadows were granted a little more influence. Once they were seated across the small table from each other, Bo shot a glance over his shoulder at the two men who were still arguing and said with a frown, "I hate this place. It's a scummy port with scummier pirates."

"What are you doing here, then?" Dallion asked.

"We hit a storm coming out of White Shores and needed repairs. This was the nearest stop along the way. I think our ship is more likely to get stolen here than it is to get proper repairs, though."

Dallion faked a laugh as he wondered how Bo had become so haughty. Was no one how he remembered them, anymore? That didn't matter, though; Bo wasn't the person that Dallion was most curious about. He asked him, "How's your sister doing?"

Bo paused at this, and for a moment, Dallion's heart seemed to freeze in his chest as a million fears for the woman flooded it. Finally, however, Bo said with a degree of caution, "She's fine. I see her every few months. She's happy."

"Where is she?"

There was another pause. This time, Dallion realized that it was because Bo was trying to decide how much to tell him about her. When he finally gave an answer, it was a vague, "She's living on an island not far from here. Big house, fancy clothes, you name it. Like I said, she's doing fine."

Dallion's heart had started to race, and he couldn't decide if it was just his imagination, or if he could really feel it beating against the shark tooth necklace that was still laying against his chest, even after all these years. He did his best to ignore that and said easily, "That's good to hear. Do you want another drink? I'll buy."

Bo finished off the one he had in one last gulp, then left the empty glass on the table and stood to go. "I need to get back to my ship. I'm a lieutenant, and they're going to be missing me if I'm gone for much longer. It was good seeing you, Dallion. Take care of yourself."

He started for the door, but as he tried to walk past Dallion's chair on his way, Dallion grabbed the sleeve of his uniform jacket. Bo stopped, but heaved a sigh that said he knew exactly what was coming next. "You're really not going to tell me where she is?" Dallion asked, looking up at him from where he was still seated. The shadows in this corner concealed one side of Bo's face, but his eyes were sharp and distrusting, even through the gloom.

He warned, "You need to leave her alone, Dallion. Katria is engaged to a good man. He owns a few islands. He's partnered with Whitefish. They'll be married in a month. She has a good life. I know that you two were fond of each other as kids, but that needs to stay in the past. She's a grown woman with adult responsibilities and decisions to make now."

Dallion let go of his sleeve to raise his hands in mock defensiveness. "It's not like that. To be honest, I'm kind of insulted that you'd think like that. I'm just curious about an old friend. I mean, I'm married, myself. I'm not interested in Kat like that, anymore."

Bo studied his face as well as the shadows would allow, clearly trying to decide if he believed that or not. He asked, "What's your wife's name?"

"Saige Moore," he answered without hesitation. "She's a good girl from Kinsmen. Gorgeous. We've got one kid and another one on the way."

Bo relaxed a little at that, even enough to say, "Congratulations."

"It was just so good to see you again after all these years, it got me curious about Katria. I'd like to send her and her fiancé a wedding gift. What island are they on?"

He struggled internally, but Dallion gave him his most earnest grin and urged, "Come on, Bo. It's for old time's sake. I'm too busy to go all the way out there to visit. I'll just have to send the gift by courier."

"Quill Island," he said, at last. "Her fiancé is Gerald Tailor. He owns that island and four more. Like I said, they're doing very well for themselves."

Dallion forced a believable smile. "I'll let my wife, Saige, pick something out for them. She's good at that kind of stuff."

Bo only nodded and placed a hand on his shoulder to give it a squeeze. "Take care of yourself, Dallion." With that, he was gone, headed for the door with his hands shoved deep in his pockets. Dallion watched him, and as soon as the door was closed behind him, he got to his feet and hurried back to the bar. Journey and Horus were still where he'd left them, but they were now speaking to the bartender. Journey was asking her about uncharted islands, but he stopped in midsentence when Dallion gripped his shoulder from behind him. Journey turned on his stool enough to see that it was him, but then turned back to the bartender to continue his question. She replied that she didn't know of any such islands, but didn't shy from refilling his drink without being asked. Once she had walked away, Dallion tugged on Journey's shoulder.

"We're leaving," he announced, but Journey and Horus only looked at him, surprised.

"We've hardly asked anyone..." Horus started, but Dallion ignored him. Instead, he leaned to whisper in Journey's ear.

"I know where Katria Laurent is," he told him. He was breathing hard, as if his excitement was almost too much to bear. "Quill Island, Journey. That's where I need to go."

"What about the *Cherub*?"

"Wherever it is, it's been there for this long. It can wait a few more days." He gave Journey's shoulder another tug. This time, Journey stood, and Dallion started ushering him toward the door.

"Are we leaving already?" Horus called after them.

"Come on," Journey told him. "Captain's orders."

CHAPTER EIGHT

ACCORDING to Brain, Quill Island was a mere ten hours away, if the winds were right. They were, and it came into view just after sunrise. Journey found that it was large for a private island, and it boasted its own lighthouse and bustling harbor. By the looks of activity in it, even so early in the morning, Quill was an industrious place. Huge blue and white banners attested to the island's partnership with The Whitefish Trading Company. Considering the bounty they'd placed on Dallion's head, it should have made the man nervous, but Journey could only find excitement on his friend's face. He told Pigeon to maneuver the *Jubilee* around to the other side of the island, where they would keep her just far enough off shore to be out of sight. He'd told the crew that this had something to do with following up a lead he'd gotten in Espoir. Journey knew that was a lie, but if anyone else on the ship suspected the same, they were hiding it well. As far as Journey could tell, even Lucien had been kept in the dark. That didn't sit well with him, but he wasn't about to call Dallion out in front of anyone else over it. For now, he'd play along.

Once the *Jubilee* had heaved to just out of sight of the island, Quick Bill and Wee Bit readied the longboat. Dallion evaded Lucien's questions about his plan and instead announced that only he and Journey were going ashore. That only made

Lucien more suspicious – Journey could tell by the furl of the man's brow and the piercing gaze he'd fixed on Dallion. He didn't object, however, and he seemed to relax when Journey assured him that he'd keep a steady eye on Dallion. Whatever he had up his sleeve, Journey was confident that he'd be able to keep him from doing anything too crazy.

Maybe.

They took turns rowing to the island and found an uninhabited swath of beach, where they stashed the longboat between two palm trees and covered it with fallen fronds. It was a steep climb up a stony hillside that bordered on a cliff, but they made it to the top without incident. Once there, Journey found himself on the edge of a small, grassy field. On the other side of it, stone and wooden buildings were laid out in the neat, straight lines of a grid pattern. The land sloped gently downward toward the harbor on the other side of the island. Atop a hill that towered over the eastern side, an impressive mansion looked out over the rest of the island around it. Its white walls reflected the morning sunlight beautifully.

Dallion started across the field, headed in the direction of the mansion, but Journey didn't follow him, yet. Dallion realized this after marching only a few yards, and when he turned back to Journey, he crossed his arms at his chest with impatience and said, "Daylight's burning."

Journey studied him with narrowed eyes. He asked, "How far are you willing to go for this girl?"

Dallion flashed him a smile that told him he would have sailed to the ends of the Realm, if he had to, but shrugged. "I'm just going to pay her a visit and see if she remembers me. But you're going to have to do the talking to get us in the house. There's no way they'll believe I'm any company's partner. Just say that you need to talk to Katria Laurent."

"This is a bad idea."

"What's the worst that can happen?"

"This is Whitefish territory," Journey reminded him, but Dallion had already resumed his march across the field. Journey followed him, finally certain that they were getting into something they shouldn't...but he'd sailed with Dallion long enough to expect that.

*   *   *

HAROLD Hackett had worked in Quill Manor since he'd been nineteen years old. He had started in the kitchen, performing menial tasks beneath the watchful eye of the cooks, but had since spent the last twenty years rising through the ranks of the house servants to become the head butler. He had served Gregory Tailor well, and now served his son, Gerald. During his two decades in the family's service, he had welcomed a great number of visitors through the front door of the mansion, but none of them had ever dared to come calling while dressed like the two young men to whom he opened the door that afternoon. The slightly taller of the two wasn't so bad, with a collared shirt and a hairstyle that spoke of frequent care. His companion, however, was a seafarer if he'd ever seen one, and one who was not likely under anyone's employ but his own. If his tanned, salt-licked skin hadn't given him away, the abundance of jewelry adorning his ears and hands certainly would have. He had the gull to give a curt bow, as if thinking that he might somehow be able to pass for a gentleman.

Hackett frowned at the sight of them as they stood in the doorway of the mansion's foyer. "I'm afraid you missed the service entrance. It's around back."

The one with the earrings flashed him a smile that he didn't trust, but he supposed it had charmed many a young girl. His companion was the one who spoke, however, and it was clear that he, at least, had received a proper education and upbringing. "I understand how unprofessional and discourteous it is to show up without an invitation, but I hope you'll forgive us. I'm here on behalf of our mutual parent company. It's imperative that I speak with Miss Laurent about an urgent matter of business."

Hackett eyed him carefully. "Miss Laurent's fiancé, Mr. Tailor, handles all matters of business. He isn't currently home."

"Her fiancé," Journey repeated, shooting a hard glance at Dallion beside him. "I see."

"It's a very urgent matter," Dallion pressed. "I'm sure Miss Laurent will want to know about it, so she can pass it along to Jerry as soon as he gets home."

Hackett's expression was one of disgust, but he stepped aside so that they could enter, instructing, "Please wait in the foyer. I'll ask Miss Laurent if she cares to meet with you."

Journey led Dallion inside. The mansion's foyer was decorated with gaudily-framed paintings of ships at sea. A chandelier hung from the middle of the vaulted ceiling, and the marble floor was shiny enough to see reflections in. The mansion that Journey shared with Saige was stunning, but this place managed to put it to shame.

"What name may I provide Miss Laurent?" Hackett asked Journey.

"John Stonewell," he answered, and if he'd hesitated for a brief moment before doing so, Hackett didn't seem to notice. Journey and Dallion watched as the older man withdrew through a large archway that led into the rest of the mansion beyond. As soon as he was gone, Journey dropped any sense of false pleasantness and glared at Dallion. "You forgot to mention that she's engaged to someone named Gerald."

"Relax," Dallion told him as he sat down on an elegant couch that rested against one of the walls and was flanked by two paintings of dramatic naval battles. "Like I said: I just want to see if she remembers me. This is a friendly visit. It isn't anything else."

Journey pointed a single finger at him, warning him not to do anything that would make himself a liar, but he knew Dallion too well to think that it would make any difference. They waited in silence for a few minutes, until the sound of footfalls reached their ears from the next room. Dallion stood from the couch, and Journey saw a great deal of anxious hope on his friend's face.

She was gorgeous. Journey hadn't known what to expect about his friend's childhood love, but the woman who stepped into the foyer possessed a deep, compelling beauty that might have brought any man to his knees. Her raven hair was pinned up in a fancy style that allowed a few ringlets to frame her face. Her olive skin was flawless, and her lovely face was the perfect setting for those dark eyes. She was wearing a green dress that accentuated her thin frame in all the right ways. A large emerald hung from a slim, silver chain around her neck. It had been cut in the shape of a heart.

She was focused on Journey, who was standing in the center of the room. He gave her a polite bow, but as she reached him and offered her hand, she said, "I'm sorry, Mr. Stonewell, but you've come at the wrong time to talk business. My fiancé is the person you need to speak to, and he's not home."

Journey placed a polite kiss on the back of her hand. Her skin was just as soft as it looked. He offered her a smile that she reflected back as he said, "I understand, Ms. Laurent. Before I leave, however, I think my colleague wanted to discuss something else with you."

Her dark eyes went to Dallion for the first time, and they narrowed slightly. He was standing near the couch, his hands clasped together before him. For a moment, it seemed like she was going to recognize him, but then a shadow of doubt crossed her face. She asked him, "Have we met before?"

Dallion didn't answer, but crossed the foyer on legs that felt weak. Journey stepped aside, and as Dallion reached Katria, she offered her hand again out of habit. Instead of kissing it, Dallion took her hand in his own and turned it so that her palm was facing up. He felt a sort of electric shock when he touched her for the first time in thirteen years, and he wondered if she felt it, too. There was something clenched in his other hand, and he placed it on her palm. Then he gently folded her fingers over it before she could see what it was. She didn't have to see it. Her eyes widened in delight and something else that Dallion could only hope was still love. Katria gaped, but no words would come. She searched eyes the color of the sea and found the boy she'd left on the beach so long ago.

"Kat…" he began, but that was as far as he got before she threw her arms around him, crying out in disbelief. He laughed and hugged her tightly. He breathed in the soft scent of her hair, but all he really smelled was the saltiness of the sea at the edge of Calico Island all those years ago.

Then, just as quickly as she'd embraced him, she let him go and stepped back, painfully aware of Hackett's alarmed gaze. He'd followed her into the foyer and had posted himself obediently in the corner. Katria took a deep breath to rein herself back in, then said with an air of professionalism, "I'm glad you were able to stop by. Gerald will be back in two days. You'll have to come back then to talk business with him."

Dallion's joy was ripped from him, and she would have seen that in his face if she'd dared to look at him again. Instead, she kept her gaze on Journey and told him, "I'm sorry."

"Me, too," Journey said quietly. Dallion whispered her name, and she finally looked at him. There were tears in her eyes that promised to smear the dark makeup around them.

"It was good to see you again," she told him with a quivering voice. "Come back when Gerald's home. Maybe we'll all have dinner together."

"Are you kidding me?" he scoffed, but Katria's only answer was to turn and start back for the archway, asking Hackett as she went to show their guests to the door. Dallion called her name again after her, but she didn't stop, and Journey set a calming hand on Dallion's shoulder. He watched as she disappeared around the corner into the next room, and a pain that he hadn't felt in thirteen years radiated from his broken heart.

*   *   *

HACKETT saw them out with an obvious sense of satisfaction, and he made sure to close the door behind them with a little more force than was necessary. Once they were alone, Journey turned to Dallion, expecting to find a miserable look on his friend's face. Instead, he found sheer determination, and that made him uneasy. He tried, "I'm sorry, Dal. Maybe it's for the best…"

"Go back to the boat," he said, starting down the steps of the mansion. The hillside before it sloped down toward the town, and a paved road wound its way down it. Dallion headed in that direction, but Journey caught up to him before he could get very far, and he grabbed his shoulder to stop him.

"This isn't the time for some sort of breakdown," Journey cautioned, but Dallion only gave a dry laugh, shaking his hand off of his shoulder to continue down the hill.

"You think I'm going to go crawl into a bottle somewhere and cry my heart out?" he asked. "You know me better than that. I'll take care of this. You go back to the boat and I'll meet you there tonight."

"Dallion…"

"That's an order, Prince."

Journey grabbed his shoulder again, but this time, he gave it a firm yank that stopped Dallion in his tracks. He turned to face him, and the resolve on his face told Journey that there was nothing in all the Realms that could change his mind about this. Even so, he pressed, "She's marrying another guy, Dal. She'd have to be insane to give up everything that she has here for someone she had a crush on as a kid. You see that, don't you?"

"It wasn't a crush," Dallion muttered. He shook his hand off once more, but didn't continue down the hill, yet. Instead, he searched Journey's eyes for understanding and said, "You told me that Saige once said she never wanted to see you again. Where would you be right now if you'd listened to her? Aren't you glad that you didn't?"

"This is different. Saige invited me back to Stonewell because she'd changed her mind. Katria just told you not to come back here unless her fiancé is home. What the hell do you think she's trying to tell you?"

"That I have to try harder," he grinned, and there was so much roguishness in the gesture that Journey was half-convinced that he would actually be able to do this.

He had no doubt that Dallion wasn't going to change his mind, however, and standing out here in front of this mansion while they argued wasn't going to help anything. Journey told him, "Don't do anything that'll land you in jail. I won't come save your ass this time."

"I'll be back before morning," he promised. Journey gave him a look that said he'd come drag him away from here if that wasn't the case. Dallion believed it.

Chapter Nine

IT was a full moon that night, and the white walls of the mansion were bathed in its ghostly light. A cool breeze was coming in off the sea, and it brushed back Dallion's hair as he scaled the stone wall that surrounded the property. He paused when he reached the top of it and scanned the moonlit patios and gardens for any signs of life. There were none. If Gerald Tailor kept anyone on staff to patrol the grounds at night, they weren't within sight. It was now or never.

He lowered himself over the other side of the wall and landed squarely on his feet. Then he ran, hunched and silent, down the gravel path of a garden that meandered between flowering shrubs and bushes that had been trimmed into the shapes of rearing horses. He crouched at the base of one of them and peered up the tall walls of the mansion before him. The windows appeared to be staring down at him like the square eyes of an immovable giant, and he was surprised by how intimidated he felt. He'd robbed plenty of places like this before…but the prize behind these windows was worth far more to him than any gold or fine wine he'd ever hauled.

Tall, twisting vines of jasmine clung to decorative trellises between most of the windows, and he supposed that was as good a way to start his search as any. He abandoned the shadows beside the bushes and darted to the wall, where he seized hold of the nearest trellis. The crisscrossed wood was sturdy and secure against the wall, and when he tested it to see if it could hold his weight, it didn't budge. He started to climb, the sweet scent of jasmine in his nose. He worked his way up to the windows of the second floor and peeked inside to find a billiards room behind the window on his right and a large study, complete with a desk and several bookshelves, on his left. He was going to try to force one of the windows open to get inside, but then a flutter of the edge of a curtain caught his eye, and he saw that a window on the other side of the next trellis had been left open to allow the night's cool breeze to make its way inside. Dallion grinned. Katria had always claimed that fresh air brought good dreams.

He gripped the edge of the windowsill to his right, and after a brief moment of wondering if he was about to fall and break a leg or two, he let go of the trellis and allowed himself to dangle from the thin ledge beneath the window. He slid his right hand over a few inches, followed carefully by his left. He repeated the process several times, making his way slowly toward the other side of the window. He was almost within reach of the next trellis when his left hand slipped, and as his body swung dangerously to that side, he got a good look at the hard, flat patio stones below. His heart threatened to climb up into his throat, but before he could panic, his left hand found the safety of the windowsill again. He let out a breath of relief as he reached out with his right hand and grasped the lattice once again.

He made his way to the open window, and when he looked inside, he found exactly what he'd expected: a spacious, well-decorated bedroom. It was dark inside, but he could make out the shadowy shapes of a couch with a tall back, a bookcase, and a fireplace that was currently cold and dead. The canopied bed that sat against one wall was what caught his attention, however, and there was only one human-shaped lump beneath the blankets on it. Her back was to the window, and her black hair was pooled in gentle curls across her pillow.

Dallion left the trellis behind and climbed through the window, lowering his boots to the floor as quietly as he could. Then he simply stood there, trying to decide what to do next. He'd spent the entire afternoon and evening thinking up a speech that he would use to sway her, but now that he was so near her, he couldn't remember any of it. That may have had something to do with the ales he'd had while coming up with that speech in a tavern at the bottom of the hill, but he'd been careful not to get drunk.

She spoke without turning, startling him. Her voice was calm, but she warned, "If I scream, a dozen servants are going to come running."

"I'd rather you didn't," he replied, and in his own voice, he heard the same, timid hope that he felt within his heart. "If you really want me to leave, I will. But I think you should hear me out first."

She sat up, letting her blanket fall to her lap, and the moonlight outside shone over his shoulder to fall across her. She was wearing a thin nightgown that swooped dangerously low, and he had to concentrate on keeping his gaze above her shoulders. The soft light played tricks in her hair, and her pretty eyes shone in it. It was strange to think that although she had changed so much since he'd last seen her – they'd parted as hardly more than children, after all – he felt as if no time had passed at all. There was a mirror in the corner of the room, and there was just enough light to reveal his reflection. In it, he found a man who had seen a great deal of action over the years, and it hadn't all been kind to him. There was a scar on the side of his neck, left there by a bullet, and the flesh there had hardened into a gnarled scar. His dark hair was tied up in a ponytail behind his head, and it clearly needed a wash. The shadow of coming whiskers on his cheeks tattled that he hadn't shaved recently, and the earrings and necklaces that he'd collected over the years weren't going to impress a woman whose fiancé owned a mansion like the one he was standing in now. When he turned his attention back to Katria, however, he didn't find any hints of disdain, and that spurred on the hope within him.

She whispered, "I never thought I'd see you again," she said. It was hardly more than a whisper. "After this long, why come to me, now?"

"You said it wouldn't matter how long it took."

Her lips turned toward a smile, but it was a wistful one. "We both said a lot of things, Dallion. But we were just kids."

There was a jolt of joy when he heard his name on her lips, but it was followed immediately by the pain that her next sentence brought him. He tried not to let her see any hint of the bizarre ride his emotions were currently taking. He sat against the windowsill, not speaking. He didn't have anything to say to that, anyway.

Katria told him, "I went back to Calico. There's no way you could know that, but I went back for you. I was eighteen. I asked around, but everyone said you'd stolen a ship and had gone off pirating. I wasn't that surprised, to be honest. You were always the rebellious type." She laughed, but there was only sadness in the sound. "I'd only missed you by a few months. I didn't have any way to track you down. So I decided that you would come find me if you still felt the same way, and I moved on with my life in the meantime."

"I was afraid you'd changed your mind," he confessed without meeting her gaze. His hands were in his lap as his butt rested against the windowsill, and he kept his eyes on them. "I thought exactly what you just said: we were just kids. Not knowing where you were was easier than finding you and having you turn me away. So I didn't look. I was a coward."

"Then why have you come here, now?"

"I ran into Bo," he said, forcing himself to look at her again. His fear of her rejection didn't make it easy. "I couldn't believe it was him, at first. I asked about you. He told me not to come find you here because he didn't want me bothering you. He said that you've made a good life for yourself."

"I have," she said, and her tone was a little sharper than she'd intended.

He continued, "Once I knew where you were, I couldn't stay away. I realized that it was worth it to see you one more time, even if you only sent me away. I couldn't help it, Kat. I still…" He trailed off before he could speak the words, and she pretended not to know what he'd been about to say.

"I have no choice but to send you away," she breathed, and the moonlight sparkled off of tears that threatened to fall from her eyes. "I'm engaged to be married. I'm doing well here, Dallion. It's an easy life."

"Is that what you want?" he asked, and this time, his tone was sharp. "You just want an easy, boring life? That's not what the girl I used to know would have wanted."

"That girl doesn't exist anymore. We've both grown up." The tears fell, at last, to course down her cheeks. She cried, "I waited for you for years, and you never came! I've made promises since then. I've given my word and I can't break it."

"I don't give a shit about promises you've made to anyone else," he growled. His hands were fists, but he knew that it was fear; not anger; that was gripping him now. "You swore to me on the beach on Calico that you would love me forever. We might have been kids, but we were old enough to know how we felt. If you don't feel that way anymore, then you should just tell me that. I'll leave. You'll never have to see me again. But I don't think you're going to say it, Kat, because I know how you felt that day, and I don't think that thirteen years is enough to ruin that."

Her lips were trembling, but she didn't speak. Dallion felt hot tears on his own face now. He didn't move to wipe them away. Instead, he pressed, "Say you don't love me anymore. If it's true, you should say it."

"You need to leave," she said, but those weren't the words he'd dared her to speak, and that was an answer in itself.

He left the windowsill and crossed the short distance to her bed. She demanded to know what he was doing, but he said nothing as he sat on the edge of the bed and began taking his boots off. She shoved his shoulder with one hand, telling him to leave again, but he ignored it. Once his feet were bare, he threw back the blankets on this side of the bed and laid down beneath them. He didn't touch her, but draped one arm over his eyes to block out the moonlight and said, "I'm tired. I'll leave in the morning."

"You can't stay here," she hissed, casting a glance toward the bedroom door. "What if someone finds you in here? You know what it'll look like. This isn't funny."

"I'll leave in the morning," he repeated.

She fell silent, and he waited for what seemed like a very long time as she struggled to decide what to do. He almost expected her to call for servants, just as she'd threatened. They would burst through the door and drag him out. Whoever the local sheriff was would charge him with trespassing and probably all of the terrible things that could be assumed by finding him in a respectable woman's bed in the middle of the night. Katria would have an amusing story to tell her fellow socialites at the next gala or dinner party she attended. Gerald would commend her on her bravery and would promise to hire a nightguard to keep her safe from riffraff in the future.

She did none of those things. Instead, she settled back into the bed beside him, and after only a moment's hesitation, she moved to press herself against his side. He took his arm away from his face to slip it around her instead, and pulled her closer. Her hair smelled of a gentle perfume that reminded him of the jasmine flowers outside. It had smelled just as sweet on the day they'd parted on Calico Island, surrounded by warm sand and the sound of the ocean. He closed his eyes and let his dreams take him back to that place, at last.

*　　*　　*

HE woke a few hours later to find her still in his arms. The moon had moved in the sky and was no longer lighting the room, and it was choked with a heavy darkness. He got out of bed and fumbled his way to the fireplace, where he felt along the mantle until his fingertips found a tinder box. He squatted down before the fireplace, and as he worked, he heard Katria stirring in the bed behind him. She said nothing, however, and he focused on lighting a fire. Finally, flames sprang up from the sparks he'd sent into the tinder, and the fire's warm light filled the room.

He turned to find that was sitting up on the bed, considering him carefully in the glow. Dallion retrieved his boots and sat down on the edge of the bed to begin lacing them up. As he did, Katria asked with a timidness that wasn't like her, "Are you leaving?"

"I need to get going so I can meet Journey before sunrise."

"Is he your captain?"

He snorted, insulted by the thought. "I'm the captain. I have my own ship and crew. She's the *Jubilee*. You're going to love her. But Journey has the longboat, and that's our ride back to the ship."

"What are you talking about?"

He finished with his boots and turned to face her on the bed. Her hair was messy around her head, but she was still the most beautiful woman he'd ever seen. He urged, "Come with me. Leave your stuffy fiancé behind and don't look back."

She shook her head. "You're crazy."

"So are you. That's why we're such a perfect fit for each other, remember?"

"I remember all the wedding plans I've been making. I remember the guest list, and the dress that's hanging up in the next room, and the honeymoon I've been looking forward to. Those are the things I remember."

He leaned closer to her on the bed, until his face was only a few inches from hers and he could smell her perfume again. He whispered, "I'm a fucking pirate, Kat. I don't have any problem with throwing you over my shoulder and taking you down to the shore by force."

Her eyes narrowed. "You wouldn't dare."

He threw himself on top of her, pinning her to the bed with one arm while tickling her side with his free hand. She squealed and tried to squirm away from him, but his bodyweight kept her from going anywhere. His fingers were separated from her flesh by only the thin material of her nightgown, and he wished more than anything that the gown wasn't there. She did her best to muffle her laughter, but it was too late. If any servants were in the hall right now, they would have heard her.

He stopped tickling her, and for a moment, they caught their breaths in silence. He was propped on his elbows above her, but everything below their waists was pressed tightly together. A few strands of his hair had come loose from their tie to dangle against his right cheek. Katria lifted her hand to brush them behind his ear. As he looked into her eyes, the words he'd been too afraid to speak before slipped effortlessly between his lips.

"I love you, Katria."

She said nothing, at first, as her brown eyes searched his blue ones. Dallion raised his eyebrows, prying for a response, even if it wasn't the one he wanted so badly to hear.

"You're crazy," she assured him once more. Then her lips parted in a daring smile.

Chapter Ten

JOURNEY had managed to get a little sleep in the longboat, but after a few hours, his body ached so terribly that he gave up and opted to sit in the sand near the waterline to watch the nighttime sea. The sun would be rising soon, and he could only hope that Dallion kept his word to be back here before then. There was a cold wind skirting along the beach now, and the drop in temperature signaled a coming storm. The waves licking the shore hadn't turned rough, yet, but he didn't doubt that they soon would. Until then, he listened to those waves and thought of Saige. What was she dreaming of right now? Did she miss his touch as much as he missed hers? He could almost hear her sweet voice in the sound of the waves, and he wished more than anything for a kiss from her soft lips.

Just as the first traces of light snuck into the world, Journey heard lowered voices from somewhere beyond the two trees that were still flanking the longboat. He got to his feet and peered through the dissipating gloom, and after a moment, two figures emerged from the darkness beyond the trees. One of them laughed, and he would have recognized that sound anywhere. Dallion had returned, after all, and he wasn't alone.

He met them at the boat, and Katria was almost unrecognizable from the woman he'd met the day before. Her hair was now in a long braid, and instead of an extravagant dress, she was wearing a pair of men's boots and pants that were far too big for her. She'd cinched the waist with a belt to keep them from falling down. Likewise, her fancy, silk shirt was too large, and Journey wondered how badly Gerald Tailor was going to miss his clothes…and his fiancée.

She knew Journey from their meeting yesterday, and she gave him a somewhat sheepish smile from across the beached longboat. Even without the fancy makeup she'd been wearing the first time they'd met, he couldn't deny that she was beautiful. Her fingers were entwined with Dallion's own, and Journey didn't think he'd ever seen the man so proud or pleased. Journey shook his head in wonder, and Dallion's smile broadened.

"Katria decided that she needs a little break from island life," he explained. "She's going to be sailing with us for a while."

"No offense," Journey told her, "but you must be insane."

Katria offered him a wink that he knew to be trouble and agreed, "That's looking likelier and likelier as the day goes on, and the sun hasn't even risen, yet."

"What are you going to tell Lucien?" he asked Dallion. "There are rules about this kind of thing. And I don't think that 'captain's privilege' is going to work for this."

"Don't worry about that. I've got a plan." He let go of Katria's hand so he could grip the front of the longboat. When Journey didn't move to help him right away, he pressed, "We need to hurry. We can't lollygag during a kidnapping."

Journey had never known of a kidnapping in which the "victim" was so willing to be whisked away, but he didn't argue the point. He helped Dallion get the boat into the water. Once it was floating, he considered the half a dozen or so yards of water between the boat and the shore. Before he could decide how they were going to get a lady across such a gap, Katria dismissed his concerns by sloshing into the salty water on her own. She seemed unperturbed as it rose up to the middle of her thighs. Journey cast another glance at Dallion to find that he was grinning again. The haughty, refined version of the woman they'd met in the mansion had been left there, it seemed.

Once they were all in the boat, Katria perched herself at the front of it, her eager eyes peering out at the open sea, and she announced, "Let's go, boys! No time to waste."

*   *   *

THEY made good time in the longboat, which was exactly what they needed to do – there was a storm coming in from the west, from the feel of it, and Lucien wouldn't be able to keep the *Jubilee* heaved to out there if it got too close. They rowed with everything they had, and a few minutes after sunrise, they were close enough to the *Jubilee* to hear one of the crewmen call from her upper topsail that he'd spotted the longboat. Before long, Dallion, Journey, and their guest were hauled up to the deck, and a small group gathered around to get a look at the enticing specimen they'd brought aboard. Before Dallion could introduce her, he found Lucien standing before him, his arms crossed at his chest.

"Who is she?" he asked without taking his eyes off of Dallion to look at her.

Dallion raised his hands in a calming gesture and announced to the crew that had gathered around, "This is Katria Laurent. She's here to help us find the cache of the *Weeping Cherub*. She's a maps expert."

There were a few murmurs at this, and Lucien raised an eyebrow. "A maps expert?"

"That's right," Dallion agreed, and looked at Katria for affirmation. She ignored the men who had surrounded them to gawk at her and looked Lucien in the eye.

"My father was a cartographer. He taught me everything I know. Captain Romilly promised me a small portion of his share of whatever treasure I help you find."

Lucien glanced at Journey to see if he'd confirm this, but Journey was gazing out over the open sea, as if he didn't want to be a part of the conversation. Dallion clapped Lucien on the shoulder and assured him, "She's good at what she does. She'll help us find our islands."

"Of course," he agreed, but there was nothing in his tone that said he believed a word of it. Dallion called for the men to get the ship ready to go, then motioned for Katria to follow him toward his cabin. Once they were gone and the others were scurrying to get the *Jubilee* under way, Lucien joined Journey at the banister and leaned against it beside him.

"Who is she?" he asked, keeping his voice low to avoid letting others overhear.

"I'm not going to take sides on this one," Journey answered, his gaze still on the sea. "Take Dallion at his word about it, or don't. Either way, she's coming with us."

"There are rules against it for a reason. A woman on board is nothing but trouble. We only made an exception for Saige because we needed her to get the money from Horizon."

"You don't believe this girl's a maps expert?"

Lucien leaned closer to him and growled, "Do I look like I was born yesterday?"

Journey laughed at that. The sound made Lucien relax a little, but he warned, "If anything bad happens because of her, I'll tell Pigeon to set course for the nearest port. I'll drag her off this ship kicking and screaming, if I have to. I don't care what Dallion has to say about it."

Journey only nodded, knowing better than to argue with him. Besides, he was right about two things: there *was* a rule against bringing women on board, and there *was* good reason for it. He hoped that Dallion knew what he was doing.

He left Lucien at the banister and helped get the ship underway. Before long, the *Jubilee* was putting Quill Island behind her.

Chapter Eleven

"OF course it's all blue," Katria smiled. She was standing in the middle of his cabin, looking around with unconcealed curiosity. "You were never very good at telling other colors apart."

"And you weren't good at not making fun of me for it," Dallion agreed. He was standing at the small table in the corner, upon which he kept a few bottles of liquor. He poured two glasses and then joined her in the middle of the cabin to offer her one. She accepted it with thanks and took a sip. She didn't know what it was, but it wasn't rum. She embraced the pleasant burn that traveled down the back of her throat.

She noticed that he was watching her, and she smiled at him after another sip from her glass. "What are you going to do when Gerald tracks us down? He owns some of the fastest ships in the region, and I doubt he's going to let me go without a fight."

Dallion finished his glass in three long gulps, then returned it to the table. "If he can hunt this ship down, he'll be doing something that none of the companies have been able to do, so far."

"You're just as cocky as I remember you being."

"And you're a better liar," he grinned. He went to the bed and stretched out on it, then turned onto his side to face her. "I don't think Lucien believed you when you told him that your old man was a cartographer, but everyone else probably did."

"What happens when I can't back it up?" she asked, coming to the bed to sit down on the edge of it. He patted the vacant part of the blanket beside him, but she shook her head.

Unperturbed, he replied, "You're either going to have to fake it or find another way to be useful around here."

"I can sail."

He chuckled at that, but she scowled. "I'm not joking. I convinced Gerald to let me go on a couple of business trips over the last year or so. I managed to get the men on board to teach me to sail. They wouldn't let me climb any higher than the lower topsail, but I learned everything I could. Besides, Gerald has a library in the mansion, and I read all the books about sailing that I could get my hands on."

"What did you learn from the books?" he teased. "Or were you just looking at their pretty pictures?"

Katria glared at him. "The *Jubilee* is a two-masted brigantine with a square-rigged main and foremast. It's more common to have one square sail above the gaff on the main mast, but you've got two. What can you get from her? Ten knots?"

"Eleven," he said, not trying to conceal his awe. "And I think I just fell in love with you all over again."

She tipped her glass toward him in a cheers motion, then took a long draw from it. As she drank, Dallion told her, "If anyone gets nosy, we'll tell them that I'm sleeping on the floor in here at night because you didn't want to sleep in the hammocks with the rest of the crew."

"Of course, we'll tell them that," she said. "You really are going to be sleeping on the floor."

He seemed surprised by this, and she laughed. The sound was music to his ears. "You think that just because I came with you on this ship, you get to do whatever you want with me?"

"No," he claimed, but then added, "I was hoping, though."

She gave him a look that said to keep dreaming. "You just pulled me out of a relationship that gave me lots of money and some pretty good sex. You don't think you're going to have to work for what you want?"

"Pretty good sex? Poor thing. How am I supposed to show you what you've been missing out on if I can't show you what amazing sex is like?"

She gave him a sly wink that made him want her even more. "You'll just have to get creative."

Dallion threw his head back and laughed. It was the only thing he could think of to do besides getting on his knees and begging her for what he wanted. Katria tossed back the rest of the alcohol in her glass, then went to the table to refill it herself.

Chapter Twelve

BERTRAND Fleury stood an impressive six foot, four inches tall. His fortieth birthday was only a few months away, but he didn't feel it. He had blond hair that he kept trimmed short, now that he was a Whitefish employee. The company had rules about hygiene and appearances. They also had rules that made him impossible to argue with, as captain. His first mate carried out most of the duties that a quartermaster would have had on a pirate ship, and he was tasked with being unquestionably loyal to his captain. Whitefish had assigned a middle-aged man named Carter to the role, and it was obvious to anyone who cared that Carter's sole purpose in life was to become captain of one of Whitefish's ships someday. That was just fine by Fleury, as it meant that Carter didn't dare defy him or even question his judgements. The rest of the crew fell in line behind him. At the start, there had been occasional grumbles about serving under an ex-pirate, but Carter had quelled these complaints swiftly and without mercy. If the wise and powerful head of The Whitefish Trading Company thought it was a good idea to make Fleury a captain, then that decision would be respected. Period.

Fleury had proven them right, so far. The number of pirate ships he'd destroyed wasn't as high as all the rumors claimed, but it was close. It was easy, since Fleury had been one of their own for years. He knew all of the best hiding places, all of the ports that were willing to welcome known pirates, and all of the easy targets that were likely to attract a pirate attack. It also didn't hurt that they'd given him the fastest ship he'd ever seen. The *Huntress* could top fourteen knots, which was fast enough to run down anything her captain felt inclined to chase. With forty cannons and a crew of almost two hundred men, she was likely the most powerful thing on the seas.

Standing near her bow, Fleury peered through his spyglass at another ship in the distance. It was difficult to tell from so far away, but he thought she was a brigantine. She was leaving Quill Island, which was a respectable port, but when he'd first spotted her, she'd been leaving from the backside of the island, for some reason. He couldn't see which flag she was flying from here, if any. Carter was beside him, awaiting his orders, and he now prompted, "Do we pursue, sir?"

There was no way that he could be certain that she was a pirate ship... but he had a feeling in his gut that said she was. Either way, it wouldn't hurt to get a closer look. He gave Carter the order, and he hurried to make it happen. Fleury took his spyglass away from his eye and turned his gaze west. A storm was approaching from that direction, sporting dark, menacing clouds and a promise of rain. The brigantine wasn't headed directly toward it, but she was on a route that would take her closer to it than was likely a good idea, if the storm happened to swing northward a few degrees. Perhaps she was a trading vessel, then, on a course determined by a captain who was dedicated to keeping a tight schedule.

There was only one way to find out.

Chapter Thirteen

JOURNEY and Lucien knocked on the door to Dallion's cabin. There were sounds of frantic scrambling from the other side. After a few seconds, Dallion's voice called for them to come in, and Journey opened the door to find Katria sitting in a chair at the small table inside. Two maps were spread out before her on it, and she was pretending to study them. Neither Journey nor Lucien commented on the fact that one of them was upside-down. There was a wooden chest at the foot of Dallion's bed, and he was sitting on it. There was a look of unbelievable innocence on his face.

"Ms. Laurent and I are going over some of the maps…" he started, but Lucien waved this off as he came into the cabin, clearly not interested in whatever lies he was going to tell.

"Pigeon says he can skirt the storm, but the waves might get a little rough."

"It would be helpful if we knew exactly where we were heading," Journey added.

Dallion shrugged. "Keep going west. Tomorrow, we'll start another grid pattern. That's the best we can do right now."

"This is like searching for a needle in a haystack," Lucien warned. "I don't think anyone's interested in spending the next six or eight months running grids."

Dallion started to respond, likely to reassure him that they would come up with something else before then, but Lil Gabe burst through the ajar door behind Lucien.

"Purple sails!" he cried, and although Katria didn't know what that meant, she saw looks of true terror the faces of every man in the room. Lil Gabe told them, "She's behind us. Jimmy Two-Tales spotted her. Horus says we need more speed."

Lucien cursed under his breath and ushered his son back through the door in a hurry. Dallion left the wooden chest to follow them. Katria dared to ask, "What is it?"

"An angel of death," Dallion answered, and the pale complexion that his face had taken on told Journey that he honestly believed that. Journey hurried after him at a jog, and he couldn't help but wonder if Katria regretted leaving the safety of her fiancée's island, yet.

*   *   *

OUT on the main deck, Jimmy Two-Tales was shouting orders as the men scrambled to coax more speed from the ship's sails. Horus was at the railing at the back of the *Jubilee*, a spyglass pressed against his right eye. As Lucien, Dallion, and Journey joined him, Dallion snatched the spyglass from his hands to peer through it himself. Horus pointed toward a tiny speck in the distance, and through the spyglass, Dallion could make out her square sails.

"She came out of nowhere," Horus grumbled. "She's moving quick. We've all heard how fast she can go…"

"We won't be able to outrun her," Lucien agreed. His tone was flat and calm, but his hands were clenched in anxious fists at his sides. "She's got at least three knots on us, if all the stories are true. And double the guns."

Pigeon called to them from his place at the helm, and his own voice was anything but calm. "Waiting on orders, boys!"

Dallion handed the spyglass off to Lucien. As he did, he noticed that Journey's gaze was no longer on the ship coming up behind them, but off the port side of the *Jubilee*. There, the world was dark with storm clouds and heavy rain. The waves out here were already getting choppy, and the temperature had dropped a few more degrees. Journey looked away from the storm to glance at Dallion instead. Their eyes met, and they saw in them that they both knew what their only chance might be, at this point. Dallion took a deep breath and held it for a moment, keeping his head clear to think this through. He judged the risks and knew that they didn't matter. Trying to outrun the *Huntress* would end with the *Jubilee* on the seabed.

Journey saw the decision in his friend's expression and let a few profanities escape his lips. Dallion called, "Make for the storm off port, Pigeon! Hit it dead center!"

Pigeon responded with a few words that were similar to the ones that Journey had muttered, but got to work turning the wheel. Lucien understood what they were doing and hurried down onto the main deck to begin barking fresh orders. Horus and Gabe followed him. That left only Journey and Dallion at the banister, and Dallion said, "Maybe you shouldn't have come along with me, after all."

"I don't doubt that you're going to get me killed one day, Dallion," he said, "but I really don't want it to be today."

"Me, neither," he agreed. "Get Brain up here. I want him to try to judge our speed to see if we can make it into the storm before they catch up to us."

"And if we can't?"

Dallion shook his head, but Journey knew the answer to his own question, anyway. This was a race they couldn't afford to lose.

*   *   *

BRAIN assured them that they could make it, but it was going to be close. The wind whipped itself into a fierce gale that threatened to tear the sails from their yards. Waves came at them like watery walls that were determined to roll them. Pigeon kept the *Jubilee* pointed into each one, and the good ship lumbered over them. The water cascaded over the decks in torrents that nearly washed men overboard to certain death. Lightning tore across the black sky above them. It was one hell of a storm.

Journey had hoped that the *Huntress* would fall back when her captain realized that his prey was crazy enough to sail directly into the gale, but it soon became clear that Fleury was just as crazy himself. Instead of shying away and pulling back, the *Huntress* pursued the *Jubilee* directly into the hellish wind and waves. The unruly sea pounded both ships mercilessly, and the wind howled like a dangerous animal. Journey had been through plenty of storms at sea while pirating with this crew, but this was undeniably the worst.

He was working with Lil Gabe and Quick Bill to secure a rope near the foremast when a massive wave crashed over the bow. All three men had lashed themselves together with a length of rope that was secured to the mast to keep from being washed overboard, but as the wall of water crashed over them, they were swept away with so much force that the rope gave at the mast. They were sent across the deck in a disorientating tumble, and Journey lost track of where he was until he was slammed against the banister on the starboard side of the ship. For a moment, the rope around his waist pulled so tightly that he thought it would cut right through him, but then that tension was suddenly gone. As the water on the deck calmed, he was able to stumble to his feet, gagging on seawater that had forced its way into his lungs. He gave the rope around his waist a tug, but there was no weight on the other end of it. He cleared enough water from his eyes to see that the rope had snapped. Bill and Gabe were gone.

He scanned the deck in a frantic search for his missing comrades, but all he found was another two dozen men who were struggling to their feet in the aftermath of the wave. Above him, men were calling to one another as they continued to wrestle with the sails, but he ignored this. Somehow, over the roar of the raging sea and the howl of the wind, he heard a voice cry out for help. He rushed back to the banister and leaned over it as far as he dared to get a look over the side. Just a foot or so below the edge of the banister, Gabe was clinging desperately to the bottom of the ratlines. His eyes were bulging with the strain it took to hold on. A few feet below him, Quick Bill was dangling from the rope around his waist. The other end was around Gabe, and the younger man didn't look like he was going to be able to hold so much weight for long.

Journey screamed for help over the howl of the wind and grasped the ratline with one hand to reach down to Gabe with the other. Gabe was too frightened to let go of the line he was clinging to, but Journey gripped one of his wrists. There was a terrible moment of vertigo as the *Jubilee* crested another large wave, and time seemed to slow for Journey. For what couldn't have been longer than a second or two, but felt like much longer, he could feel every drop of seawater on his face and arms, feel every creak of the wooden ship beneath him, and see the depths of Gabe's fear in his bulging eyes. His stomach rolled as the ship started her decent down the backside of the wave. Journey felt his chest sliding over the top of the banister until his stomach laid across it instead. He called over his shoulder for help again, but his voice was lost in the wind.

The *Jubilee* finished her descent and rocked violently upward as she met the trough at the bottom. Quick Bill was struck with a blast of seawater, and Gabe let out an agonized howl as the rope pulled violently against his waist. One of his hands lost their grip on the ratline he was clinging to, and his other hand would have done the same, if not for Journey's grip on his wrist. The water had brought Quick Bill out of whatever daze he'd been in, and he began thrashing and screaming for help as his body was slammed repeatedly against the side of the ship. His struggles made things worse for Gabe, who couldn't seem to reassert his grip on the ratline.

The *Jubilee* started up the next wave, and Journey felt the banister slip down his stomach and to his hips. There was no question as to whether he was going over the side, but if he could just hold on long enough for Gabe to be able to grip the line again with his free hand…

A pair of hands grasped the bit of broken rope that was still tied around Journey's waist, stopping his deathward slide over the banister. He couldn't see who it was, but Dallion's voice rang out above the whipping wind and water, and Journey had never been so glad to hear him before.

"Don't you go over!" he ordered, as if Journey had a choice if the waves decided to take him. Dallion tried pulling Journey back onto the safe side of the banister, but Gabe wouldn't let go of the ratline he was clinging to, and Journey didn't let go of his wrist. A second pair of hands joined Dallion's on the rope around Journey's waist, and Dallion told him, "We'll pull on three!"

Journey told Gabe to let go of the ratlines, and for a moment, the young man's panic and fear kept him from doing so. Then another wall of water slammed Quick Bill against the hull and nearly pulled Gabe from it, anyway, and that convinced him. He forced himself to let go just as Dallion reached the count of three, and Journey held onto Gabe's wrist with everything he had. They moved upward, and after two or three seconds, Journey's feet were back on the deck. Gabe's hands were now close enough to the top of the banister so that the second pair of hands – Horus' – could grasp one of them.

"Bill's at the bottom!" Journey warned them, but the wind howled even louder, as if determined to keep that a secret. Dallion peered over the banister to find that Quick Bill was, in fact, dangling from the bottom of the rope below Gabe. As he watched, another wave made its way down the hull, and the water tried once more to take Bill with it. Gabe cried out in pain as the rope around his waist yanked him downward again. Journey and Horus were pulled with him, until their chests collided painfully with the banister. The edge of it tore Gabe's hand from Horus' grasp, and Journey felt his own grip on Gabe's other wrist begin to slip.

"I can't hold him!" Journey cried, and even as Horus leaned as far over the edge as he dared to try to grab onto Gabe again, Journey knew that it wasn't going to be enough. The next wave that struck Quick Bill was going to tear Gabe from his grasp, if it didn't take him and Horus along with them.

Dallion was over the side of the banister before Journey's frenzied brain could register what was going on. He held onto the ratline with one hand, and in his other, a bit of metal flashed. Journey realized with dismay that it was the blade of a knife…but they had no other choice. Dallion, dangling from one hand beside Gabe, cut the rope hanging from his waist with two quick swipes of the knife. A hundred and sixty pounds were gone in an instant, and Journey pulled Gabe up with all his might. Horus grasped Gabe's other arm and joined in the effort, and in the blink of an eye, Gabe was over the top of the banister. All three men crashed onto the deck, where yet another wave of water washed over them. It wasn't nearly as bad as some of the others had been, and after just a few seconds, Journey was able to stand again. He left Horus and Gabe in a heap to scramble back toward the banister. Dallion was still holding onto the ratline, but he'd lost the knife to the sea below. Quick Bill was nowhere to be seen.

Journey reached down to offer Dallion his hand, and he accepted it gratefully. He helped him up over the banister, but the ship lurched at the last moment, and they both spilled onto the deck. As they righted themselves, they spotted Horus as he helped an injured Gabe toward the nearest hatch, where he would finally be safe.

"Damn!" Dallion roared, slamming both of his fists against the deck. He had managed to get into a sitting position, and he rapped the back of his head against the banister behind him. Quick Bill had been a good man, and he'd deserved a better fate than the one he'd just been handed.

Journey told himself that there would be time to dwell on that later. For now, he forced himself to his feet, cradling an arm that felt as if it had been dislocated during the struggle, and got moving to answer Jimmy Two-Tale's call for help with one of the sails.

There was still a storm to survive.

Chapter Fourteen

BY the time it was over, everyone on board the *Jubilee* felt as if the squall had lasted a hundred years. They were exhausted, battered, and soaking wet. There were a number of minor injuries reported, as well as a broken leg that one of the men had suffered when he'd fallen from somewhere on the main mast. Journey's shoulder was dislocated, as he'd feared. Wee Bit and Horus helped him put it back into place, and that hurt even worse than the initial injury had. Lil Gabe was in much worse shape, although he hadn't suffered anything too serious and was expected to pull through alright. He was told to stay in the crew's quarters for a few days to recover. Considering all that had happened, they were fortunate to only have lost one man.

The best news of all was that there was no sign of the *Huntress* when the sea finally calmed and the storm had moved on. That wasn't surprising, according to Pigeon. He and Brain estimated that they had been blown more than fifty miles off course. This was verified when they spotted an island off the port bow that Brain identified as Gale Rock. Considering what they'd just experienced, it was a fitting name for the place.

The *Jubilee* had suffered some damage, but it wasn't anything that couldn't be repaired at sea. Lucien oversaw a funerary service for Quick Bill, and everyone except Dallion attended.

He'd shut himself up in his cabin, and that was where he stayed for the next few days. Not even Katria could lift his spirits. Journey was too busy helping out with repairs on the ship to have time to try. At the end of the third day, however, Katria approached him and asked for his help in at least getting Dallion to come out of his room. He agreed to make an attempt, but when he knocked on the door, Dallion called for him to go away.

He went inside, anyway. Dallion was sitting at his table, a half-empty bottle of rum before him. There was also an array of maps, and there were Xs through large swathes of them. Dallion grumbled something about coming in here without permission, but Journey ignored this and sat down in the chair across the little table from him. Dallion took a swig from the bottle of rum before offering it to Journey, but he shook his head.

He said, "Katria's worried."

"She doesn't have anything to worry about," Dallion muttered, and took another drink from the bottle. "Everything's fine."

"Then why have you been holed up in here for the past three days? This can't just be about Quick Bill. You've lost plenty of other guys before him."

"It was rough to have to cut him loose," he said, "but that's not what's driving me nuts. Look, if that storm hadn't been there, we'd all be having our eyes plucked out by fish right now."

"Charming."

"It's true." Dallion swept a hand over the maps before him. "We're running out of time. We shook the *Huntress* for now, but they know we're in the area, and they're not just going to give up. Any minute, somebody could run through that door screaming about purple sails again. And what are we going to do if that happens?"

Journey propped his elbows on the table and cradled his head in his hands. It had been a long few days, and he didn't have an answer for the question at hand. Dallion must have reminded himself of this, because he took a moment to settle down and then asked, "How's your shoulder?"

"Sore, but I'll live. Lucien says that Lil Gabe is going to be alright, too. He was up top for some fresh air today. He looks okay."

Dallion nodded, but it was clear that his attention had returned to the maps on the table. He wondered aloud, "How do you find a needle in a haystack?"

Journey didn't have an answer for that one, either. Instead, he told him, "Morale isn't great right now, and it doesn't help that you won't come out of this cabin."

"Morale isn't great *in* the cabin, either," he murmured. "We need a new plan. Get Lucien, Horus, Pigeon, and Watts in here for dinner tonight. We need to come up with something better than this."

"And Katria?" he asked. "Your maps expert?"

Dallion looked up from the table to find a slight grin on Journey's face, and he couldn't help but laugh. "Do you think anyone buys that?"

"Not a single soul."

"As long as they don't care enough to call me out on it, that's fine. I'll see you at dinner, alright? Bring Brain, too. We need all the help we can get."

"Try to stay sober until then," he advised, standing, but Dallion took another drink from the bottle to spite him. Journey heaved a sigh and made his way out the door. Some things never changed.

*   *   *

THE dinner that was served in Dallion's cabin that night wasn't anything fancy, as Catfish was rationing the ship's supplies in anticipation of the lengthy search they still had ahead of them. Seven men and one woman crowded around the long table that Dallion had set up for the occasion, and they set about making all of the jerky, boiled eggs, bread, and mangos disappear from the dishes before them. At the center of the table, the worn map that Watts had given them was laid out for everyone to view.

Dallion, sitting at the head of the table, stopped the chatter around it by announcing, "We need a new plan. Unless we get really lucky, wandering around the open ocean to find these islands is going to take years."

Lucien and Journey both bit back I-told-you-so retorts. Horus pushed back in his chair with a huff and said, "Look, I don't want to sound too negative about this, but I don't think that sticking around this area is a good idea, anyway. The *Huntress* is still out here somewhere, and she'll be looking for us."

"We were lucky last time," Pigeon added. "And I'm not just talking about escaping Fleury's ship. I've sailed through plenty of storms in my life, but never anything like that."

"With you at the helm, we weren't in any danger," Dallion assured him, but Pigeon's frown remained.

Lucien asked, "What does our 'maps expert' have to offer us?" All eyes went to Katria.

She was sitting with Lucien on her right and Journey on her left, and they both noticed as she tensed slightly. Even so, she said with a confidence she shouldn't have had, "I believe that the map Mr. Watts gave you is genuine."

"Of course, it's genuine," Watts said from his place between Pigeon and Horus. "I paid five hundred marks for that map. The man I bought it from gave me his word that it was real. He swore on his father's grave."

"I can swear on my father's grave that I'm a unicorn," Lucien grunted. "That doesn't make it true."

Journey had been silent until now, but he finally spoke up to suggest, "If the stories about Stonecraft and the *Weeping Cherub* are true, then it's history. We need a historian. We need someone who knows how to tell historical fact from fiction. Someone who remembers."

"Remembers what?" Dallion asked as he refilled his cup with rum. "Remembers what the islands were like a couple of hundred years ago? Unless they can remember *where* they are, I don't know how that will help. I mean, islands don't change much."

"They sink," Brain said from the foot of the table, and that gave everyone at the table pause. Brain's attention was on the egg that he was peeling, his fingers meticulously removing every shard of the shell.

Journey asked him, "What do you mean, Brain?"

He shrugged his shoulders, suddenly shy from being the center of attention. His face reddened, and he wouldn't take his gaze from the egg in his hands, but he explained, "They're like ghosts. They're not islands, anymore, and you can't really see them. But that doesn't mean they're not there."

Dallion leaned over his end of the table, his blue eyes focused on Brain as he continued to peel the egg. "What do you know about these ghost islands?"

He only shrugged again, but Journey was the nearest one to him, and he set a comforting hand on Brain's shoulder. Brain struggled with his bashfulness some more and finally said, "Pigeon had to go around the shallow parts by the island with all the trees. The one that wasn't on Pigeon's map. The shallow parts by it are the ghosts of the other islands. I paid attention to where they were. They're in the same places as the islands on Watty's map. The one with all the trees is the island that's circled."

Pigeon was on his feet in an instant, leaning over the table to get a closer look at the map in question. Lucien, Horus, and Journey all did the same. Dallion asked with wonder, "You're telling me that the other islands on Watty's map sank into the sea? Is that what you're saying?"

Brain nodded and ate half of the boiled egg in one bite. Dallion pressed, "You knew this all along, Brain? Why didn't you say anything?"

Brain shrugged a third time. "You asked me if I knew of any islands that looked like the chain on the map. I don't. They're not islands, anymore. They're just shallows that Pigeon has to move the ship around."

"He's found it," Pigeon marveled, looking at Dallion with wide eyes. "He's actually found it."

Dallion began to laugh, and it was a thunderous, joyful sound. After a moment, most of the others in the cabin joined in.

*   *   *

RATIONS be damned. There was a celebration that night, and everyone on board the *Jubilee* drank far more than his usual share of rum and ale. It wasn't wise, especially with the *Huntress* skulking through nearby waters, but it provided the boost to morale that they'd so desperately needed. Drinking games were played right out on the deck, and lamps were kept burning to make up for the lack of moonlight from a cloudy sky. As the night wore on and more alcohol was consumed, impromptu wrestling matches cropped up, along with footraces along the main deck and the occasional shanty that was wailed by a chorus of drunken voices.

Dallion made a rambling, slurred speech about how much he appreciated the hard work of the crew, after which he promptly challenged anyone who thought they could best him at poker to prove it. So many men took him up on it that they had to break it up into multiple games, and a tournament began. Gabe was well enough to join in, and he was soon in a three-way tie for first place with Dallion and Wee Bit.

Journey took part in the revelry for a while, but eventually withdrew to the bow, where it was quiet enough to think straight. Thomas was the only other person over here for the moment, and he was snoring loudly from the coil of rope he'd passed out on top of. Journey leaned against the banister with his cup of rum and drew in a breath of the fresh, salty air. It would have been a lie to say he hadn't missed the freedom of the sea…but there were things he loved a little bit more, now. They were waiting for him on Stonewell, and he missed them terribly.

Lucien's voice spoke up behind him before Journey knew that he was there. "No interest in poker, Teach?"

Journey shook his head as Lucien joined him at the banister. He rested his elbows on top of it, as Journey was doing, and they shared a moment of quiet contemplation, watching the calm sea below as it was parted by the bow.

Lucien drew in a deep breath, held it for a few seconds, and then let it out. He asked, "Do you miss it while you're on your island?"

Journey smiled a little. "You just read my mind."

"I haven't thanked you for saving my boy, yet," he told him, still watching the water below. Journey judged by his speech and demeanor that Lucien was one of the few sober men left aboard.

He shrugged. "Anyone else would have done the same."

"I'd like to think that's true, but it's not. You could have died, but you didn't let him go. Gabriel owes you his life, but he's probably too young and dumb to understand how serious that is. So I wanted to let you know that I do. I owe you."

"Gabe's a good man, Lucien. Like his father."

He chuckled at that, but it was more of a sad sound than a joyful one. "I can't take any credit for that. I didn't raise him. I didn't even know he existed until a few months ago. His mother left a letter for me in Port Kelsey to say he wanted to know about me. I hadn't heard from her since the handful of nights we'd spent together all those years ago. Three nights were all we shared, but…" He drew in another deep breath and let it out, his eyes on the nighttime sea. "I never forgot her. Anyway, I tracked him down and offered him a place with the crew. You're right: he's a good man and an even better sailor. If I ever see his mother again, I'll pass your praise along."

Journey tried to imagine a life in which he didn't know his own child, but shut the idea out almost as soon as it sparked in his head. Mirelle was the best thing that had ever happened to him, and he didn't want to think of living without her. His thoughts were interrupted, anyway, as a loud cheer erupted from one of the groups playing poker farther down the deck. Dallion stood and took a bow. Lucien cast a glance over his shoulder at this, then turned his attention back to Journey and said in a lowered voice, "He's obsessed with this damn treasure, and not in a good way. He's desperate."

Journey nodded slowly before looking back at the man, himself. Dallion had sat back down to resume the card game, and there was a cocky grin on his face as he said something to the other players. Journey said, "He's scared of the *Huntress*."

"He's right to be," Lucien agreed. "And finding the treasure might be his ticket out of piracy, but his desperation is making him careless. We knew that the *Huntress* could have been anywhere, but we decided to go to an island in the middle of a major shipping route to pick up a 'map expert.' The next thing we know, we're seeing purple sails."

"That was out of a different kind of desperation," Journey said. He finished the last of the rum in his cup, hoping that Lucien wouldn't ask him to explain that.

He didn't have to. Lucien spotted Katria as she approached them, and the slight weave in her walk across the deck told them how much she'd had to drink tonight. Lucien muttered, "With this many drunk, lonely men on a ship, having a tipsy woman aboard is going to mean trouble."

"Everything has been alright, so far."

He grunted in disapproval, and as he stepped away from the banister to leave, he said to Journey, "Keep an eye on the girl."

Katria passed him as he made his way back toward the others on the main deck, and they exchanged pleasant enough hellos. Then she came to stand in the place that Lucien had just left, and she asked Journey, "Should I call you Journey or Teach? I've heard the crew call you both."

"Either," he answered, wishing that his cup had more rum in it. He didn't dislike Katria – it was very much the opposite, in fact – but Lucien was right about there being rules against bringing women on board for a reason. He'd heard the lewd comments some of the men had been making about her, and it was only a matter of time before Dallion heard something, as well. If a fight were to ensue, he didn't doubt that Lucien would keep his word and drop the young woman off at the nearest port, and Dallion's reaction to that would not be pretty.

She must have seen some of this concern on his face, for she asked him, "I'm not exactly welcome on this ship, am I?"

"It isn't like that," he answered immediately, but after a moment, he admitted, "It's kind of like that."

She laughed – a melodic sound that he liked a lot – and slapped him playfully on the shoulder. "See? Honesty isn't so hard. I thought you'd be a little better at it, since Dallion tells me that he doesn't trust anyone on this ship more than he trusts you."

"He seems to trust you, too," he said, considering her. The lanterns on the deck were doing their best to dispel the nighttime darkness, but there were still shadows across her face. They danced prettily. "I'm curious about your intentions."

"Concerning?" she asked, but her smile said that she knew what he meant. He didn't clarify, and after a few seconds, she confessed, "Nothing's set in stone. I don't know how much you know about me, but Dallion and I knew each other as kids. We cared about each other a lot back then." She shrugged. "Some things don't change, I guess."

He still didn't respond, so she continued, "At any rate, we're on friendly terms, but not what you're probably thinking. Not yet. I need to think things through a little more. I just left my fiancé, I have no home, no money, and no friends, besides Dallion." She hesitated, but then said, "I'd hoped that I could also consider you a friend, since you're like a brother to him."

"I want him to be happy. I just don't like the way he goes about doing it sometimes."

She laughed again, and it reminded him of Saige in a way that made him homesick. She said, "I'm sure your wife probably says the same thing about you. Dallion tells me you're married to a woman somewhere out near Kinsmen. She doesn't mind you being so far away from her all the time?"

"This is a one-time thing."

"I don't know about that," she teased. "It seems to me like this is in your blood. Mrs. Teach might need to get used to her man being away."

"Why are you out here, Katria?" he asked her suddenly. She sobered and looked out at the sea for a little while. He gave her time to think it through, and when she answered, he believed that she was being honest.

"I grew up without my parents, because my dad died when I was a baby and my mom was always off with the next 'love of her life.' My grandmamma raised me. So when my mom made me leave Calico to go live with her, it took me away from everything I'd ever known. I didn't like my new life. Her new husband had some money, but not as much as he'd made her think. He sort of tricked her. He wasn't very nice. Sometimes, he'd hit her. And he tried to get a little too close to me, if you know what I mean. But he had a bad heart and he died, and then my mom had all his money. She spent it on silly things, and before I knew it, we didn't even have enough to buy food with. So I left as soon as I was old enough to get out of there. I hopped around the islands a little. I worked in taverns or as a nanny to rich families. I faked all my references and changed the way I talked so that I'd sound more educated than I really am. I eventually met Gerald, and he liked the idea of having a younger woman around to show off and…enjoy. I agreed to be with him because after everything else, I'd finally found something stable and safe. I had everything I needed on his island, and the only cost to me was having to bed him once or twice week." She was frowning, but now she brightened as she said, "But then Dallion showed up. It took him a lot longer than I'd hoped, but he finally came and found me. I realized that I didn't need my life to be stable and safe, anymore. I love having freedom, and I'd tried to change that about myself while I was with Gerald. But I don't have to do that, anymore. I can be as free as I want to be now. I can do anything I want. It's a good feeling to have."

He knew what she meant. Even though he'd met Dallion and had become a pirate under the worst circumstances, it hadn't taken him long to fall in love with the freedom that such a life had to offer. He hadn't stuck around and become a part of the crew because he'd had no other choice; this *was* his choice, and he'd never regretted making it.

She asked him, "Well? What's your judgement? Be honest."

"I think that you haven't been given many opportunities in your life to do what makes you happy," he decided. "You have a chance now, and you'd be crazy not to take it."

"Dallion says you're smart," she mused, "but I think he really means you're wise."

"Dallion says a lot of things," he grinned, finally stepping away from the banister to go find some more rum. "Most of it's bullshit."

The sound of Katria's laughter followed him across the deck.

Chapter Fifteen

KATRIA woke the next morning with a headache that she cursed last night's rum for. The blankets on Dallion's bed were almost warm and soft enough to coax her back to sleep, but after some internal debate, she decided to open her eyes. Morning light was weaseling its way through the window in the rearmost wall of the cabin. It fell across the floor to reveal the mound of blankets that Dallion had been sleeping on each night since she'd come aboard, but they were currently vacant. Katria vaguely recalled her drunken trek to bed sometime after midnight, but she wasn't sure if Dallion had come into the cabin after that, or not. She wondered with some amusement if he'd slept out on the deck all night.

She forced herself out of bed, despite her aching head's objection, and wasn't surprised to find herself still dressed from the previous day. She used her fingers to tame her hair as well as she could in the reflection of the window's glass, then headed through the cabin's door to face the day. On the deck, she found that the crew was already hard at work, as if the amount of alcohol they'd consumed last night hadn't been as substantial as she knew it had been. The men who had been cheating at poker and howling sea shanties all night were now working hard to set the sails and keep the ship sailing smoothly. Katria spotted

Dallion, Journey, and Lucien standing near the foremast, and she headed in that direction, weaving around busy crewmembers along the way. As she drew closer, however, she saw in the frown on Dallion's face that the conversation he was having with Lucien and Journey was a tense one. She turned around and placed her back against this side of the foremast to stay out of their sight while she listened in.

Journey had been saying something about having patience, but Dallion interrupted, "I can't believe we're finally this close, and you two don't want to get there as soon as we can."

"We need more food and supplies," Lucien said sternly. "You saw the trees and brush on that island. Do you really want to try to tackle it without spades and axes?"

"Stopping at Espoir will barely cost us an extra day," Journey added. "I know you don't want to waste that time, but we need to be smart about this, Dal."

Dallion was silent as he considered the options, and Katria could easily picture his expression of irritation. Finally, he conceded, "One stop in Espoir, and then we're on our way. If either of you want to go anywhere else after that, you can both swim for it."

Lucien muttered something about tossing Dallion over the side, but he must not have been interested in listening, because he appeared around the foremast on his way across the deck. He stopped when he noticed Katria standing there, however, and he told her, "It's not nice to eavesdrop."

She gave him a sheepish grin, and although he tried to return it, his current mood only allowed him a half a smile. She started to give him a clever excuse for listening to their conversation, but he must not have been interested in hearing about that, either, for he turned once more and headed down the deck. Katria struggled to ignore the sting that brought and decided to leave him alone for now.

She visited the galley and talked Catfish into letting her fix a late breakfast, then spent the much of the rest of the day soaking up the sun from the bow. Nice or not, she found herself eavesdropping on plenty of other conversations between pirates as they worked. She overheard Wee Bit and Thomas discussing their doubts about her experience as an expert in maps, which was entertaining. She also heard exaggerated tales about a few of the crewmen's love lives, which was even more amusing. By late afternoon, her headache was gone and she felt like herself again. She offered to help out with some of the chores around the ship, and just as she was beginning to suspect no one was going to take her up on it, Horus handed her a mop and a bucket. Swabbing the deck wasn't exactly the sort of task she'd hoped for, but it was better than nothing, and she got to work right away.

It was almost dinnertime and she was still swabbing her way around the mainmast when Brain approached her and announced happily, "Captain Dallion wants to talk to you in his cabin."

She was tempted to spurn his invitation, just as he'd walked away from her earlier, but before she had time to weigh that decision, Brain added, "He said please."

Katria set aside the mop – and the anger she'd felt earlier – and headed that way. She hoped that he didn't intend to tell her he didn't want her doing chores with the rest of the crew, and she rehearsed a chastisement for him in her head, if that was the case.

When she opened the cabin door and stepped inside, however, she found the interior to be lit with plain candles, instead of the usual lanterns. The small table had been moved to the middle of the room, and there were two place settings on it. Three more candles graced its center. The usual clutter that the cabin often contained had been tidied, and there was a fragrance in the air that could only have been some sort of cologne. Katria came to a stop just inside the doorway, surprised and somewhat alarmed.

Dallion was sitting on the edge of the bed, but he stood to greet her. She saw that he had washed his hair, and he was wearing a stylish waistcoat that she never would have expected to have seen him in. He was freshly shaven and wasn't wearing his usual necklaces or rings. To anyone who didn't know him, Dallion could have passed for a wealthy island owner, instead of a pirate at sea.

He gave her a dashing smile, but was there also a hint of nervousness in it? She thought so. He came to her and placed a polite kiss on her cheek. She was taken aback by how deeply it made her blush. She asked him, "What is this?"

"This is me being creative," he said, going to the door behind her to close it. "That's what you said I had to do, isn't it?"

She didn't answer, trying to decide if this was all an elaborate prank. He went to the table and moved one of the chairs for her, and she decided to let him try to woo her, if that's what he wanted to do. She sat down, thanking him, and considered the food on the plate before her. Under ordinary circumstances, she wouldn't have thought of sea turtle and potatoes as a romantic meal…but he was trying, and she could give him that.

He sat down across the table from her. There was a bottle of red wine near its center, and he set about pouring them each a glass. As he did this, she dared to ask, "What brought this on?"

"I've been thinking about you – about us – and I realized that I've been awful."

She raised an eyebrow, but accepted the glass of wine when he offered it to her. She took a sip, then asked over its rim, "How so?"

"I convinced you to come out here with me, but I've ignored you for the past few days. That isn't fair." Katria supposed that anyone else who knew him may have been surprised by his sincerity. Not her, however. She had seen him at his most vulnerable before, and it was refreshing to know this side of him again.

"We've talked," he continued, "but not about anything important. I've been distracted with all this *Cherub* stuff, and I forgot that I have something even more important than that right in front of me."

She didn't know what to say to that, so she sipped her wine some more, instead. Dallion started on his potato, and for a while, they ate their meal in silence. Finally, however, Katria said, "I've heard the crew talking about what happened with the storm. They say that it was your idea to sail into it, and if we hadn't done that, we wouldn't have survived."

"I don't want to talk about any of that right now," he said. "I want to talk about you. I haven't seen you in thirteen years. What have you been doing?"

She told him. She surprised herself with her candidness. She told him about her stepfather, her mother, and the various jobs she'd held to keep herself fed and clothed. She didn't shy from speaking about past lovers, and he didn't seem perturbed. She told him of her dreams and her fears, her hopes and her failings. She spoke so earnestly that he accepted every word as the truth, and it was. By the time she was finished, their plates were empty, and Dallion refilled their glasses.

He asked, "What about Gerald?"

She sighed, swirling the wine around in her glass. "What about him?"

"Do you think he's going to take you back after running off with me?"

She recognized that as a candid way for him to ask if she was planning to stick around or not, but decided not to give him an answer. After all, she didn't know what her future held, and she couldn't even answer a question like that for herself. Instead, she sipped from her fresh glass, then said, "We've talked enough about me. It's your turn. What have you been doing for the last thirteen years?"

"Trying to stay out of the noose," he said, and although he tried to make it sound like a joke, she knew it wasn't. "I was young and dumb when I started pirating. Don't get me wrong, it's a lot of fun, but it comes with a price, and that price is steep. I've already been caught once. Commercial Horizon put me on trial and were getting the rope ready for me. Journey's the only reason that it didn't happen. Ever since then, I've been wondering why I keep doing it. The truth is that nobody pirates for long, because they either get out while they can, or they get killed. At this point, I'm on borrowed time."

"Is that what this hunt for legendary treasure is all about?" she asked.

He nodded, and there was a sadness in his eyes that she didn't like seeing there. "I'm going to miss it," he confessed. "This is the only life I've known since I left Calico. The *Jubilee* is my only home. But now that you're here, I'm hoping I've got something that I can love even more than this ship."

She couldn't help but smile at that. "You can be really charming when you want to be."

"Honest, too," he assured her. He took a drink of wine, and when he set the glass back down, he brightened. "Do you remember the night before Bo was going to leave to go work for Western Straights? The three of us met the Baker twins down at Wicker's."

"We all had too much to drink that night," she said. "You and I were far too young for them to have been serving us, but old lady Wicker knew that it was my brother's last night on the island, so she let us drink."

"And dance," he added. "Guy Marion and his cousin were playing violins there that night. We kept asking them to play slow songs, and we danced to every one."

"We weren't very good," she laughed.

Dallion stood from his chair and stepped around the small table to offer her his hand. "I've had some practice since then," he said. "Let me have another shot at it."

Katria hesitated for only a moment before placing her hand in his, but as she stood, she reminded him, "There's no music to dance to."

He took a bow, anyway, and then placed his other hand on the small of her back. He began to lead her in slow circles, and as they danced, he hummed a soft melody that she vaguely recalled from their childhood on Calico Island. Her hand was warm in his, and she liked the feel of his other one on her back. He led her in a few basic steps, slowly pulling her closer until they were pressed together and she could rest her head on his chest. She closed her eyes as they moved and listened to the steady beating of his heart. The sound of his humming was like a dream of an old memory, and her heart ached over the years that had separated them.

After a few minutes, his steps slowed, but she held onto him tighter and whispered, "Don't stop."

He stopped, anyway, letting go of her hand to tilt her chin upward with one finger. She looked up into his eyes and found them to be full of the love he claimed was still there. He planted a soft kiss on her forehead, and she was tempted to tell him that wasn't where she wanted it. Instead, she asked him, "What do you want from me, Dallion?"

"I want you to marry me," he replied, and there was so much sincerity in his voice that it somehow didn't sound like a crazy idea, at all. "Not for money, because I'm not rich. And I don't have a mansion or a bunch of islands, so not for any of that, either. I want you to marry me because you can't imagine one more day of your life without me. I want it to be because you love me again, like you used to."

She lost the fight against the smile that wanted to bloom on her lips, and she confessed, "I never stopped."

He kissed her lips, at last, and she tasted the salt of the sea air on his. Her heart began to race as she found herself kissing him back. She didn't object when he started moving them both toward the bed. Without breaking their kiss, her hands began to undo the buttons on the front of his waistcoat.

Chapter Sixteen

THE stop in Espoir was as quick as Journey had promised. Lucien took six men ashore to fetch the needed supplies. Journey waited on the dock for their return, meaning to help them haul everything aboard, but when they arrived, he noticed one man was missing. As Lucien joined him near the gangway, he asked, "Where's Watts?"

Lucien looked to Catfish, whom he'd sent Watts off with, for an answer. Catfish complained, "That shady bastard told me he'd seen a good deal on eggs in the market. We agreed to meet up in ten minutes, but he never came back. I gave him good money to get those eggs with. I'm guessing he's spending it in a whorehouse as we speak."

"I hope you're wrong about that," Lucien told him, and Journey felt a sinking feeling in the pit of his stomach. He supposed Watts could have gotten tied up with something else in the market, of course…but he couldn't shake that feeling that something was wrong. Lucien told Catfish, "Get everything loaded up and tell Horus to get the ship ready to go. If Watty isn't back soon, we'll leave without him."

Catfish muttered something about the lost money again, but got moving to do as asked. Lucien called for Wee Bit, Thomas, and Jimmy Two-Tales to help the others get to the supplies loaded onto the ship. As they worked, Lucien motioned for Journey to follow him to the end of the dock to wait for Watts to appear. They watched other sailors come and go, but there was no sign of him. As if wanting Journey to tell him he was wrong, Lucien suggested, "He could have decided to jump ship."

It wasn't uncommon for men to do that when stopped in a port, but Journey said, "He's too invested in this hunt for the treasure. He's almost as determined about it as Dallion is."

"What is it, then? Did he run into some sort of trouble?"

If that was the case, there was little to be done about it, but Journey knew he didn't have to tell him that. Instead, they waited in silence for a while, watching as Catfish and the others finished taking the fresh supplies aboard. Just as they finished the job, Journey spotted Watts. He was coming at a run, his feet thumping against the wooden dock, and he nearly knocked an elderly man over as their shoulders collided in his rush. Watts stumbled, but kept his feet. He was panting hard when he finally reached Journey and Lucien. He started past them with a simple nod in greeting, but Lucien placed a firm hand on his shoulder, and he stopped.

"I know I'm late," Watts panted. "I'm sorry. I got mugged on my way here. There were three guys. I didn't stand a chance."

Journey and Lucien both studied him, trying to judge his sincerity. His hair was mussed, but that may have been from the run here. There was a small, red mark on his left cheek that could have been left there by a fist. Lucien demanded, "They took all the eggs?"

"The eggs, the rest of the money Catfish gave me, and all of my own money, too. They took everything." He shook his hand from his shoulder. "If you don't mind, I just want to get on board so we can get out of this place. You couldn't pay me enough to come back here."

Lucien let him go. Journey watched him head up the gangway, and if he was faking the slight limp he was now walking with, it was a believable act. Once he was out of earshot, Lucien said, "I like to think I'm good at reading people and knowing if they're lying, but that boy is always so shifty that it's impossible to tell."

"Mugged for a few dozen eggs," Journey muttered, watching as the man in question disappeared onto the ship.

Lucien frowned. "Do you believe him?"

"I don't know what to believe, anymore."

"I'll make him work off the debt with extra chores. I'm going to keep a closer eye on him, and I want you to help me do that. If I find out he's lying, he'll swim for it."

Journey had never seen Lucien throw a member of the crew overboard, but he disliked Watty so much that he wouldn't have been surprised to see it happen. Horus called down to them from the deck that the ship was ready to go, and they headed up the gangway, Lucien barking out orders as they went.

*   *   *

PIGEON had marked the location of the forested island on a map when they'd first discovered it, so he knew exactly where to head. The wind was favorable for the first few days, but then it died out. For the next two days, the *Jubilee* was unmovable. She floated listlessly on the still water, a testament of grace and speed that had been brought still by powers beyond her control. The crew kept themselves as busy as they could, but there were only so many chores to be done in a day spent stationary. Eventually, boredom overtook nearly everyone, and no number of card games or footraces along the deck could stave it off. Journey took up a book and found a patch of shade near the mainmast, where he sat down with Lil Gabe to embark on reading lessons. He opened to the first page of the book that he'd scrounged up in Dallion's cabin, and he helped Lil Gabe plod through the first two pages.

While Gabe started the third page, Journey's attention was pulled away as he overheard Wee Bit suggest to a few others that they play a game called "Test Brain." It was something the crew had used to pass the time for years. A dozen men gathered around Brain near the mainmast, and Journey asked Lil Gabe to take a break, setting the book aside to watch. No matter how many times he'd seen this done, he'd never stopped being amazed by Brain. Thomas started it off by calling out, "Cape Kelsey."

"Twelve days, nineteen hours, and four minutes," Brain answered immediately, as if he'd practiced it. Without a map, none of them had any way to verify Brain's estimate, but it hardly mattered. He may have never been able to master spelling his name or tying a bowline knot, but none of them doubted his ability when it came to this.

Jimmy Two-Tales proposed, "Carine Island."

"Twenty days, three hours, and seventeen minutes." Brain gave him a smug grin. "Unless you mean South Carine. That's twelve hours and thirteen minutes farther away."

They went on like that until every man standing there had taken a turn. Brain spotted Journey sitting in the shade of the masts and offered, "Do you want to know how far away Stonewell Island is, Journey?"

"No," he answered, and his tone had been a little sterner than he'd intended. Brain blinked, clearly stung, and Journey quickly corrected himself with, "I'm sorry, Brain. I just don't want to think about how far away it is."

"Because you miss Saige?" Brain asked quietly, but before Journey could respond to that, the corner of the page in the book beside him rose slightly, then fell back down. He glanced at it, his heart leaping, and after a few seconds, the page stood up again. The same breeze that was playing with it also brushed over his face. Lil Gabe must have felt it, as well, for he sprang to his feet, his hands raised in the air.

"Wind!" he exclaimed, and the other men who had been gathered around the mainmast let out a cheer. Lucien had been speaking to Pigeon about something near the helm, and he called out across the decks for the crew to get to work. They scrambled to catch the wind in the sails. Journey abandoned the book he and Lil Gabe had been reading and seized the nearest ratline, preparing to climb up. Before he could do so, Katria arrived beside him, and she offered him a playful salute that couldn't have been more out of place on this ship.

"Give me some orders," she told him, and he almost laughed, thinking it was a joke. Her face couldn't have said she was more serious, however, and she reinforced this by adding, "I want to help."

He nodded toward helm, from which Lucien was shouting his orders. "You can ask Lucien to give you something to do…"

"Lucien isn't going to let me lend a hand, and you know it. You're the first mate, aren't you? You can give me orders, like I'm part of the crew."

"You're *not* part of the crew."

She raised her chin in defiance. "I know how to sail. Just give me a chance to show you."

He was tempted to tell her that it wasn't going to happen, but then he thought of his daughter, Mirelle, and how he would want her to be treated aboard a ship if he ever taught her to sail. Besides, Katria had spent enough time boasting about how much she knew about sailing. It was time for her to prove it. He pointed toward the bow and said, "You see that small, triangular sail in front of the foremast?"

"It's called a jib," she replied, and in an instant, Journey understood just how frustrating it must have been for her to have been patronized this entire time. The fact that she hadn't gotten furious about it was a testament to her patience.

He instructed, "Make sure the luff of that staysail is secure on the forestay."

"Aye!" she cried eagerly, and sprinted toward the bow to carry out the order. Journey cast a glance back toward the helm and found that Lucien was watching him with a scowl on his face. Journey gave a shrug. Lucien shook his head…but he didn't shout across the deck for Katria to stop, and that was something. Instead, he turned his attention back to handing out commands to a few other men nearby, and Journey was glad. If Katria knew what she was doing, there was no reason to keep her from doing it.

As that day wore on, it became clear that Katria truly did know what she was doing. She knew all of the necessary terminology and could follow instructions from anyone who gave them. Even better, she wasn't afraid to get dirty or work up a sweat, and her natural nimbleness was an asset when it came to climbing the ratlines or perching herself near the top of the masts. Journey found that most members of the crew adjusted to having her working beside them quickly, and it wasn't long before Jimmy Two-Tales was giving her tasks to do on the deck and Wee Bit was asking for her help adjusting the bowlines. By the time the sun went down, even Lucien had to admit that she gone beyond merely earning her keep.

*   *   *

AT last, Pigeon estimated that the forested island that was their destination would show up on the horizon in a matter of hours, and Journey couldn't have been happier. The end of this adventure would mean that he could return home...but it was also more than that. The feverish exhilaration that Dallion possessed about finding the hidden treasure had turned out to be contagious, and Journey was its latest victim. He'd been dreaming about heaps of gold and precious jewels for the last few nights, and if everything they now suspected was right, then they were within hours from finding the treasure's resting place. It was theirs for the taking.

He was taking a break from a few tasks that Lucien had assigned him when he saw the first sign of wreckage. He'd been leaning against the banister near the *Jubilee*'s bow, looking out over the welcoming expanse of sea before them, when he happened to glance down at the small waves that were being pushed aside by the ship's hull. There, barely visible in the surf, was a piece of wood that was too straight and flat to have been a natural branch of any sort. He watched it slip past the ship until he lost sight of it, his curiosity hardly peaked. That changed when he caught sight of the next board, and then the next. His eyes scanned the surrounding waters and picked out more debris: a wooden barrel, a half a dozen more boards, and something that was too long and straight not to have been a mast.

"Starboard bow!" Journey called, scanning the surrounding waters for any sign of purple sails. His skin crawled with the imagined sensation of being watched from afar.

A few men came running to get a look at what he'd noticed. Dallion and Lucien, who had been engaged in some sort of philosophical discussion about whether or not it was bad luck to bring a woman aboard a sailing vessel, shouldered their way past the other men to join Journey at the banister. As they watched, more and more debris drifted past. Journey caught sight of a shark's fin in the water, and he knew what came next. Just as he'd feared, corpses began to float by. There were dozens of them. They floated limply, as lifeless as the drifting boards that had once made up their ship's hull. They were dressed in clothing comparable to what was worn by the crew aboard the *Jubilee,* instead of matching uniforms that would have denoted a company's employ. These men were pirates. Journey was as sure of that as he was of his own name.

One look at Dallion's face told him that he was certain of the same thing. His eyes searched the horizon for the *Huntress*. Horus was standing nearby, and Dallion hissed at him, "Get somebody up on the foretop. Hurry!"

Horus started off at a jog, but came back after only a few steps and pointed at the foremast. Dallion saw that Katria was already scurrying her way up it to get a look at the surrounding waters. If the Huntress was still around, she would spot it.

Lil Gabe was standing on the other side of Lucien, and he suggested, "It could have been an accident. Or a different ship. It didn't have to be…" He trailed off, not quite brave enough to speak the name of the ship they all feared.

Dallion ignored this and said to Lucien, "Get some men on the cannons, just in case. We'll search for survivors, but I don't think we'll find any."

He was right. There were no survivors amongst the floating bodies, but there was also no sign of the *Huntress*, and that was good. They managed to haul a few loose barrels out of the water and found that they were filled with unspoiled food, and that was also good. When their search was complete, Pigeon resumed his course toward the forested island, but Dallion told him to turn westward, instead. He gave no explanation for this, but posted a few men on deck whose assignment was to keep an eye on the horizon for the purple sails that would undoubtedly mean their deaths.

Dallion gathered Journey, Lucien, Katria, and Horus in his cabin. They were all on edge – the tension in the room was thick enough to choke on – and Dallion was the worst of them all. He paced the length of the cabin with his hands laced behind his back, his brow furled and his steps hurried. Lucien and Horus sat down at the small table and watched their captain pace, while Journey leaned tiredly against one of the bedposts. All of the excitement he'd felt about the treasure had been sapped from him, and he didn't doubt the same was true for the others.

Katria was sitting on the foot of the bed, and now she said, "Dallion, you have to stop pacing before you drive us all crazy."

He either didn't hear her or didn't care, for he continued marching back and forth, back and forth. He asked, "Why does he do it? What makes Fleury want to hunt us down and kill us all? He was a pirate. Why would he turn like this?"

He hadn't asked anyone in particular, but Horus offered, "Money. I don't know how much Whitefish is paying him, but I'm sure they're making it worth it."

"And prestige," Journey added. "They've given him command of the fastest and most powerful ship in the region. Whatever he was sailing before, it can't hold a candle to what he has, now."

"It doesn't matter why he's doing it," Lucien said, dismissing all of this with a wave of his hand. "All that matters is that we need to stay out of his way, and we haven't been doing that very well, lately. Everywhere we turn, there he is."

"What do we do?" Katria asked, but none of the men in the cabin had an answer for her.

Dallion stopped pacing and stood with a hand over his eyes. He felt a headache coming on. He said without taking his hand away, "White Crest is two days west of us, maybe a little more. There are at least a dozen smaller islands just off her northern shore. The waters between them should barely be deep enough for the *Jubilee*. Fleury won't expect us there."

"No kidding," Lucien grunted. "White Crest is Commercial Horizon territory."

"Horizon mostly sails galleons out of White Crest," Journey reminded him. "They can't enter the shallows on the north side of the island."

Dallion pointed a finger at him in a you-got-it gesture. Horus asked, "So we'll just anchor there for a while and hope that Fleury moves on?"

"Not quite," Dallion said, finally taking his other hand away from his eyes. There was a look of determination on his face that none of them felt up to the task of questioning. "I'll take a few men and charter a small boat in White Crest to bring us back here. We'll be flying legit colors, so the *Huntress* should leave us alone. We'll search the island and head back to White Crest after a couple of days, whether we find what we're looking for or not. If we have to, we'll charter a whole fleet of boats to move the treasure, but I don't want the *Jubilee* anywhere around here. Not until we know that Fleury is gone."

"And if the treasure isn't on the island?" Horus asked, but Dallion's determination wasn't shaken.

"It's there," he assured him. "I know it is."

Chapter Seventeen

IT was decided that Journey, Katria, Horus, Jimmy Two-Tales, and Watts would accompany Dallion to search the island, which Brain had taken to calling Tall Island, since all of the others in its chain had been lower and were now underwater. The name was as good as any, and Pigeon even labeled it as such on his maps. It was frustrating for everyone to have been this close, only to turn west and sail away again, but they knew that Dallion was right: it wasn't safe for the *Jubilee* out here. The sooner they could stash her somewhere out of Fleury's reach, the better.

White Crest was a bustling place, but only on the southern side of the island. To the north, dangerous shoals threatened disaster for unsuspecting ships. The smaller islands that dotted the seascape here were uninhabited, but offered stunning, white beaches and tall, shady trees that beckoned passing sailors like sirens tempting them toward their doom. If not for their desperation, Pigeon would never have been willing to navigate a ship through these waters. He gripped the helm so tightly that his knuckles turned white. Lucien, Horus, and Journey called out to him from the bow, where they were looking out for dangers. Katria and Wee Bit did the same from atop the masts.

Somehow, they managed to get the *Jubilee* safely tucked between two of the small islands. A nearby sandbank meant that another ship could only approach from one direction. Lucien didn't like being so trapped, but Dallion convinced him that this was the best hiding place that they could have hoped for. The tall, thick trees on the surrounding islands blocked them from view of passing ships that were brave enough to come this close to the shallows. It was a perfect place to stay out of sight.

Dallion, Journey, Horus, Katria, Jimmy Two-Tales, and Watts piled into the longboat, taking two large sacks of supplies along with them. As before, Katria perched herself at its bow. Wee Bit had gifted her a shirt and a pair of pants of his own, and they fit her much better than the clothes she'd stolen from her ex-fiancé. She still needed to wear a belt to keep the pants up, and the red shirt was knotted in the back to keep it snug against her sides, but there wasn't a man in that longboat who could have denied how gorgeous she was, nonetheless. Her raven hair was in a braid, and the breeze over the sea tugged a few curls loose to play with them. When she glanced over her shoulder to offer Dallion an adventurous smile, Journey saw the grin that the smitten man gave her in return, and he knew that Lucien would have been troubled by it. Dallion was in over his head with this girl, and there was no question as to whether the ship and crew came first for him, or if she did. It wasn't even close.

Watts and Horus rowed the boat to a small patch of sand on the north side of White Crest's main island. They pulled it up the shore to stash it above the high tide line, concealing it with branches and leaves that they scavenged from the surrounding brush. That done, they began the hike over craggy hills toward the south end of the island, where the port was. Dallion and Katria walked ahead of the others, speaking in low voices that were punctuated by Katria's occasional laughter. The other four men followed behind them, and as Horus fell in step beside Journey, he spoke in a low tone that wasn't meant to be overheard by anyone else.

"I don't like it, Teach," Horus grumbled. "He's full of shit about the girl, and don't pretend that you don't know it."

"Does it matter?" Journey asked. "If she can help us find what we're looking for, then we should be glad to have her."

"She's not an expert on maps, if that's what you're talking about. I don't think she's an expert on anything, unless you count running away from home to play pirate."

"She can sail," he reminded him.

Horus gave a grunt in disapproval, but Journey knew it was only because he couldn't argue that point. Katria *could* sail, and she'd carried more than her own weight aboard the ship, so far. Still, Horus muttered, "There are rules about girls for a reason."

Journey wondered how many more times he was going to hear that same sentence used about Katria. He didn't have an argument against it. He only hoped that Dallion knew what he was doing.

The port town on the southern end was called Crestline. It was only as busy as it often was because the next place to trade for anyone heading farther west was nearly a full week away. There were plenty of merchants coming and going from Crestline, but Dallion didn't want any of them. Merchants were often on the payroll of one of the companies, and the less they had to do with them, the better. Instead, Dallion sent Horus and Jimmy Two-Tales to find an inn with a few available rooms for the night, then headed off with the others to find the tavern nearest to the docks – a guaranteed place for the seediest characters and juiciest gossip.

The tavern was called the Golden Conch, and it was a two-story-tall building that overlooked the port and all of the ships that came and went. As Dallion led Journey, Katria, and Watts inside, they were met with lively music from the far corner of the room, where a pair of men were expertly coaxing a spirited tune from a guitar and a drum. A dozen small tables were set up in a circle around an empty space in the center of the room, and a handful of men and women were currently dancing. Dallion led his companions past all of this and sat down at one of the few vacant tables that sat against the far wall. He tossed a generous number of marks onto the table and called for drinks, which the bartender brought soon enough. For a moment, they simply sat around the table without speaking, sipping their drinks and taking in the music.

Journey found his thoughts turning to the two-day voyage ahead of them, and all of the things that might be waiting for them on Tall Island. He was startled by Katria, who had finished her first drink, and now slammed the bottom of the empty glass against the table hard enough to make all three men start. "We should be celebrating!" she informed them. "We're two days away from more riches than any of us have ever imagined. Why does everyone look so bleak?"

"Some of us have been searching for a lot longer than you have, Miss," Watts grumbled. His eyes kept darting toward the front door, and he was bouncing one leg nervously beneath the table…but such things weren't unusual for this man, and Journey reminded himself of Lucien's words: Watts hadn't given them a reason not to trust him, yet.

"Why aren't you chasing the ladies around, Mr. Watts?" Katria asked him. "Do you have a girl of your own somewhere?"

He shrugged his shoulders, but wouldn't look her in the eye. "I've never been the kind of man that ladies are taken with, to be honest."

She gave him a look that said not to be ridiculous and came around to that side of the table to offer him her hand. He seemed alarmed by the gesture, but Katria's smile reassured him.

"It's rude to refuse a dance," she pressed. Watts shot a quick glance in Dallion's direction, but he didn't seem perturbed by what was happening. Watts stood and let Katria grip his hand, and she led him toward the middle of the room, where other dancers were making use of the upbeat music.

Dallion watched them spin around in a few circles before turning his attention to Journey. He was grinning, and Journey braced himself – a grin like that on Dallion's face always meant trouble. He said, "We're getting married."

Journey had been taking a sip of his ale, but now he spat it back in the glass in surprise. He studied his friend's face for any sign that he was joking, but Dallion seemed too pleased with himself for that to have been the case. Journey asked, "What are you talking about?"

"Marriage. You know – two people, in love, having kids, driving each other crazy. Like you and Saige."

"I just…never expected that from you."

Dallion shrugged and jerked a thumb over his shoulder, toward the pairs of dancers. "You've just never known me around her. She's my Saige, Journey. She's the love of my life. I should have gone looking for her as soon as I left Calico, but that doesn't matter, now. You think it was a coincidence that we ran into Bo like we did? We're meant to be together. I've never been more sure about something in my life."

"You said that the time we were playing cards in Port Kelsey, and you wanted me to bet everything I had on a queen turning up for a four of a kind…"

"That big guy with the tattoos was cheating," he reminded him, but then waved this off. "It doesn't matter. Look, I need you to back me up on this. When this treasure ordeal is over, I'm going to settle down, but I want to keep the *Jubilee*. I'm going to need the crew to be on my good side to get them to agree to that, and it isn't going to happen if they think I'm ditching them for Katria."

Journey's expression told him that he thought he was insane, but he asked with marked patience, "Why do you need a ship if you're going to retire, Dal?"

"I just do," he said, but wasn't quite able to explain it any better than that. He didn't have to. Journey knew that as much as Dallion claimed to love Katria, he also loved the *Jubilee*. He also knew something else, however: there was no way that the crew would be willing to disband just because Dallion wanted to quit. If the treasure was enough to make them all so rich that they could stop pirating altogether, then they might agree to it…but even then, Journey suspected that some of them would want to continue living this life until they died. It was simply in some men's blood to do so.

Before he could tell him any of this, Katria and Watts returned to the table, out of breath and grinning like fools. Watts plopped down into the chair beside Journey's again, but Katria offered her hand to Dallion. As he stood, he pulled her close and planted an eager kiss on her lips. Journey sighed. So much for discretion.

He and Watts watched as Katria and Dallion joined the merriment in the center of the room, spinning and laughing and trying to keep up with the swift rhythm the drum player was laying down for them. Watts' eyes followed Katria as she twirled, his eyes wide with admiration.

"I need to find myself a woman like that," he mused, still not taking his gaze off of her.

Journey set aside his empty glass and reached across the table to steal Dallion's. As he did, he warned, "I'm not sure there are any other women like that."

Watts laughed, as if Journey had been joking, but neither of them doubted his words. Watts told him, "I've heard your own wife is just as pretty. Hair like fire, if I've heard right."

"You've heard right," he agreed, and finished off the last of Dallion's ale. He noticed Watts' expression turn slightly sad, and he asked, "What's wrong?"

"Nothing," he said, saying the word so quickly that it could only mean that it was a lie. He shifted in his chair and drummed his fingers against the table a few times. Finally, he said, "You shouldn't be out here. You're not like the other guys.

You've got a family to go home to. If anything happened to you…well, there are people who would miss you."

Journey wasn't sure how to take that. He studied the nervous man beside him, but Watts wouldn't look at him. Instead, he stood and said, "I'm going to go get some fresh air. I'll be back later."

With that, he was gone. Journey watched him head for the front door, scooting between twirling dancers and nearly knocking one woman over as they crashed into one another. Then the door was closed behind him, and Journey couldn't shake the feeling of uneasiness that the man had left him with.

The two-man band ended their song and announced that they were taking a break. Katria returned to the table, where she sat down beside Journey and reached for her cup, only to remember that it was empty. She flashed him a wily smile and asked, "Are you buying the next round?"

"Did you forget to take some of your fiancé's money with you when you let Dallion whisk you off in the early morning hours?"

She threw her head back and laughed, but scolded, "Don't be like that, Journey. I wasn't whisked anywhere. I'm here because I wanted to come. Am I crazy for leaving behind an easy life and running off with a bunch of pirates? Maybe." She leaned toward him with a playful glint in her eye and assured him, "But if I'm crazy, so are you."

He didn't have a witty comeback for that; she was right, after all. Before he could say anything, anyway, Dallion returned to the table, carefully balancing an armload of overfilled cups. He was trailed by the two men who had been playing music only moments before. As they all sat down, Dallion began handing out the cups and announced, "These guys look like our kind of people. I thought they could help us out and we could share a few drinks."

Journey considered the two men in question. Dallion was certainly right about one thing: they looked like fellow pirates. One was wearing a gray hat with a large feather stuck in it, and the other had a handkerchief wrapped around his head. In a swanky tavern on an island of reputable merchants and company men, Journey supposed he shouldn't have been surprised that Dallion had somehow managed to find the only other pirates around for a hundred miles.

Dallion motioned to each person at the table in turn. "Journey. Katria. Michael. Dashane."

"Call me MJ," the man he'd called Michael replied, and he dropped a wink at Katria across the table. She narrowed her eyes at him over the rim of the cup Dallion had handed her, but she couldn't hide her smile.

Dashane, the man in the hat, downed half of his drink in two gulps, then set it aside to ask Dallion, "What sort of help are you looking for?"

"A ride." He'd lowered his voice to avoid being overheard by any of the tavern's other patrons, and everyone at the table leaned closer to hear him. "We're trying to get to a little island east of here. Two days there, two days back. No questions asked, and no company flags."

MJ and Dashane shared a look at that, and for a moment, Journey was hopeful that the two had an available ship somewhere nearby. Dashane frowned, however, and told them,

"Our ship's the *Dancing Cherie*, and she's due back to pick us up two weeks from now. We can give you a ride for free, but you'd have to wait until then. And I don't know if it's a good idea for you to be hanging around here for that long."

"Why not?" Dallion asked.

Dashane held up a finger in a *wait here* gesture and left the table to head to the bar. He plucked a paper from a small stack near the end and returned to the table with it, and he offered it to Dallion. His stomach tightened and his heart missed a beat as he read the words written on it: *Wanted: Captain Dallion Romilly and crew of the brigantine JUBILEE. Known associates: Journey Travert and Lucien Cole. Reward if captured ALIVE. – Captain B. Fleury, Whitefish Trading Co.*

MJ asked Dallion, "That's you?"

"That's us," he muttered. "Where'd these come from?"

"They're all over the place. If you believe the rumors, Captain Fleury has it out for you. You almost wrecked his precious *Huntress* in a storm, and he took it personally. He's been asking around about your ship, and someone must've told him your names."

"Like I said," Dashane told them, "We're willing to give you a ride, but I don't think you want to wait around here long enough for it."

Katria snagged the paper out of Dallion's hands and crinkled it into a ball, then tossed it over her shoulder carelessly. She said without worry, "Fleury must be desperate if he's asking for help. It doesn't matter, anyway. We'll find a faster way."

Dallion grinned at her, and although Journey had expected the wanted poster to worry him, Katria's carefree reaction seemed to have trumped that. Katria smiled back at him, and Journey understood that they truly were as perfect for each other as Dallion claimed.

MJ offered, "There's the *Sally*."

Dashane nodded. "The *Springtime Sally* is a little schooner that hauls fish around here. Her captain is William Mannerly. Trustworthy guy."

"Our kind of trustworthy, anyway," MJ clarified.

"He might take you for cheap. I just hope you don't mind the smell."

Dallion slapped his hands against the table. "It's a done deal. We'll track down Mannerly and his *Sally* in the morning. Right now, I think we could all use a drink. I'm buying."

No one at the table had any complaints about that.

Chapter Eighteen

WITH Dallion's money spent on alcohol, it came down to Journey, Horus, and Jimmy Two-Tales to pool their money to pay for the rooms at the inn down the street. Journey lay awake in his room for a long time, wondering over their luck. They were only two days away from finding out if Dallion had truly been crazy this entire time. Despite all the grief Journey had given him, he hoped he was right about this. If he was, they were all going to be rich beyond their most optimistic dreams. He didn't care as much about that as he did about the fact that this meant Dallion was going to be able to retire. And it wasn't just Dallion; Lucien, Pigeon, Wee Bit, Brain, Thomas, Horus, Jimmy Two-Tales…they were all going to be able to settle out of this lifestyle and live good, long lives. As long as the treasure really was where Dallion thought it was, at any rate. And as long as they didn't see any purple sails.

He let those thoughts wander as he lay in the dark and listened to the muffled music still coming from the tavern next door. It was long after midnight and Journey was nearly asleep when the door to his rented room opened, and Watts' silhouette appeared against the light out in the hallway. He shuffled inside and closed the door behind him as quietly as he could. He let out an audible squeak in surprise as Journey spoke up from the darkness, saying, "There's a blanket and a pillow on the foot of the bed for you."

Watts mumbled what may have been a thanks. Journey listened in the darkness as Watts retrieved the offered bedding and tossed it onto the floor beside the bed. He collapsed onto it, and after a moment, he let out an exhausted sigh. Journey closed his eyes to resume his pursuit of sleep…but curiosity got the better of him, and he asked, "Where have you been, Watty?"

He was silent for a few seconds, and it was long enough for Journey to wonder if the man was going to pretend to have already fallen asleep. Finally, however, he answered, "I found a game of dice going on down the street, and I joined in. Stayed out a little later than I'd meant to."

"Did you win?"

"Broke even."

If he was lying, this time, he was getting better at it. Journey recalled Dallion's trust in the man and struggled to set aside his own misgivings. If they really did find the treasure they so desperately wanted, it would be because of Watts and his map. He would be to thank for any good things that came out of this entire ordeal. Journey resolved to keep that in mind.

"Goodnight, Watty," he said into the dark room. The only response was a small snore. Journey closed his eyes to follow him down into sleep.

*   *   *

IN the next room, Dallion held Katria close beneath the blankets in their rented bed. His thoughts were on stacks of gold bars that were surely waiting for him on Tall Island, but he was pulled from such fantasies as Katria placed a gentle kiss on his bare shoulder. He grinned up into the blackness filling every inch of their room. Even if the haul of the *Weeping Cherub* wasn't on Tall Island, he already had his life's greatest treasure beside him. She'd taken to wearing the shark tooth necklace over the last few days, and that had somehow made it real for him. Katria wasn't going anywhere. Against all odds, she was here to stay.

She whispered, "What if Brain is wrong about the islands?"

"I don't think Brain's ever been wrong about anything in his life."

"How did he become a part of your crew, anyway?"

Brain had been around for so long that it was strange to think back to a time when he hadn't been there. Dallion said, "We were planning to raid a little town called Grainger about a hard day's sail north of the Isle of Runes. The whole town sits right along the shoreline, and the water is deep all the way up to the beach. It was just begging to be raided, so I figured I'd give them what they were asking for."

"How many stories of yours start off like this?"

"Lots. Anyway, the day before the raid, I took Lucien and a few other guys with me into town to look it over. Right in the middle of town, there was this little courtyard, and that's where they kept their stocks and pillory. There was this guy with his head and his wrists locked up, and some kids were throwing rotten fruit at him. He was begging for them to stop. I mean, he was sobbing and screaming. I'd never seen a grown man break down like that, and I…I don't know. There was just something about him that made me feel bad for him, you know? So I asked one of the kids what he'd done to get stuck in the pillory like that, and they said he stole a blanket off of someone's washing line. It wasn't even for himself; he took it for a little girl who said she was cold. I mean, I've stolen a lot of stuff in my life, and I probably deserve to swing from a rope for it, but that blanket was the first and only thing that Brain had to have taken that wasn't his. He didn't deserve to be treated like that. Besides, Brain is different from most people. Not in a bad way. Just…different."

Katria smiled, thinking of all of the quirky traits she'd noticed in the man since she'd met him. Dallion continued, "Anyway, we came back that night to raid the place. We hauled everything we could carry out of Dumont's house, right down to the fancy silverware. The whole time, the cannons were firing on the *Ocean Sprite* – that was my ship at the time – and wrecking all the buildings in range. People were running and screaming. It was chaos. But then I got to that courtyard again, and Brain was still stuck in the pillory. He looked so scared, with the cannonballs blasting everything around him, and I didn't even think about it. I just smashed the lock and let him out. I told him to run, but he just kind of stood there, like he didn't know where to go. I headed for the beach, and he followed me. Lucien said we needed to drop him off at the next port we got to, but Brain…he has this way of growing on you, and when we put in at Port Kelsey, I didn't make him leave. He's been with me ever since."

Katria rested her forehead against his shoulder, still smiling. "You're a good man, Dallion, whether you try to be, or not."

"That's not what Fenwick Dumont thought about me when he put a bounty on my head after the raid. I think he was mostly just pissed off about the bottles of eighty-year-old wine I took from his cellar."

"And all his silverware."

He laughed at that – a carefree, hearty laugh that would have made Fenwick Dumont furious to hear, if he'd still been alive to do so. Dallion pulled Katria tighter against him and closed his eyes to sleep. There was still a grin on his face as he started to dream.

*   *   *

THEY were up early the next morning, and they all set off together to find the *Springtime Sally*. It wasn't hard; they simply followed the stench of fish once they'd reached the docks. Aside from stinky, the *Sally* was also old and warped, but Captain Mannerly boasted about her speed and soundness. They found him to be a stern, surly old man, but he agreed to take them to their destination for next to nothing – according to Mannerly, the unnamed island they wanted to go to was in an area that was prime for fishing this time of year, and he meant to turn their excursion into a lucrative one. They set sail later that morning, and it wasn't long before Journey, Horus, Watts, and Jimmy Two-Tales were recruited to help Mannerly's sailors with occasional tasks. They didn't mind, as it helped pass the time, and Katria even leant a hand when the regular crew didn't grumble too much about it. Dallion managed to befriend Mannerly, whom he discovered was originally from an island near Calico, and the two spent a great deal of time swapping stories of sailing exploits. Mannerly wasn't technically a pirate, but he'd had his fair share of illegal dealings in his day, and he wasn't shy about sharing the tales with his new friend. At night, Journey and Horus would join them to play cards, and the trip to Tall Island passed swiftly.

It was early afternoon when the aged schooner reached her destination. The *Sally* had no longboat, so Mannerly personally took control of the helm to bring the ship as close to the shoreline as possible. It left roughly thirty yards for Dallion and the others to swim, but Mannerly supplied them with a wooden barrel to float their supplies in for the excursion. Horus and Watts were put in charge of getting the barrel to shore. One by one, the members of the *Jubilee*'s crew leapt over the side of the *Sally* to begin the swim. Dallion was the last to go, and he made certain that Mannerly was in agreement over the plan from here: the *Sally* was to wait here for two days, rain or shine. Dallion considered leaving one of his men on board to make sure that the ship didn't take off and leave them stranded, but Mannerly seemed to be a man of his word, and Dallion decided to trust him.

The shoreline of the island was rocky and rough, but beyond that, the land became softer and covered in green moss. The trees were crowded closely together, their upper branches blocking out the sky above to create a shadowy, cooler climate from the one that surrounded the island. The pirates emptied their wooden barrel on a large, flat stone near the shore and took stock of the supplies they had brought along with them: enough food and fresh water to last such a small group at least three days, two lanterns and plenty of oil, a few sheets that would serve as bedding or shelter, a crudely-drawn map of the general shape of the island, compliments of a joint effort between Pigeon and Brain, a machete, two axes, and three spades. The handles of the spades had been broken to allow them to fit into the barrel, and no one looked forward to having to use them, if it came down to that.

Dallion judged the time by the sun and announced, "Let's explore the shoreline first. Look for any sign that someone else has been here before. The growth on this island is old, so look for anything that might be a little younger. Jimmy, Horus, and Watty will go one way along the shore, and Journey and I will go the other way. We'll meet somewhere on the far side of the island. Katria, you'll stay here and set up camp so we can have a fire and a place to sleep tonight."

Katria set a hand on her hip, and all five men visibly braced themselves. "Leave the woman behind to make camp while the boys go exploring? Are you serious?"

"Camp is important," he scoffed, as if insulted by her being insulted. "Besides, we're not going to find anything right now, anyway. We're just going to get a good look at the shoreline, and we'll all decide what to do after that."

She crossed her arms at her chest, but seemed resigned to stay behind. Still, she warned, "If I make everyone a bed for the night, don't be surprised if you find a scorpion in yours."

"Don't call yourself names like that," he grinned, and laughed as she plucked a piece of wood from the ground near her feet and threw it at him. He ducked as it sailed past his head, then started down the shoreline, calling for Journey to go with him.

The other three men headed in the opposite direction, and Katria watched them all go, fuming.

*   *   *

THE island wasn't huge by any standard, but the thick vegetation and treacherous rocks along the shoreline made their trek a painfully slow one. They crashed through thorny brush and thick foliage, staying as close to the water as they could. Horus' group found a small river flowing in from the ocean, but they followed it to find that it tapered off into a swampy patch no more than fifty yards inland. By the time the two groups met up on the far side of the island, it was early evening, and they'd found nothing of interest. They met at the foot of a large, natural tower of stone that jutted up above the treetops. The base of it swept down to the water on this side, sinking steeply into a small lagoon that they hadn't noticed the first time they had passed the island aboard the *Jubilee*. Its waters were separated from the sea by a sandbar that likely hadn't been there until the water levels had risen, sinking much of the island below the surface. The lagoon's water was so clean and blue that most of the men couldn't help but wade out into it. The sandy bottom dropped out beneath their feet quickly, but the water was warm and had very little salt. When Dallion stripped off his shirt and boots, most of the others followed his lead, and they were soon splashing around in the light of the setting sun.

Journey found a ledge near the base of the stone tower and climbed up onto it. From here, he had a breathtaking view of the sunset over the ocean. The sky bled beautiful hues of pink and purple that were reflected in the calm waters. There was a cool, steady breeze up here, and it brushed his hair back pleasantly. From here, it was hard to imagine that there might be a murderous ex-pirate looking for them, or any of a dozen other worries. Right now, it was just the breeze and the sea, interrupted only by the sound of his friends splashing in the warm water below. He would have been lying to tell himself that he didn't miss moments like this on Stonewell.

Eventually, they dragged themselves out of the lagoon and agreed to head back to camp. Instead of returning along the shoreline, they opted to make a direct line through the heart of the island. The trees created a green, living ceiling above their heads, and their trunks grew so closely together in some places that it was difficult to pass through. They spoke very little as they made their way slowly back to the southwestern shore, their focus on looking for any sign of past human activity. They found traces of a campfire and the remains of someone's fish dinner, but they were far too recent to have been left by anyone hiding the treasure they were seeking. They could only hope that it hadn't been discovered already.

By the time they left the foliage and stepped out onto the short stretch of open ground before the ocean, the sun had set and twilight had arrived. They found that Katria had moved all of the supplies a short distance down the shoreline, where the ground was relatively level and high enough to keep the tide from reaching them. She'd done well to build the camp. There were six beds made of green twigs and branches. They surrounded a fire that she'd built within a ring of stones. It was roaring, and as they approached, Katria threw a few more pieces of wood on it. Then she stood back, sweeping an arm around the campsite, and boasted, "Welcome to the finest camp in the region, gentlemen."

A delicious aroma reached their noses, and they were impressed to find four fish baking on flat stones on one side of the fire. Horus and Jimmy Two-Tales cheered. There would be no dried goods for dinner tonight.

Journey kept a watchful eye on the anchored *Sally* until the last of the sun's light gave way to darkness. The gloom swallowed the ship up, but he was confident that her captain would continue to keep his word. Probably, anyway. They enjoyed the fresh fish, and then sat around the fire for a little longer, lost in their own thoughts. Above them, the stars were allowed to steal the show as clouds hid the moon away. The salty breeze off the sea kept the flames of the campfire dancing, and the only sound was that of the waves gently licking the edges of the island. Journey felt as if this was another of those moments that he was going to miss when he went back to Stonewell for good.

After a long time, Katria pulled them all from their thoughts by asking, "What will you do with your share?"

"Retire," Horus answered without hesitation. He'd been picking at his teeth with a cleaned fish bone, but he now tossed it into the fire. "Settle down somewhere quiet, like Port Darry or Windway. Spend my days raising goats and not worrying about money."

"Carine Island," Jimmy Two-Tales offered. "It's quiet there. Property is cheap. I've got a sister who lives on Carine. She's raising four kids on her own, now that her husband's dead.

I'm going to head out there and help her out. I'll build a house and never have to work again in my life. Maybe I'll find a girl and have kids of my own."

Katria looked at Dallion, eyebrows raised, but the only answer he supplied was a telling grin. He countered, "What about you?"

"A house," she answered. "I want a house of my own, where I don't have to depend on anyone else. I don't even care where it is. Wherever the water's warm and the sunsets are pretty. One of Gerald's friends has a swimming pool, and I liked that. Maybe I'll have one. And I'll have a chair on the beach that I can sit in, and I'll watch the sunsets with a drink in my hand."

"And kids?" Dallion asked, his eyes reflecting the firelight. He was sitting across the fire from her, and she looked over its dancing flames to meet his gaze, a soft smile on her lips.

"One or two," she answered, and a wide grin crossed his face. If the others suspected what was going on here, they pretended not to.

"What about you, Teach?" Jimmy asked. Journey didn't answer, at first, staring into the fire as its flames danced and swayed. He knew that it was bad luck for a person to plan on spending money before they even had it…but he decided to do it, anyhow. His plans were too dear to him not to.

"I'm going home," he said, his gaze still on the fire. In them, he saw Saige's red hair. He missed her more than usual. "I'm going back to my wife and daughter. We'll hire more hands from Kinsman and pay them well. We'll raise Mirelle to be a good woman, like her mother, and if my kids ever tell me that they're thinking about pirating, I'll lock them in a room until they're too old to sail."

The others around the fire laughed at this. Only Watts was silent, and Katria pressed, "What about you, Watty?"

He started when she spoke his name, as if he'd been so lost in thought that he'd forgotten anyone else was here with him. "I…I don't know. I guess I'll just go back to the island I was raised on and retire. I still have a sister and some cousins there."

"Where?"

"Matin. It's on the northern edge of the region. It gets cool there in the winter. I like that." He was staring down at his hands in his lap, and he didn't look up from them as he added, "We shouldn't get ahead of ourselves. We haven't found anything, yet. It's bad luck…"

"I don't care about bad luck," Dallion declared. "The treasure's here. I can feel it."

They all hoped he was right.

Chapter Nineteen

JOURNEY woke in the middle of the night from a terrible dream. He'd been on the deck of the *Jubilee*, but the ship was otherwise deserted. The sun had just begun to set, turning the sea beautiful shades of pink and red. On the western horizon, almost blending in with the sky, was a set of purple sails. An acrid smell of smoke was in his nose, but he didn't see any. He willed his legs to carry him to the helm, where he would turn the *Jubilee* away from those approaching sails, but he found himself moving toward the bow, instead. His feet drifted over the smooth wood of the deck so effortlessly that he felt like he was floating. They took him to the banister, and he leaned to look over it at the water around the *Jubilee*'s hull.

Dozens of corpses were floating in the water around the ship. The majority of them were bobbing facedown, but there were a few that were floating on their backs, and their pale, lifeless faces stared up at him. He recognized them all: Lucien, Horus, Jimmy Two-Tales, Wee Bit, Katria, Brain, Pigeon. There were even a few who couldn't possibly have been here, as they had died long ago, but Old Rube, Tawny Paul, and Quick Bill's bodies were bumping along the wooden hull as the gentle waves moved them slowly past. To his horror, he spotted a shock of red hair in the water, and he couldn't stop his eyes from turning toward it. She was facedown in the water, but he knew the fancy dress was Jubilee Travert's.

He managed to tear himself from the sight, but when he looked to the horizon, instead, he found that the purple sails had grown much closer. From here, he could make out the vague shape of the *Huntress'* captain standing at the bow. Dying sunlight reflected off the spyglass in his hands. Journey called for the cannons to be readied below deck, but there was no one there to answer. They were all dead, doomed to float in the water until the sharks and other sea life decided to do something about it.

Dallion's voice spoke his name from behind him, and Journey felt his body turning in the same, slow motions that had brought him to the bow. Dallion was standing just a few feet away from him, but his voice sounded so far away that it was hardly audible.

"We don't all have mansions waiting for us, Prince," Dallion told him. Someone was standing behind him, crouching so that he wouldn't be seen, but Journey could see enough of him to recognize him as Landon Travert. Landon began to laugh, and that laughter was accompanied by the sound of Saige calling his name, her tone one of fear and pain. Journey searched the deck in terror, but there was no sign of her.

"We need to get back to Stonewell," he said to Dallion, but he didn't seem to hear him. Instead, he began to make his way toward the banister at the edge of the deck. Landon was gone, now, but the sound of his laughter still remained, soiling the air with its ringing taunt. Journey reached out for Dallion, but no matter how hard he tried, he couldn't grasp his arm. Dallion reached the banister and leaned over it. Without hesitation, he lifted his feet from the deck and tumbled over the side. A terrifying splash sounded as he met the surface of the water below.

Journey was still reaching after him, but now a hand grasped his shoulder, and he turned to find Saige. Her hair was wet with seawater and laid flat against her head. She was crying, but it was impossible to tell her tears apart from the drops of water running down from her hair.

"The purple sails!" she warned, and her voice sounded just as far away as Dallion's had. "Journey, watch for the purple sails!"

He tore his gaze from her frightened face to look over his shoulder for the sails. They were here, towering over the *Jubilee* at an impossible height, and Saige let out a piercing scream as the first sound of cannon fire shattered the world around them.

That was when Journey woke, and he did so with a gasp that threatened to pull more air into his lungs than they were capable of holding. He was sitting upright on his bed of leaves before he was entirely awake, and it took him a moment to recognize where he was. The starlight revealed the fire pit, which currently only hosted dying embers, and the other five makeshift beds around it. Horus, Jimmy, and Watts were asleep in theirs, snoring softly, but Dallion and Katria were nowhere to be seen. Journey didn't doubt that they'd snuck off to be alone somewhere, but considering the dream he'd just had, their absence still made him uneasy. He looked out over the water to see if the *Springtime Sally* was still anchored where she should have been, but it was too dark out to see that far.

Journey took a few deep breaths to try to slow his heart in his chest. The sound of Saige's scream was still ringing in his ears. He forced himself to lay back down on his bed of leaves. The stars above him twinkled prettily, and he allowed himself to wonder if his wife was looking up at them right now, too. Perhaps their soft light was coming in through the bedroom window, resting on her smooth forehead and cheeks. His side of the bed was empty, but he swore to himself that it wouldn't be like that for much longer. This paranoia about purple sails had to end.

He closed his eyes to try to sleep again, but his thoughts wouldn't let him. After a little while, he heard Dallion and Katria return, whispering to one another and doing their best to keep their childlike giggles from getting loud enough to wake the others. Journey pretended to be asleep and listened as they settled down on their respective beds of leaves. Then they were silent, and after a few minutes, Dallion's breaths had settled into low snores.

There was no more sleep for Journey that night, however.

*   *   *

THEY were up before the sun, making breakfast in nothing but the light of the fire that Jimmy Two-Tales got going again. As the sky brightened in the run-up to sunrise, Dallion gathered everyone and announced the latest plan: he, Journey, and Jimmy would return to the natural stone tower they'd found yesterday and climb to the top of it to get a good look at the rest of the island. After that, they would begin searching that end of the island. Katria, Horus, and Watts would begin scouring the east side, starting at the shoreline and working their way inland. So far, the *Sally* was still anchored where they'd left her, but they all felt the need to work with speed so that her captain wasn't tempted to change his mind about waiting.

Dallion's group reached the tower in good time, but as they stood at its base and peered up at its sheer sides and mossy stones, Jimmy Two-Tales shook his head and announced, "Nope."

"Too tall?" Journey asked him.

"You jackasses can climb all the way up there if you want to, but I'm not taking the risk of falling and breaking my neck."

Dallion elbowed Journey's side and grinned. "Come on, fellow jackass. Daylight's wasting."

It wasn't as hard a climb as they'd feared, since they found that the eastern side of the tower wasn't as sheer as the rest of it. There were ledges that they could use to climb, and they set about doing so. Jimmy watched them for a while, until they were high up enough to make him dizzy. Then he set about searching the surrounding woods in a loose grid pattern.

Journey led the way up the stones, and as he climbed from ledge to ledge, he called down to Dallion a few yards below him, "I just want to let you know that no matter how the rest of the search of this island plays out, I'm going home when we're done."

Dallion gave him a dissatisfied grunt, but didn't argue. Journey said, "I don't care if that makes you mad, Dal. I have a family waiting for me. I know I said I could stick around with you for three months, but I've changed my mind. I need to go back as soon as I can."

"We can fight about this later," Dallion grumbled as he strained to reach the next ledge above him. "Let's just get to the top of this thing alive."

They managed to do so. The treetops were at least twenty feet below the peak of the tower, which they were relieved to find was flat and wide enough for them to rest on. A cool wind rustled Journey's hair as he hauled himself over the ledge, breathing hard. Dallion reached the ledge, as well, and Journey grasped one of his hands to help him over it. Their arms and legs ached terribly, but the view from here was impressive enough to keep them from caring too much about that. The entire island stretched out below them. Tree branches swayed gently with the wind, moving back in forth in a way that almost made it look like the forest was breathing. Journey and Dallion watched this for a few minutes without speaking, and they caught their breaths as they sat beside one another a few feet from the edge. Just off the far shore, the *Sally* rocked softly on the waves.

"You're serious about retiring, aren't you?" Journey asked suddenly.

He'd pulled Dallion from his thoughts, and he looked at him, surprised. "What?"

"You're not going to come up with some excuse to keep pirating after all of this?"

Dallion scoffed, as if such an idea was unimaginable. "That's what this is all about. I told you that when I first asked you to come out here with me. Besides, you heard Katria last night. There's no room in our plans for piracy."

Journey nodded, but then said, "If we don't find this treasure..."

"We will."

"But if we don't, you still need to retire. Saige and I can help you buy a little bit of land so that you and Katria can make a life together. I want your word that you'll let us help you if that's what it comes down to. Agreed?"

Dallion's face was unreadable, but Journey gave him time to decide how to react. After what felt like a long time, the corners of Dallion's mouth turned up toward a grin, and he teased, "I remember the day that you came scampering into the Hoary Witch in Port Kelsey, looking like you hadn't eaten in a week and smelling like it had been even longer since you'd last had a bath. You'd spent a long time trying to track me down to ask for my help."

"And you did help me," Journey agreed. "That's what I'm trying to offer you, now. I'm trying to save your life. That's the only reason I agreed to come all the way out here, in the first place. I want your word that you're done pirating after this."

Dallion considered him, trying to judge how serious he was about it. He must have decided that this wasn't a joke, for he offered his hand for Journey to shake. He grasped it, but also threw his free arm around Dallion's shoulders in a rough hug. Dallion hugged him back. When they let each other go, Journey got to his feet and took in the sight of the waving forest again before saying, "We should climb back down. I don't see anything useful from up here."

"You're always giving up so easily," Dallion said. He pointed to a place near the center of the forest, where some of the trees were a little shorter than the others around them. "See that?

The smaller trees are new growth compared to the tall stuff. I don't know why they would have had to cut some trees down…"

"It's not there," Journey said. He sounded out of breath again, or as if his chest was tight, for some reason.

Dallion frowned. "You don't know that. It's as good a place to start looking as any."

"Dallion," Journey breathed, and this time, there was no mistaking the sound in his voice. It was awe.

Dallion looked up at him to find that Journey had turned his back to the forest that was stretching out over the island. Instead, he was looking down into the lagoon at the base of the northern side of the tower. Dallion was on his feet in a second. He stepped as close to the edge as he dared and followed Journey's gaze downward. There, beneath the clear, calm waters of the lagoon, was the recognizable shape of a ship. It was on its side, but it appeared to be a four-masted galleon. A big one. From here, they could make out the silhouettes of the masts and the graceful curve of her hull toward her bow. The top of her main mast had been only twenty yards from where they had been swimming the previous afternoon.

"It's the *Cherub*," Dallion said, his voice hardly more than a whisper that the wind up here stole away. Journey almost couldn't believe it. Surely, this was a mirage of some sort. The shadows on the floor of the lagoon were playing tricks that just happened to make it look like there was a ship down there…but he knew in his heart that that wasn't true. The shape at the bottom of the lagoon was a ship, and not just any ship. She was the *Weeping Cherub*, and she was cradling a greater treasure than he'd ever dared to dream of.

"It's the *Cherub!*" Dallion exclaimed. This time, his voice carried over the lagoon. He jumped into the air, pumping his fists in celebration, and Journey had to catch the back of his shirt to make sure he didn't fall off the edge of the tower. Dallion whirled and threw his arms around him in a celebratory hug as his words were overtaken by a deep, wild laugh. Journey joined in, and their laughter rang out over the surrounding trees of an island that certainly wasn't used to the sound.

Chapter Twenty

THEY climbed back down so quickly that they both nearly fell multiple times. Somehow, they managed to keep their hold on the small ledges along the way, and they made it to the ground without falling. They rushed to the edge of the lagoon and strained their eyes to see any sign of the ship below its calm water. It hid its secret well – it was impossible to see the ship from here. Both men sat down at the water's edge and hurried to unlace their boots. As they did, Journey pondered aloud, "How did they get her here? If all of the other islands sank, then this island should have been twice the size it is, now. This lagoon might not have even existed."

"Who cares?" Dallion asked. There was a triumphant eagerness in his voice that Journey felt bubbling inside himself, as well. "Maybe the lagoon was a small valley back in the day. They could have moved the ship over land, if they'd cut a big enough path through the trees. I've heard of it being done before, but never for such a big ship."

"We should go find the others to let them know."

Dallion's only response was to stand and take his shirt off, tossing it aside. There wasn't anything in all the Realms that was going to keep him from getting in this water right now. He left his gun atop his shirt and waded out into it, calling for Journey to follow him. He did so, pausing only to leave his own gun and shirt behind with his boots. They swam out to the middle of the lagoon, where the main deck should have been, and took deep breaths to get ready for the dive. There had been no way to tell how deep the ship had been from atop the tower, and they could only hope that it was reachable with just the air in their lungs.

Journey watched Dallion's head slip below the water, then immediately followed. They swam downward, leaving a trail of bubbles in their path that hurried up toward the surface. Once Journey's eyes adjusted, he found that the water down here was likely the clearest he'd ever been in. It wasn't quite as salty as the ocean that was so near it, but it was enough to sting his eyes for the first few moments. What those eyes reported to his brain was almost too good to be true: a hulking beast of a ship that appeared to be entirely intact, at least from what he could tell from here. They were descending over its hull, but they adjusted their course toward the deck. Silt from the bottom of the lagoon coated the hull, but as Journey's hands and feet disturbed the nearby water, it was brushed away to reveal wooden boards that had been beneath these waters for a long, long time. They were shadowy at this depth, but he could still make out the individual lengths of them.

They reached the banister that ran along the main deck, and as they gripped it to peer down over it, they found the silhouette of one of the main hatchways. It was closed, secured with what appeared to be a length of chain. Considering how long it had been submerged, Journey doubted that it would present much of a problem. The important thing was that the chain was still here, now, and that meant that the ship likely hadn't been disturbed throughout the years. The treasure was still waiting within.

They spent the next hour diving over and over again, returning to different parts of the ship each time. All of the hatchways were secured. The helm had become detached from the ship at some point and was laying in the silt on the floor of the lagoon. The sails were gone – either removed by Captain Stonecraft and his crew before leaving the ship here, or destroyed by years spent beneath the water. Otherwise, the *Cherub* was in such good condition that it almost seemed as if she was still seaworthy, if there was a way to get her back to the surface. There wasn't, however. This was her final resting place, and although her treasures would soon leave Tall Island, the *Cherub* never would.

Eventually, both Journey and Dallion were too exhausted to continue diving, and they returned to dry land. Journey set about putting his boots and shirt back on, but Dallion laid on his back on the soft moss at the water's edge for a moment. The sun warmed his wet skin, and he grinned up at the cloudless sky above him.

"We found her, Journey," he said. The giddiness hadn't left his voice, and Journey wasn't surprised. They'd done what should have been impossible, and their lives were about to change forever.

Chapter Twenty-One

ON the other side of the island, Katria and the others continued their search. They'd decided on yet another grid pattern that was efficient, but hadn't turned anything up. They stopped in a small clearing that had been made when one of the larger trees had fallen over recently, and they sat on the mossy ground while they ate a lunch of dried meat. Watts had been especially gloomy all day, and he listened without input as Katria and Horus discussed their next move. They decided to move farther inland, toward the very center of the island, but the lack of any clues so far was disheartening.

Katria finished her last piece of dried beef and stood to wipe bits of moss and dirt from her pants. Horus stood up beside her, saying, "One of us should try to find the others in a few hours. All the lanterns are back at camp, and if we need to keep searching after dark, we're going to need them."

"Are you afraid of the dark, Horus?" Katria teased. "Don't worry. I'll protect you."

Horus started to taunt her in kind, but his words were stopped by a sound they all heard: cannon fire. It echoed through the trees around them. Horus, a weathered seaman, ducked low out of reflex, but the noise didn't make sense. The *Sally* wasn't equipped with cannons, so it couldn't have had anything to do with her. Unless…

Before Katria and Horus could ponder this further, Watts was on his feet, drawing a knife from a loop on the back of his belt. He threw himself at Horus. He wasn't expecting the attack, and he went down hard, screaming as Watts drove the blade of his knife into his lower back. Horus tried to scramble away, but Watts straddled him and stabbed him again, this time in his left side. The knife came out covered in slick, red blood.

Katria had been too shocked to move, at first, but now she recovered and searched frantically around her for anything that could be used as a weapon. Horus managed to twist onto his uninjured side in the dirt and was barely able to catch Watts' wrist as he tried to drive the blade into his chest, this time. He was still on top of him, but was struggling to keep Horus from bucking him off. He drove a fist against the wound in Horus' back, making him scream in agony again. It also made him lose his grip on Watts' wrist, and he shoved the blade into him once more. Horus managed to twist out of the way in time to keep the knife out of his chest, but its blade sank deep into his right shoulder. Horus roared in fury and pain.

Watts pulled the knife free and raised it high, meaning to give him a finishing slice across the throat, but then Katria brought a stone down against the top of Watts' head. He rolled off of Horus, seeing stars, and fell over when he tried to get to his feet. Horus dragged himself across blood-covered moss to cower against the trunk of a large tree. Katria put herself between him and Watts, although there would be little that she could do if Watts decided to use the knife on her, next. She held the stone above her head in both hands, prepared to bring it down on the man's face if he got too close to her.

Watts fumbled to his feet and glared at Katria, his knife out in front of him to ward off any attack that she might have in mind. A thin line of blood was running down his forehead, and it trickled into his right eye. He wiped at it, but continued to glare with his other eye.

"What's wrong with you?" Katria demanded. Her brain hardly registered the fact that there had been two more cannon shots during the scuffle, but now it was silent. Her anger over what had happened finally trumped her fear, and she took a menacing step toward Watts. She was pleased when he stumbled back a few steps, keeping the knife raised.

"I don't want to kill a woman, but that won't stop me if you come any closer!" Watts growled. "Sit down on the ground. Do it!"

She didn't move, at first, struggling to get her anger in check, but Watts convinced her by taking two steps toward her and swiping the knife through the air to show that he meant business. Katria dropped the stone, then sat down and scooted backward until she bumped into Horus. His pained moans told her that he was still alive, for now, but he would be no help if Watts decided to try to kill her.

"You're going to stay right here," Watts told her. His head was still bleeding, but he'd managed to get most of it out of his eye, now. "If you stay here and be quiet, you'll probably be alright. But if you try to follow me, I'll slit your throat from one ear to the other."

"You bastard," Katria managed past the lump in her throat. There were tears of shock and rage in her eyes, but she didn't let them fall. "What have you done?"

"Don't follow me," Watts warned, and then he was gone, crashing through the brush at a run. Katria turned her attention to Horus. He had managed to get himself into a sitting position with his back against the trunk of the tree. The front of his shirt was soaked with blood from his shoulder, but it was nothing compared to the amount of blood coming out of his side. Katria untied the knot in the back of her shirt and then tore a strip of material from the bottom. It didn't want to give, at first, but she put all her strength into it, and the fabric finally surrendered. She folded it with hands that weren't quite steady and pressed it against the wound in Horus' side. He cried out in pain, but she held it there firmly.

"You're going to bleed out if we can't get this to slow down," she told him. The tears in her eyes were falling, after all, and she wiped them away with her free hand, further angered by their presence.

"The cannons," Horus said between gritted teeth. "The *Sally* is under attack. If it's who I think it is…"

"I know," she said, not wanting him to speak the other ship's name. "Keep pressure on this hole in your side, Horus. I have to go find the others."

"Watty took off toward the camp," he said, squeezing his eyes shut as he put his hand over his injured side so that she could let it go. He groaned in pain, but then managed, "Go north. You need to catch them before they get back to camp, too."

"Don't die," she pleaded, and left him there to rush into the surrounding woods. She crashed through low branches that tore at her face and hair, but they couldn't slow her. Her feet pounded against the moss and stones beneath them, and she slapped away the leaves and twigs that got in her way. Her heart was pounding in her chest, but she couldn't afford to give it a break. She was in a race, and the lives of people she cared about were at stake.

*   *   *

WHEN the first boom of a cannon sounded, Journey was sure that he'd imagined it. The *Sally* was an unarmed fishing vessel, after all, and not even the lowliest pirates would have had much reason to try to attack her. But Dallion had been finishing with the laces on his boots, and the way that he stopped, cocking his head to the right to listen, convinced Journey that he'd heard it, too. They were both silent, and after a few seconds, the sound came again.

Dallion looked at him, his eyes wide, and the startled look on his face told Journey what he suspected. Dallion scrambled to put his boots on, hissing, "How the hell did they find us?"

Journey didn't have an explanation for it. The fear he'd felt from his dream threatened to seep back into him, but he pushed it away. He collected his gun from where it was sitting on the ground and checked the clip. It was full. He said, "If they're sending men ashore, it should take them a little while to do so."

"Not very long," Dallion cautioned. He finished putting his boots on and did the same with his shirt. Standing, he said, "We'll split up. You track down Jimmy Two-Tales. I'll go find Katria, Watty, and Horus on the eastern side. Remember where we saw the newer trees from the top of the tower? We'll meet up there."

They both cast a longing look over the calm water of the lagoon. Dallion said gravely, "Whatever happens, we can't lead those bastards here."

"I don't think that's our biggest worry right now," Journey said, but Dallion didn't argue. He watched Journey slip into the woods, and after one last glance in the direction of the hidden ship, Dallion did the same.

Chapter Twenty-Two

GRITTY sand and rocks crunched beneath Bertrand Fleury's boots as he stepped out of the longboat and onto the beach. Behind him, the *Springtime Sally* was listing dangerously far onto one side, and it wouldn't be long before she sank. The *Huntress'* cannons gave one final blast, then fell silent. Fleury grinned in satisfaction, but then turned his attention to the vacant camp on the beach. A thin whisp of smoke was still drifting up from it. Six beds had been fashioned out of leaves and twigs, and a handful of supplies had been left among them by their unsuspecting owners. A dozen of Fleury's men were hauling the two longboats ashore, and Fleury called for two of them to search the little camp.

There was a ruckus in the wall of vegetation just past the camp, and a man suddenly burst through it. His blond hair was a sweaty, tangled mess atop his head, and blood was smeared across his forehead. Fleury placed his hand on the gun on his hip, but didn't draw it, yet. The bloody man clasped his hands before him, like a schoolboy who was about to ask his headmaster for something. To Fleury, he was undiscernible from any other wretched, ratty pirate he'd put an end to in the service of the Whitefish Trading Company.

"Captain Fleury?" the man asked.

Fleury set aside his disdain, for now, and said, "You must be Laurance Watts. I received the messages you sent from White Crest and Espoir. You said I'd be able to find the pirate ship called *Jubilee* here. The schooner I just sank isn't her. If you value your life, you'll have a good explanation."

Watts' hopeful expression turned to one of near-panic. "The ship you want is in the shallows off White Crest. She's tucked away between a few of the little islands on the north side. The plan had been to bring her here, but they were afraid that you'd spot her."

"Did I waste a trip to this little spit of land, then?" Fleury asked, and his right hand twitched toward the gun on his hip once more. It was a silver revolver with a long barrel, and Fleury suspected the desperate man with a bloody face might start to cry in fear if he drew it from its holster.

"No, sir," Watts said quickly, and swept his arm around the camp. "The *Jubilee*'s captain is here on this island. Some of his crew are here, too, and that includes his first mate."

Fleury's eyes narrowed. "Dallion Romilly and Journey Travert are both here?"

Watts gave an eager nod. "Yes, sir. I know that you expected the whole ship, but can I still get my pardon? The *Jubilee* is as good as yours, now that you know where she is. She's cornered in those shallows."

Fleury took a good look at the nearby wall of forest, and the beginnings of a grin returned to the corner of his lips. "As soon as I have Romilly and Travert in my custody, you'll get your pardon, Mr. Watts. I suggest you help us track them down, just in case I'm thinking about changing my mind."

Watts was on the move in an instant. He marched directly into the shadows of the trees. Fleury trailed him, motioning for his men to follow.

Chapter Twenty-Three

DALLION nearly missed her. Katria was moving as quietly as she could through the trees, but he spotted her red shirt through the brush. He called her name as loudly as he dared, and she must have heard him, for she skidded to a halt, her feet slipping on the green moss beneath them. She'd been coming in his direction, but she seemed to be alone. They crossed the short distance to one another, both of them panting. As Katria reached him, she threw her arms around him in a fearful hug.

"It's alright," he told her, but they both knew that wasn't true. If it really was Fleury who had attacked the *Sally*, then it would be foolish not to expect him to send men ashore to hunt them down. There was nowhere to run.

She stepped back to look all around the surrounding forest with wide eyes. "Whatever's happening, Watty's in on it. He attacked Horus and left him for dead. I don't know where he went."

That made more sense than he wanted to admit, and Dallion cursed himself for not listening to Journey and Lucien's concerns about the man. His heart sank as he realized that Watts also knew the location of the *Jubilee*. The way they had stashed her in the shallows had made her a sitting duck. That sparked a flame of fury in Dallion's chest, and he lashed out, punching the nearest tree trunk hard enough to promise bruised knuckles. A stream of obscenities began to flow from his mouth, but Katria shushed him, looking around with those fearful eyes again.

Dallion reeled himself back in to tell her, "I swear, if I get my hands on that scrawny son of a bitch…"

"We should be more worried about his friends getting their hands on us. We need to get back to Horus as soon as we can. He's lost a lot of blood."

"Horus is going to have to wait," Dallion muttered. He started toward the center of the island without explanation, and Katria hurried to keep up. Their footfalls sounded very loud in the otherwise silent forest.

*　　　*　　　*

JOURNEY had found Jimmy Two-Tales napping between the upturned roots of an old, dead tree. It was something that Lucien would have walloped him for if he'd found him like that, but it was far from Journey's most pressing concern. Jimmy had been sleeping so soundly that he hadn't even heard the cannon fire, so Journey caught him up on what was happening as they made their way toward the center of the island at a jog. Journey did well to estimate the location of the newer growth that Dallion had pointed out to him from atop the stone tower. It was thirty yards or so in diameter, and the trees here were slightly shorter than the average height of the rest of the trees on the island. They were spaced a little farther apart, as well, and it was possible to get a glimpse of the sky between some of their branches.

Dallion and the others hadn't arrived yet, so Journey and Jimmy placed their backs against opposite sides of one of the centermost trees to keep watch. They strained their ears to hear any sign of movement in the surrounding brush, but heard nothing…until, faintly, their ears registered the sound of a twig snapping somewhere nearby. It had come from the direction that Journey was watching, and he braced himself for whatever might appear out of the surrounding forest. After a moment, he glimpsed an approaching person through the thinner trees and recognized Watts. He was headed north, his head high and his eyes alert.

Journey called his name, and Watts froze, as if he'd been caught doing something he shouldn't. He recovered after only a moment, however, and looked relieved as his gaze fell on Journey. Watts headed that way, and Jimmy came around the other side of the tree to meet him, too.

"You have no idea how glad I am to see you two," Watts said, and Journey couldn't tell if that was merely relief in his tone, or some sort of giddiness. He put a finger to his lips in a shushing motion, and Watts lowered his voice to ask, "Where's Dallion?"

"He went to find you," Journey told him. He was hardly looking at him, instead opting to keep his eyes scanning the wall of thicker forest that surrounded the area they were in. "Where are Horus and Katria?"

"We got separated. We all panicked when we heard the cannon fire."

"It's the *Huntress*," Jimmy whispered, pressing his back against the tree once again. His eyes were huge and his hands were clenching and unclenching at his sides. "There's no one else that would be blasting holes in ships out here. We need to find a place to hide. Where the hell is everyone else?"

"They can't be far off," Watts said, and to the horror of his comrades, he raised his voice to call out Dallion's name at the top of his lungs. Journey was across the few yards between them in an instant. He grabbed the front of Watts' shirt and shoved him backwards a few steps, making him bump into a tree behind him. Journey kept him there and hissed that he was going to get them all killed.

Watts raised his hands to show that he'd meant no harm, but there was something in his eyes that Journey didn't like. There was some slyness in them, as if he knew something that Journey didn't. As if to affirm his suspicions, Watts told him, "Settle down, Teach. This'll all be over soon."

Journey's jaw dropped as he realized that they'd been had, but before he could fully grasp that as reality, a man he didn't recognized stepped through the brush from the direction that Watts had come from. He was tall, with a firm jawline and piercing eyes. He was dressed in a Whitefish uniform that boasted the insignia of a captain on his shoulders. His blond hair was trimmed close to his head beneath his large, white hat. Even without those things, Journey would have known this man for who he was. Bertrand Fleury was here, at last.

There was a pistol in Fleury's right hand, and a shaft of sunlight made its way through the trees to shine off its long, silver barrel as he pointed it at Journey. His voice was deep and gravelly, and it seemed to echo off the surrounding trees as he instructed, "Step away from Mr. Watts. I won't ask you twice."

Journey forced his hands to let go of Watts' shirt, and he took a few steps back, raising his hands to shoulder level in surrender. His gun was tucked into the back of his pants, but he wasn't foolish enough to grab for it. From where he was still standing with his back against the tree, Jimmy allowed a terrified moan to escape his lips.

Watts scurried like the jackal that he was to Fleury's side. There was a triumphant grin on his face that Journey would have liked to remove with his fists. Fleury didn't take his eyes or gun away from Journey, but asked Watts, "Names?"

"Journey Travert and Jimmy Two-Tales," Watts said, pointing to each man in turn. He paused, however, and then confessed, "I don't know Jimmy's real name."

"You lying snake!" Jimmy roared, some of his fear shifting into anger. To his dismay, at least a dozen other men began to materialize from the surrounding forest. They were all in Whitefish uniforms, and the rifles they were carrying were top-of-the-line.

Journey kept his hands up and ignored the newcomers to keep his gaze on Fleury. He was just as furious as Jimmy was, but when he spoke, he was glad to hear only calmness in his own voice. "Captain Fleury, I presume?"

Fleury gave a quick bow that somehow infuriated him more. Even as he did so, his gun never wavered from its target. "One and the same," he said, and didn't bother trying to hide his conceit. "I'm technically here to represent Whitefish Trading Company, but I've gone out of my way to find you and Captain Romilly to settle a personal score. Where is he, by the way?"

"Dead," he lied immediately, but Watts gave a fervent shake of his head.

"He's lying," Watts tattled. "He's on the island somewhere."

Journey was tempted to try for his gun, anyway, but he wouldn't aim for Fleury. Instead, his last moment of life would be spent shooting the traitorous blabbermouth named Laurence Watts, and it would be worth it. Instead, he asked the man, "What did he promise you, Watty? What have you sold us out for?"

"A full pardon," Watts sneered. "Whitefish is going to give me a paper that says I can't be tried for piracy or any other crimes in the past. I won't have to worry about being caught and hanged."

"In other words, you've sold out just as much as he has," Journey said, turning his fiery gaze on Fleury. "If you wanted out of the life, you could have just retired. But that wasn't good enough; you had to turn on the people that are only doing the same things you once did."

"I've made my peace with my past," Fleury said, but there was something in his tone that said that may not have been completely true. He pointed at the ground at Journey's feet and ordered, "On your knees. Keep your hands nice and high."

"If you reach for your gun, he'll shoot you," Watts added, but Journey gave him a look so piercing that it shut him up.

Once Journey was on his knees, one of Fleury's men approached him with caution. Part of his gun was visible above the waistline of his pants, and the man snatched it out. Journey didn't fight him. Two other men seized Jimmy by the arms and forced him to his knees beside Journey. They bound their hands behind their backs with lengths of rope. As one of the men tightened the knots around Journey's wrists, Fleury told him, "There are rumors that you're an island-owner, boy. And I saw that ring on your finger. Why's a rich, married lad like you sailing with a bunch of pirates?"

Journey didn't answer, keeping his eyes on Watts. They bore into him so hotly that Watts wouldn't look at him. He shifted his weight from one foot to the other and kept his gaze on the ground, instead. Fleury waited until his men were sure that the ropes were secure before motioning for them to step away from their captives. Then he came to stand beside Journey and set the barrel of his gun against his left temple. Journey's breath caught, but he still didn't take his gaze off of Watts.

"What now?" he asked, and there was only the slightest tremor in his voice.

"Now, we call the rest of your pals to join us," Fleury said, and Journey cursed himself as he realized that he had unwillingly become bait.

Chapter Twenty-Four

DALLION and Katria had almost reached the area of the forest where they'd planned on meeting the others when a voice they didn't recognize rang out. It was coming from just ahead of them, and Dallion grabbed Katria's hand to pull her behind a nearby tree. They pressed their backs against its rough bark and held their breaths to listen to the stranger's voice.

"Captain Romilly! Unless you show yourself, I'm going to shoot two members of your crew! Don't waste their lives, Romilly! Come on out!"

Katria immediately began asking whispered questions, but Dallion shushed her. He closed his eyes, trying to hear his own thoughts over the sound of his racing heart. They needed a plan, something that would give them a chance to get off of this island…

"You have one chance to save their lives, Romilly!" the voice called through the trees. "This isn't how you want your first mate's life to end, is it?"

Just like that, all of the options that he'd been hoping for disintegrated. A strange sort of peace came over him, brought on by a certainty that he was going to meet his end today. All of the cards were down, now, and the game was up. He'd never thought that he would find himself so tolerant of his own death, but now that it was the only possibility, he felt a serene sense of acceptance.

When he opened his eyes, Katria was watching him closely, clearly waiting for him to suggest a way out of this. Instead, he turned so that he faced her squarely. He took both of her hands in his and gave them a reassuring squeeze. "I'm going to go handle this. I need you to go back to Horus and keep him safe. Stay hidden and don't make a sound. Got it?"

Fleury was shouting something again, but she ignored it to tell Dallion, "If you go out there like he wants, he'll kill you. He isn't going to let you leave here alive."

"I'll be fine," he said, but they both knew that was a lie. He let go of one of her hands so that he could stroke her cheek. He saw that there was something besides fear in those brown eyes of hers: love. "We'll be together again before you know it," he told her. "For now, go to Horus…"

She threw her arms around him before he could say more than that, and she whispered in his ear, "I've come this far with you. I'm not going to let you go meet Fleury on your own."

"I won't be on my own. Journey's down there. He and I have gotten out of worse scrapes than this together. Don't worry."

"I can help you."

"I love you," he said firmly, taking a half a step back so that she had to take her arms from around the back of his neck. He placed his hands on either side of her face and took a long, loving look at her. He said with a sad smile, "You're the best thing that's ever happened to me, Kat. That's why you have to stay safe, alright? Stay hidden. I'll come find you after I take care of Fleury."

"Please…"

He placed a kiss on her lips before she could argue further. She kissed him back, and after only a moment, he could taste the salty tears that had started streaming down her cheeks. From his place nearby, Fleury was calling out about a last warning, but Dallion hardly heard him. There was so much more that he wanted to tell this woman…but he had run out of time.

Dallion let her go and stepped back, giving her a reassuring grin that she probably didn't buy. Then he forced himself to turn away, and he took the first step toward Fleury's voice and his fate.

*   *   *

JOURNEY'S hopes were beginning to rise that Dallion wasn't within earshot of Fleury's threats. If he didn't arrive on time and Fleury shot him, then the sound of the gunfire would warn Dallion, Katria, and Horus of where the danger was. Fleury and his men would scour the island, but if they were able to find a good enough place to hide…

Those hopes were dashed when Dallion's voice called out for Fleury to hold his fire. Everyone's attention went to a space between two trees that was choked with green growth. Dallion pushed his way through it and stepped into view. His gun was in his hand, but it was raised above his head in surrender. Three of Fleury's men hurried to him, and he didn't fight them as they seized the gun and set to work tying his hands behind his back.

With that done, they led him roughly by the arms to Fleury, who grinned with satisfaction as Dallion was forced to his knees between Journey and Jimmy Two-Tales. Watts stood off to the side, beaming, but Dallion ignored him to focus on the man who had become his nemesis.

"Captain Romilly," Fleury crooned, taking his aim off of Journey to turn the gun in his direction, instead. "It took a lot of patience and talent to find you. Whitefish has a bounty of over ten thousand marks on your head. That would have been reward enough for killing you, but that stunt you pulled with the storm off Quill almost sank my ship, and I don't take things like that lightly. Now, you're going to pay for it."

Dallion gave him a bored look and said to Journey beside him, "He sounds pretty pompous for a guy who couldn't even cut it as a pirate anymore."

Fleury didn't bother taking that bait. Instead, he asked Watts, "Where are the rest of the crew?"

Dallion's eyes met Watts' own, and Dallion mouthed the word *Please*. He didn't expect it to work; Watts had betrayed them all, already, and there was no reason to think that he would care enough to spare Katria's life. Watty hesitated for a moment, however, and Dallion silently willed him to think about the kindness she had shown him. He recalled her dancing with him in Crestline, letting him spin her around and around in circles. Watty now held Katria's life in his hands, and if Dallion could have done so, he would have begged him to spare her.

His heart leapt as Watty said, "It's just the three of them. There isn't anyone else."

Fleury whirled, surprising them all, and strode the short distance to where Watts was standing. He brought his gun against the left side of Watts' face with a painful *crack* that could only have meant a broken cheekbone. Watts cried out and went to his knees on the mossy ground at Fleury's feet, and raised his hands above his head to ward off any further attacks.

"I don't tolerate liars!" Fleury barked, and for the first time, Dallion saw the pirate that this man had once been: wild, vicious, and fearsome. The calm demeanor that his role aboard the *Huntress* demanded of him had been stripped away, and if Dallion hadn't been certain before that he was going to kill them all in cold blood, this convinced them.

Watts cowered at his feet, sobbing as he placed one hand over the injured side of his face. Fleury squatted down beside him and said in a calmer voice, "There were six beds around the fire pit at the camp I arrived at. I see four men. Where are the other two?"

"Dead! I killed them both when the cannons first started firing." To prove this, Watts held the sleeve of his shirt out for him to see. From where Dallion was, he could see the bloodstains on it, and although he hated to think that Horus was bleeding out somewhere on the island, he hoped that the blood on Watty's sleeve would be enough for Fleury to believe him.

It must have been, for Fleury visibly relaxed, and he left Watts alone. He came to stand before his three captives once more. Dallion kept silent as he watched him sooth the front of his uniform with the hand not holding the gun, and it was clear that he was getting himself back under control. His composure returned after only a few seconds, but Dallion wasn't going to forget what it was like for him to lose it anytime soon.

"Now," he said, "Mr. Watts has told me where I can find the *Jubilee*. It was smart of you to hide her in shallow waters, but it won't stop me. The rest of your crew will be dead soon, but I have another plan for the three of you." He eyed each one of them, starting with Jimmy and ending with Journey. There was victory on his face, but it was a cold look. "I'm going to take you with me to go sink her. You're going to watch while I send her to the bottom, even if I have to tie you to the foremast to make sure you get a good view. And once she's been blasted into a thousand pieces, I'll fish the survivors out of the water and let you watch as I slit their throats, one by one."

A sobbing noise escaped Jimmy Two-Tales' lips, but Dallion refused to show a reaction. Beside him, Journey asked rather gently, "Is that what you did to your own crew when you changed sides?"

Fleury answered with a cold, stony stare that was as chilling as it was hard to read. His professional demeanor threatened to break again, but he kept himself in check and managed to say through gritted teeth, "I was going to kill the three of you after all of that, Mr. Travert, but I think that you've earned something worse. Whitefish owns an island that grows sugarcane. A lot of sugarcane. The workers aren't there by choice. They're convicted criminals who've been sentenced to a life of hard labor on the island. It's a prison, you see, and I know the man who runs it. I'm going to deliver you to him, and I'll pay him good money to make sure you disappear there. I'm going to make sure that the three of you are worked…and worked…and worked. They'll work you until you die. The rest of your pathetic lives will be spent slaving away for the benefit of Whitefish Trading, while you dream of the days when you were free to sail the seas. That's the only fate that's awful enough for the likes of you. And when you're lying in the dirt one day, gasping your last, pathetic breaths, I hope that you remember my face and know that I've won. After all the pain and horror you'll have faced, you'll know that *I won*."

Dallion faked a loud yawn. There was another flash of Fleury's uncontrollable rage, and he lashed out with the gun. He was trying for Dallion's cheek, just as he'd done to Watts, but he saw it coming and managed to turn away enough to escape the worst of the blow. The barrel connected with the side of his head, and although it was painful, it wasn't nearly as bad as Fleury had meant it to be.

Fleury struggled with his temper for a moment, most likely fighting the urge to simply point the gun at Dallion and pull the trigger. Instead, he turned and marched back to Watts, who had managed to get to his feet, still weeping. Too late, he realized that Fleury was leveling the gun at him. The shot echoed off of the surrounding trees, and Watts collapsed in an instant. A bloom of red blood spread across the front of his shirt, stemming from the hole that the bullet had placed over his heart.

A few of Fleury's men shared looks of surprise, and one of them dared, "Captain, he was supposed to get a full pardon…"

"For piracy," Fleury agreed, straightening the front of his uniform once more. "I killed him for being a piece of garbage. I'd say that justice has been served. Any objections?"

None of his men would meet his gaze, and Fleury must have taken that as a no, because he started south, toward the shore. Before disappearing into the thick of the forest, he ordered his men to bring the three remaining pirates. Journey, Dallion, and Jimmy Two-Tales were hauled to their feet, and they dreaded every step they were forced to take.

*   *   *

KATRIA watched from where she was crouched in the bushes as Dallion and the others were led away. Once the last of Fleury's men were out of sight, she allowed herself to breathe normally. She was trembling – she'd been certain that she was going to witness Dallion, Journey, and Jimmy's deaths – but by the grace of some higher power, that hadn't happened. She'd managed to hear most of what Fleury had been saying, however, and the future he planned for them wasn't much better. She considered following them to the shore, but what could she do after that? She had no way of helping them escape from all those armed soldiers. A feeling of helplessness threatened to overtake her, but she shut it out. They were still alive, which meant there was still hope. And that meant that it was up to her to do something.

She waited for a long time to make sure that none of Fleury's men were going to double back for any reason. Then she slipped quietly out of the brush and among the thinner trees to Watts' body. He had fallen in an unnatural, twisted position. His eyes were wide and his mouth was agape, as if frozen in perpetual alarm. Katria tried not to look at his face as she fished the knife from his belt. She searched his pockets for anything else that might be useful, but there was nothing except a few, crumpled marks.

She thought she heard a twig snap nearby, and she froze, crouching low beside the corpse. After a full minute without a repeat of the sound, she decided that her nerves were playing tricks on her and got moving again. She headed in the direction in which she'd left Horus, hoping that the injured man was still alive.

They were going to need each other if they were going to survive on this island until they were rescued…if that happened, at all.

Chapter Twenty-Five

LUCIEN sat at the small table in Dallion's cabin with a game of backgammon before him. Pigeon sat across from him, trying to decide his next move. Boredom had driven them both to this desperation. Lucien despised the game and had never understood why Dallion and Journey enjoyed it so much, but there was nothing else to do on the ship right now. It had been three days since Dallion and the others had set off without the rest of the crew, and he'd run out of tasks to assign everyone to keep them busy. They were currently holding wrestling competitions on the main deck, but even that was starting to get old, now. These were men of action, and they didn't know what to do when their hands weren't occupied.

The last three days had given him plenty of time to think, and there was one thing that didn't sit right with Lucien: Watts. He'd never been one for putting too much faith in wild hunches or inklings, but there was something about the man's behavior that made Lucien uneasy. He went over his past conversations with him in his head, and the one he kept coming back to was the day they had left Espoir with fresh supplies. Watts had seemed sincere in his apology for returning late to the ship. Lucien recalled the man's messy hair and breathlessness as he'd told him the tale about being mugged while purchasing supplies. The three mystery men had made off with the boxes of eggs and the rest of the marks in Watts' pockets. Surely, the limp that he'd returned with hadn't been a ruse…but the more Lucien thought about it, the more certain he was that the limp had disappeared by the following morning.

Pigeon finally took his turn, making a decent move on the game board. Then he sat back in his chair with a sigh. "Tell me the truth, Lucien: what do you think the odds are of them coming back with good news?"

"Somewhere between zero and less than zero," he muttered as he rolled the dice on the board. "But you never know. Dallion has surprised me before."

"At this point, I'm ready for them to come back, with or without the treasure. Sitting still like this is driving me crazy."

Lucien didn't comment on that, but moved one of his checkers and ended his turn. As he waited for Pigeon to make his move, his thoughts turned back to Watts again. Journey had been helping him keep an eye on the man, but they hadn't noticed anything unusual in his activities on the ship. There was no reason to feel as uneasy about him as Lucien currently did.

Even so, he asked Pigeon, "Have you noticed anything strange about Watty lately?"

Pigeon considered for a moment. "He's friendlier than he used to be. I think a lot of the crew has started liking him a little more than they used to."

"Does that include you?"

Pigeon shrugged, but also frowned. "I don't have any reason not to like him, but…"

"But you don't trust him?" Lucien pressed.

Pigeon shrugged again, then moved one of his checkers on the board. "It's hard to trust most of these guys, isn't it? But with Watty, it was like he didn't want anyone to get to know him too well. And then all of a sudden, he's buddying up to everyone. I've played cards with him a few times lately. He's still awkward as hell, but he tries to joke around and have a good time. He didn't even get mad when he lost a bunch of marks to Spits a few days ago. He just shook his hand at the end and told him he'd gotten lucky."

"When was this?"

"Not too long ago. It was the night after we left Espoir with all the supplies."

Lucien had been reaching to move one of his checkers, but his hand paused just above it. His eyes were narrow as they studied Pigeon across the table. "You're sure it was the same night? It wasn't before then?"

Pigeon shook his head. "I remember some of the guys giving him a hard time about being late getting back to the ship. Wee Bit and Big Al were telling him he needed to learn to tell time. Watty took it alright, though."

Lucien sat back in his chair, the backgammon game temporarily forgotten. Watty was a liar, at the very least, since he'd claimed that all of his own money had been lost in the mugging on Espoir. He was likely a thief, as well, since it could be assumed that some of the money he'd lost to Spits had been at least a portion of what Catfish had given him to purchase eggs with. So if he hadn't been mugged and he hadn't been busy buying eggs, what had he been up to that afternoon? What had made him so late getting back to the ship? Catfish had suspected

Watty had gone to find the nearest whorehouse, and that would have explained things…but that didn't sit right with Lucien, either. He heard Journey's voice in his head asking if they trusted the man.

"I hope they get back here soon," Pigeon complained, and although it was still Lucien's turn, he rolled the dice on the board between them. "All I can think about is seeing purple sails. I feel like a sitting duck."

Lucien couldn't have agreed more, and that finally decided it. He pushed the backgammon board aside on the table and said, "Go get one of your maps, Pigeon."

He brightened. "Where are we going?"

Anywhere that's not the last place Watty saw us, he thought, but didn't tell him that. Instead, he merely repeated his request for the map, and Pigeon left the cabin to fetch it.

Chapter Twenty-Six

KATRIA rested on a flat rock at the edge of the water. The sun was hanging low in the west, and it would begin to set before long. She stared out over the empty ocean that had her trapped. She'd never hated the sea before, but she was getting there now. As beautiful and enticing as it was, she'd started to suspect that it was going to mean her death on this tiny speck of green in all the blue.

It had been two weeks since the *Huntress* had departed with Dallion, Journey, and Jimmy on board. The last of the supplies they'd brought here with them hadn't lasted them very long, but Katria had kept herself and Horus alive by fishing and collecting berries from various bushes that she'd found on the island. It had rained twice in the last two weeks, flooding a low spot in the ground with enough fresh water for them to survive on. It was muddy and needed to be boiled first, but that was alright. She'd fashioned bandages out of one of the sheets they'd brought with their supplies, and Horus was doing okay. He was still weak and not much use to help with their survival, but he hadn't died, yet, and Katria was glad. Being stuck on this island was bad enough. Being stuck here alone would have been so much worse.

She stood, brushing the sand off of her pants, and started her daily walk down the shoreline. Every bit of metal that they'd brought with them here was lined up along the water's edge in the hopes that sunlight would reflect off it and attract a passing ship. She'd spent hours trying to shine axe heads, spades, and tin cups for this purpose, but it had turned out to be futile, so far. This island was far outside of any shipping lane, and she wasn't surprised that she'd yet to spot a single ship on the horizon. Despite this, she continued to check each bit of metal every afternoon to make sure that none of them had fallen over and tumbled from the places she'd left them atop rocks. It gave her something to do, and that was important. Every time she found herself sitting idly, her thoughts turned to desperate ones about Dallion. She was powerless to help him or the others, and that knowledge was going to drive her insane, if she wasn't careful.

She walked the length of her metal signal line and was satisfied that none of them had budged since the day before. She started back toward camp, where she would ask Horus to tell her another story about the various adventures of the *Jubilee* or the ship that he had served on before that one, called the *Golden Wake*. The *Wake* had been captained by a middle-aged man named Edward Horner, and Horus had served as his boatswain for two years before the man was killed in a fight against a frigate that sailed beneath a Commercial Horizon flag. Horus had promised to tell her the tale of how he had come to leave the *Wake* for the *Jubilee* tonight, and Katria was eager to hear it. Like her daily walks along the shoreline, Horus' stories were helping to keep her sane.

She'd made it halfway back to camp when a splash off shore made her look in that direction. There was a pod of dolphins that came near the island most afternoons, and as she watched, one of them jumped again. Something far beyond the dolphin caught her attention, however, and she stopped walking, shielding her eyes from the afternoon sun with one hand to get a better look. It was a ship, but it was still so far away that it was no more than a small dot on the horizon. It was the first one she'd seen since getting stranded here, and her heart leapt with hope that she couldn't keep at bay.

She scrambled to fetch a nearby axe and hefted it above her head, tilting it back and forth to try to catch the sunlight in it. She had no idea if it could be seen from this distance, but she was far too desperate not to try. Slowly, very slowly, the tiny dot grew larger as the ship drew closer, and she realized with surprise that it was coming directly toward the island. She continued to tilt the axe back and forth, whispering, "See me. You have to see me."

She saw a glimmer of sunlight off of something aboard the ship, and her desperation assured her that it was a spyglass. They'd seen her. They must have, for they were still coming straight toward her. She cried out in relief, dropping the axe to the ground at her feet, and took off toward camp. Horus was dozing on a bed of leaves she'd rebuilt for him just this morning, but he was startled awake as she cried his name. She arrived in camp at a run and went to her knees beside him. She threw her arms around his shoulders in an ecstatic hug.

"There's a ship!" she announced, and she didn't mind the tears in her eyes, this time. "They've seen me, Horus! They're coming!"

His expression of relief was a hesitant one, and she understood why: the approaching ship could have been the *Huntress* returning to finish them off. Her excitement couldn't be quelled by such fears, however, and she let him go to run back to the shoreline. She climbed up on one of the higher rocks there and waved to the approaching vessel, calling out toward it, "Keep coming, boys!"

The ship was too far away to hear her, yet, but as it grew closer, her jaw dropped. She recalled Fleury telling the others about his plans, and she'd been trying to come to terms with the fact that the *Jubilee* had been destroyed, by now…and yet here she was, sailing along like there was nothing in all the Realms that could stop her. She let out a triumphant shout, her fists pumping above her head. She climbed down from the rock and hurried back to Horus to share the news, but she could tell by the look on his face that he already knew. She threw her arms around him in another hug, and this time, he hugged her back. They were saved, and they would soon be in the company of friends again.

Lucien and Thomas rowed to shore in a longboat. As soon as Lucien's boots were on dry land, Katria threw herself at him with enough force to make him stumble. He kept his feet and let her squeeze him tightly, even putting an arm around her in an awkward, yet comforting, hug. He considered the camp over the top of her head. Horus was struggling to get to his feet. Without a shirt on, his bandages were easy to see. Lucien asked Katria, "What happened here?"

"Fleury," she answered, letting him go to step back. Thomas finished securing the longboat and joined them on the shore as Katria explained everything that had happened. When she was finished, she asked with real amazement, "How did you keep the *Jubilee* away from him?"

"Gut instinct," Lucien muttered. "He must have been surprised to show up at Espoir to find us gone. We left two men on one of the smaller islands to wait for you to return. But you never came back, and after a while, it wasn't hard to figure out that something had gone wrong. We took the risk of coming out here to find you, but we need to get moving. We don't know where the *Huntress* is, now."

"We need to find her. Fleury didn't say where the island is that he's taking Dallion, Journey, and Jimmy to. We need to figure out where he went."

Lucien didn't answer this, and Katria felt a pang of panic in her chest. She pressed, "Lucien? We have to find them…"

"We'll talk about all of that on the ship. The longer we stay here, the more danger we're in."

She decided not to argue that. Instead, she returned to Horus to help Thomas get him into the longboat. With Thomas rowing, they were soon on their way back to the ship, and Lucien asked, "No treasure?"

Horus and Katria both shook their heads, but Lucien wasn't surprised. Considering how much of a disaster this excursion had turned out to be, it would have been too much to ask for anything good from it.

*   *   *

AS soon as they were back aboard the *Jubilee*, Lucien called for Pigeon to get them as far away from Tall Island as possible. Brain,

Wee Bit, and Spits helped Horus below, where he would be able to rest and dress his wounds with clean bandages. Lucien started for Dallion's cabin, ignoring Katria as she called for him to stop. She caught up to him before he could leave the main deck, however, and grabbed his arm. Lucien was almost a full foot taller than her and twice her strength, but he let her stop him, all the same. Turning to her, he found anger on her face.

"What's the plan?" she dared him, but judging by her fury, she already knew what it was.

Lucien looked around to find that nearly two dozen members of the crew were gathering around them, and there was uncertainty written all over them. Lucien raised his voice so that they could all hear him and announced, "The captain has been arrested by Fleury and taken aboard the *Huntress*. Teach and Jimmy Two-Tales are with him. Fleury means to take them to a prison island somewhere. He has a two-week head start on us. Even if he didn't…" He didn't finish. He didn't have to.

Catfish was among the men who had gathered around, and he took his hat off to clutch it solemnly before him, as if he'd just been informed of his friends' untimely death. Katria looked all around at the others to find that most of them were sporting similar expressions of sadness. She cried, "They're not dead, yet! We can't just write them off and go on with our lives! We have to go find them!"

All of the men glanced around at one another at that, and she was glad to see at least some shame on their faces. Catfish soothed, "We'd all like to go after them, missy, but it's the *Huntress* we're talking about. If it was any other ship…"

"It doesn't matter what ship it is, Catfish. How many times have those men risked their lives for you?" She picked Lil Gabe out of the crowd and pointed an accusing finger at him. "Journey almost died saving you in that storm, Gabe. You'd be dead right now if he hadn't risked his own life. And you've all told me dozens of stories about the times that Dallion got you out of dangerous situations. He's been a good captain to you for all this time, and now you just want to turn your backs on him when he really needs you?"

"None of us *want* to do that," Thomas argued. He was standing between Spunky and a crewman that Katria didn't know, but they were both nodding in agreement with him. "But we don't want to hurry off to our deaths, either. The *Jubilee* is a good ship, but she doesn't stand a chance against the *Huntress*. We'd all die."

Katria took in a deep breath, trying to calm herself down. She said with a little more control, "All we need to do is figure out which island he took them to and go there to get them. If we can do that without running into the *Huntress* at all, that's fine. But we can't just give up and run away. We can't."

The looks on their faces said differently, but all eyes went to Lucien for the decision. Katria had ever seen the man look so worn out before. His shoulders were slumped and his lips were pursed so tightly that they were little more than a thin line above his chin. After a few moments of contemplation, he said, "We could ask around about the island Fleury mentioned..."

"For what?" Catfish scoffed. "So Fleury can hear about us sticking our noses in it and come after us for it? It's like I said: if it was any other ship, it would be different. We need to be smart about this."

"How many of you learned to read because Journey showed you how?" Katria demanded. "How many times did Jimmy Two-Tales lend a hand with your chores? How much good money has Dallion put in your pockets over the years? If you don't care about anything else, I know you care about the money! Where would most of you be if you didn't have this ship? It's because of Dallion and Journey that you even have the *Jubilee*!"

Not a single person there would meet her gaze…except Lucien. Katria pleaded with him, "You and Dallion have been through so much together. You can't just leave him to rot, now, Lucien. We have to do something."

"It isn't worth the risks," Thomas said quietly. "The captain would agree."

Katria ignored him, her dark eyes still pleading with Lucien. There wasn't much hope in his voice when he announced, "We'll put it to a vote. Thomas, go let everyone below know. Everybody has a say in it."

Thomas hurried off to do so, and Katria's hopes were rekindled. Surely, the majority of the crew would be willing to risk as much for Dallion and Journey as they'd risked for them over the years. There was no way that they would vote to abandon them.

Fifteen minutes later, as a deck full of pirates surrounded her with their hands raised, she was proven wrong. Only a handful of them had voted to try to rescue their missing comrades: Lucien, Wee Bit, Brain, Lil Gabe, and Pigeon. The rest were united in their desire to turn tail and flee from what they deemed certain death.

Katria looked around at all of the gathered men her as they finally lowered their hands. She felt angry tears stinging her eyes, but she refused to let them fall. Instead, she pointed a finger at Catfish and hissed, "Coward!"

"Katria…" Lucien started, but she ignored him, turning in a circle to point at each and every man around her.

"Cowards!" she declared. "All of you! Your bellies are so yellow, I'm surprised you're not afraid of your own shadows. You're a bunch of worthless, spineless, awful cowards!"

The looks on the faces of many of the men surrounding her turned quickly from sad determination to anger. Lucien grabbed for Katria's wrist, but she slipped nimbly from his grasp and raised her voice to be heard by even more of the crewmembers. "Aren't you cowards ashamed to know that a woman is a hundred times braver than any of you? Dallion should have taken on a female crew, instead of a bunch of gutless, pathetic deserters like you!"

She would have gone on in her fury, but Lucien caught her arm and bent to put his shoulder beneath her breasts. Then he lifted her, setting her stomach over his shoulder, and carried her like that toward Dallion's cabin. She squirmed wildly as she demanded to be set down, but he kept going. They left behind a crew of grumbling men.

Lucien threw the door of the cabin open and strode inside. He slammed the door closed behind them, then went to the bed and dumped Katria onto it. She roared in anger, but stayed laying on her back on the soft blankets. Lucien stood at the edge of the bed, his arms crossed at his chest, and demanded, "Are you crazy, or just a fool?"

"This is bullshit!" she spat, sitting up.

"There's nothing I can do. The crew voted to leave, so we'll leave. We'll head for Port Kelsey and lay low for a while. After that, maybe they'll change their minds."

"That's not good enough," she said, trying to get off of the bed. Lucien shoved her shoulders, however, pushing her back down onto it. She swatted his hands away, but didn't try to get up again. Instead, she peered up at him with fearful desperation and begged, "He thinks of you like an older brother, Lucien. He would never leave you like this. Don't make me try to find him on my own. I need your help. Dallion needs your help. Journey needs it, too, and he saved your son's life. You owe him. You owe it to all three of them."

Lucien opened his mouth to argue, but there was no point in doing so. After all, they both knew she was right.

Chapter Twenty-Seven

THE brig aboard the *Huntress* was a cramped, dark space that was void of any hope, but as bad as that was, Journey could only assume that their destination would be worse. He lost track of the days, but after what may have been an eternity, he and the others were marched back onto the deck by Fleury's men. It took a while for Journey's eyes to adjust to the bright sunlight, but once they had, he found that the *Huntress* was now resting at the end of a long, wooden dock. At the other end of the dock was an island full of tall fences and several tall, stone guard towers. From what he could see over some of the fences, the island was also home to a sprawling sugarcane farm – one of the largest he'd ever seen. He supposed he should have felt despair at the sight of the prison that was waiting for him, or at the very least, fear. Instead, a strange sort of numbness had come over him, as if this wasn't real, and he would soon wake up from this terrible nightmare.

He followed Dallion and Jimmy Two-Tales as they were marched down the gangway at gunpoint, and they were immediately ushered into a large, stone building at the far end of the dock. The room they stepped into had no windows and was at least fifteen degrees hotter than the air outside had been. It was empty, save for a handful of benches that lined the walls, but Journey and the others were told to stand in the middle of the room. Fleury was already waiting for them there, and his lips were stretched in a disturbing grin. A portly man with a balding head was standing beside him. He was dressed in an expensive suit that seemed out of place among the old, sagging benches and dusty floor.

Once his newest arrivals had come to a stop before him, the balding man offered them a smile they didn't trust and said, "Welcome to Dove's Roost, gentleman. This island is the property of the Whitefish Trading Company, and it's also your new home. You'll be expected to work in the fields from sunrise to sunset. No excuses and no exceptions. You'll be given a meal each morning and each evening in the bunkhouses. There's also a bathhouse that you're allowed to use once a week. No fighting, no loitering, and no talking back to the guards. There are about two-hundred other criminals here, and I suggest you try to get along with them as well as you can. Understood?"

"We haven't been sentenced for any crimes," Journey objected.

The balding man glanced at Fleury, who continued to grin as he said, "I'm not going to take the risk of the three of you getting let go on some sort of technicality or bribe. You're entering the records here under fake names, and no one will ever be the wiser. Dove's Roost is where you'll disappear forever. This is where you'll eventually die and be buried." His grin stretched wider. "I've already told you: I've won."

Journey expected some sort of reaction from Dallion at that, but he surprised him by staying silent. One glance at the man told him he was feeling just as hopeless and defeated as

Fleury wanted. Journey couldn't blame him. He felt the same way.

Their clothes were taken from them and replaced with plain, brown clothing made of the roughest, itchiest material they'd ever felt. Dallion was allowed to keep the earrings in his ears, but all other jewelry was confiscated. Journey's stolen wedding band left a small, untanned circle around his finger. A number was branded into their shoulders with a hot iron, as if they were cattle, and as Journey screamed through the searing pain, he pictured Saige, alone in the mansion on Stonewell, waiting for his safe return. He would have given absolutely anything to have been there, now.

*   *   *

THREE nights later, they huddled together in the corner of their assigned bunkhouse. It was a long, wooden building with a dirt floor and more than a hundred bunkbeds. Most of the other prisoners were captivated by a raucous game of dice going on in the center of the building's only room, and that meant Journey, Dallion, and Jimmy Two-Tales had their first opportunity to speak privately since their arrival here. They all squatted down behind the last row of bunkbeds, and they took turns peeking up above the nearest bed's straw mattress to make sure no one had noticed them over here. They'd learned quickly that the island was full of men willing to snitch on one another in exchange for special treatment from the guards, and the swollen, bruised eye that Dallion was currently sporting had been a lesson in not attracting the guards' attention.

Journey waited for an especially loud bout of laughter from the other prisoners to quiet down before saying lowly, "The first shift change is at noon. They don't leave their posts until the next guard shows up to relieve them."

Dallion nodded. "It's the same way down at the docks. I got a good look at the harbor today. The only way in or out is to go between two watchtowers. They can see everything from up there."

"I haven't seen anyone watching the northern shoreline, yet."

Jimmy snorted a hopeless laugh. "That's because they don't have to. I was on that side this morning. There's a line of jagged rocks that stick up out of the water about a hundred yards off the shore. It goes almost all the way around the island."

"We don't know that for sure," Journey reminded him. "None of us have been over to the eastern side, yet."

Jimmy gave him a look that said he was dreaming. "It's going to be the same thing over there. There's a reason Whitefish uses this place as a prison, Teach: it's already built like one. All they had to do was stick a couple of towers in the only place where ships can come in or go out."

"We might be able to get over the rocks when the water is calm…"

"For what? So we can drown a half a mile on the other side?"

"We could all just lay down and die," Dallion suggested, and the anger in his voice made both Jimmy and Journey fall silent. "Is that what you want? You think we should just give up and accept that we're never going to get off this piece of rock? Are you already done, Jimmy?"

He dropped his gaze and kept it on the patch of dirt floor between them. Once it became clear that Dallion was waiting for a response, Jimmy muttered, "I didn't say that."

"Fighting isn't going to help our situation," Journey warned, but to be honest, he felt just as frustrated as Jimmy Two-Tales now sounded. The rocks were going to keep the *Jubilee* out, if she even came to find them. And how could she? No one knew where they were. Their names weren't going to show up on any records, and Fleury and his crew certainly weren't going to tell anyone what had happened to them. Despite how certain Dallion seemed to be that they were going to figure out a way to get off this island, Journey was starting to doubt that such a miracle was possible.

From the doorway at the other end of the bunkhouse, a guard's voice called, "Lights out!"

The other prisoners abandoned their game of dice and scrambled to their beds. Journey and Jimmy both stood to do the same, but Dallion caught them each by the shoulder and looked first one man in the eye, then the other. He said sternly, "I'm going to get us out of here."

Jimmy mumbled something about believing him, and that was going to have to be good enough, for now. Dallion let them go, and the three of them hurried to their assigned bunks. Journey collapsed onto his just as the guards began putting out the lanterns that hung on the walls. He stared up at the bottom of Dallion's bed above his and watched as it grew darker and darker with each lantern flame that was extinguished. Finally, it was too dark to see the splintery boards above him, and he listened as the guards made their way back outside. There was a *bang* and a *click* as they closed the bunkhouse's only door and locked it. Then there was only silence.

The straw mattress beneath him was one of the least comfortable things he'd ever laid on, and his filthy, coarse clothing made him itch, but he was too exhausted to care. The grueling labor he'd been tasked with since his arrival here had taken everything out of him, and there was only more of the same waiting for him when the sun rose. He was tempted to let himself slip into hopelessness, but decided to keep that feeling at bay for another night. Instead, he closed his eyes and thought of Saige and Mirelle, and before he knew it, he was asleep.

That was how he made it through the next night, as well, and then the one after that. Days began to melt into one another, and time slowly lost its meaning. The routine of the island took over: wake up, eat tasteless gruel, work, work, and work some more. Plead with the sun to go down sooner so the workday would be done. More tasteless gruel. Sleep. Over and over it went, but each night, Journey dreamed of his family on Stonewell, and he somehow kept from going mad.

Chapter Twenty-Eight

SIX months later, Katria woke in the soft bed in the guestroom she'd claimed as her own for the night. For a moment, she thought the bed was gently rocking, but that was just because she'd gotten so used to living and sleeping on a ship. Hardly any of her time was spent ashore, anymore; there was too much to be done on the sea. She threw the blankets back and got out of bed. The sun was already half-risen in the east. Its warm light was spilling through the window in the far wall to greet her. She dressed, but then paused at that window to look out for a moment. Outside, Stonewell Island was a dozen shades of green and a chorus of cheerful birdsong. The brightening, summer sky was cloudless. Looking out at such a view, it was almost enough to convince someone that all was right in the world, and there was no such thing as absent lovers.

Katria drew the curtain across the window to block out the view and all of its lies. She headed downstairs, where she was met with the smell of sausages and fresh bread. It was the busiest time of morning for the servants in the place, it seemed, for she passed a half a dozen of them as she made her way to the dining room. She found Saige at the table, nursing her two-month-old baby. The child was bundled so tightly in her white swaddling blanket that only one small fist was visible from here. There was a plate of untouched eggs and sausage on the table before Saige. There were two other places set, but it seemed that Katria had beat Francis down to breakfast this morning.

Saige greeted her with a smile that Katria saw through. The woman's husband had been missing for half a year now. The infant in her arms might never meet her father, although Katria was determined to make sure that she did. She sat down at one of the vacant settings and helped herself to a few sausages from the dish in the center of the table. As she did that, Saige told her, "I had fresh supplies delivered to the dock. You should be all set for a few weeks, at least."

"Thank you," she answered between bites of sausage. "We're going to need it. I've got a good tip about another island. It sounds promising."

"How far away is it?"

"About two weeks from here," she replied, but that was a stretch. The trip might take two weeks under perfect conditions, but there had been a strong headwind coming in the opposite direction for the last few days, and if it didn't let up soon, it was going to take much longer.

Saige seemed relatively pleased with the answer, however, so Katria didn't elaborate. Instead, she finished the sausage on her plate and then stood, leaning over the table to reach across it. Saige shifted the baby in her arms to free up one of her hands, and she took hold of Katria's.

"I've got a good feeling about this one," Katria told her. It was something she'd said a few times before about other possible islands, but Saige believed her. She had no other hope to go on, after all. "We're going to find them, Saige. Journey's going to be back here before you know it. Alright?"

Saige squeezed her hand hard enough for it to hurt. In her eyes, Katria found desperation and sadness, but also courage. "Whatever it takes," she reminded her. This was also a line that had been spoken between them several times over the last six months. Saige had been funding the search for the three kidnapped pirates, and Katria knew she was determined to continue doing so until the men were found or the family funds were bled dry.

Katria nodded, and Saige let her go. Katria turned to go, but before she could take more than a couple of steps toward the door, a small figure appeared in the doorway, still clad in a tiny, yellow nightgown. Mirelle was clasping a wooden doll to her chest, and she stroked its hair with one hand. The girl had taken to Katria immediately when she'd first shown up here, but her mother had been more reluctant. She'd come around, however, when Lucien had backed up her claims, and Katria supposed that she and Saige were now friends. It was a friendship forged out of desperation and heartache, but it was something.

"Auntie Kata," the girl said, using her best pronunciation of her name. "Daddy?"

Katria felt a stab of pity deep in her heart, and she gave her the same answer she'd given all the previous times the child had asked. "Not yet. He'll be home soon, okay?"

She pouted. When Saige motioned for her to come to her, Mirelle did so. She pressed her face against her mother's side as she slipped her free arm around her eldest child's shoulders. Mirelle began to cry, her sobs muffled against Saige's dress, even as she soothed her with loving words. Katria stepped quietly out of the dining room, the sounds of the girl's cries clawing at her heart.

Her pace was quick as she made her way to the docks. She arrived to find the last of the supplies being loaded onto the ship. It was Journey's sloop, *Lady Swift*, and she'd certainly been living up to her name. Lucien and Pigeon had modified her rigging themselves, and she was now the fastest ship of her size that Katria had ever seen. It would have been a lie to say that she didn't miss the *Jubilee*, however, and she knew that must have been doubly true for Lucien and the others. The last they'd heard, the *Jubilee* was somewhere near Port Kelsey. Horus had recovered from his injuries and had since been voted captain. Only a handful of Dallion's crew had left with Katria to pursue their lost comrades. The vast majority of them had stuck with Horus and the *Jubilee*, and considering the lack of results that the search had yielded, so far, it was hard to blame them.

Brain greeted Katria with a hug as she stepped on board the *Lady Swift*. She hugged him back, just as she always did, but he pulled back after only a moment, concerned. "You're sad," he told her, as if she may not have noticed.

She gave him a wistful smile and tried to sound cheerful. "I'm not sad. I'm just ready to get going again."

"We're just about ready to get underway," Lucien agreed, leaving a conversation with Pigeon at the helm to join them near the *Lady's* single mast. As Saige currently owned the ship, she'd had the right to name a captain, and she'd chosen Lucien. To some surprise, he'd accepted. They sailed beneath a green banner that sported the Travert family crest. As strange as it seemed to everyone involved, they were currently a legitimate crew aboard a licensed vessel. It was odd to think of themselves as safe from the *Huntress*…though they still hadn't quit checking the horizons for purple sails.

Lil Gabe and Wee Bit were getting the sails ready, so Katria joined them to lend a hand. One of Saige's dockworkers untied their ropes from the dock for them, and then they were on their way. Katria watched Stonewell slowly fade from view behind them, Mirelle's heartbroken tears on her mind.

Chapter Twenty-Nine

HUNDREDS of miles away, Journey slipped his bare feet into the cool, salty water on the northern shoreline of Dove's Roost. The full moon was half-concealed by nighttime clouds, and the surface of the ocean was as black as he'd ever seen it. A gentle breeze was rustling some of the sugarcane leaves behind him, but his focus was on the open water ahead. Dallion was standing in the water on his right, and his eyebrows were raised to silently ask if he was ready. Journey took a deep breath of the midnight air, braced himself for the danger ahead, and gave a nod. Together, they set their hands on their makeshift raft. It had been cobbled together with broken crates, barrels, and whatever else they'd managed to smuggle out to the shoreline without being noticed. It had taken three weeks to collect enough junk for them to lash together this five-by-three-foot raft, and it had nearly been discovered by guards twice. Their only supplies were in a small sack that was tied to the middle of the raft, and it contained portions of their meager rations they'd managed to stash away over the last week or so, as well as a canteen that was half-filled with drinkable water. Journey knew that they were crazy for what they were about to attempt, but it was better to be crazy than trapped on this island for one more day.

They waded farther out into the water, pushing the raft before them. Small stones and bits of seashells pressed painfully against the bottom of Journey's feet as he went, but he was so full of adrenaline that he hardly noticed. His heart was racing in his chest. Somewhere out there, among the dark ocean and carefree breeze that skirted across it, Stonewell was waiting. He had another child waiting to meet him, if all had gone well with the birth. As the water got deeper and he and Dallion began to swim, keeping the raft out in front of them, Journey fixed an image of Saige in his head, just as he'd done each night since arriving in this horrible place.

They moved through the water in silence, steering their raft through the small, gentle waves that came their way. The clouds cleared above them to allow the moon's silvery light to wash over them. In it, they could make out the dark, jagged shape of the line of rocks ahead of them. The sound of the waves crashing against the far side of them reached their ears, but Journey refused to worry about that, yet. Dallion must have decided to do the same, because he panted, "Nice and steady. This is the easy part."

"How's your hand?"

"Fine," Dallion replied, but judging by the grimace currently on his face, that was a lie. He'd nearly lost a finger when the cane knife he'd been using in the fields had slipped, and although that had been nearly a month ago, now, it still pained him to do much with that hand. He changed the subject by offering, "The drinks are on me at the first tavern we can crawl into."

"I'd settle for a comfortable bed and a real meal."

"Soon," Dallion assured him, and the conviction in his tone gave Journey hope, despite the odds they were facing.

The sound of the waves against the rocks was very loud, now, and the water on this side was beginning to get choppy. Dallion called above the noise, "Get on top and start paddling."

Journey hauled himself out of the water and onto the raft, nearly tipping it over in the process. Once he'd settled on his knees, he took up a makeshift paddle they'd fashioned from a pair of barrel staves. He dipped the end into the water and started to paddle slowly and firmly. Dallion continued to push the raft from the back, and the little raft made its way through the churning waters without much trouble. Once again, Journey felt that faint bit of hope grow a little more.

The moon disappeared behind another cloud for a moment, and when it reappeared, its ghostly light revealed the line of rocks that were jutting up out of the water. Some of them were tall, sticking out at least four feet above the surface, but there were occasional gaps between them that the waves were able to push some water through. Journey used the paddle to steer the raft toward one of these gaps, and as they grew closer, he stopped to offer his hand to help haul Dallion out of the water. The raft rocked so far to the left as he climbed up on top of it that water rushed over the top of it, but Journey scrambled to put all of his weight on the opposite side, and the edge of the raft crashed down onto the water hard. Once they were both on top of it, Dallion grabbed the second paddle they'd brought with them and stuck the end of it in the water. He paused before doing anything else and looked at Journey in the moonlight to ask, "Ready?"

In answer, Journey put his paddle back in the water, and they timed their strokes together to make the raft move through the growing waves as smoothly as possible. Thick, white seafoam was churning around the rocks, and some of the waves threw it up into the air. It landed on top of the raft and the two men on it, but they wiped it from their faces and kept going. They eased the front of the raft into the small gap between the rocks, and Dallion called out over the loud roar of the waves on the other side, "Keep her steady!"

He couldn't have asked for a more impossible task. As soon as the front of the raft was in the roiling water between the rocks, it was shoved violently to the right. The barrel keeping that corner of the raft afloat was smashed against the rock there in an instant, and shards of wood flew up in the air to join the tossing seafoam. Journey was thrown forward, and he nearly tumbled into the rougher waters on the other side of the gap. Instead, his shoulder caught painfully on the jagged edge of the rock, and it was enough to stop him from falling off the raft. Dallion was yelling something from just behind him, but his words were drowned out by the sound of the raging sea on the far side of the rocks.

The raft began to move backward, and Journey's hopes started sliding with it. He tightened his grip on the paddle in his hand and jammed it down into the water, only to feel the end of it wedge itself between two rocks. The raft rose up on the next wave forcing itself through the gap, and with a loud *crack*, the makeshift paddle snapped in half. Journey tossed the top half aside in frustration, and he reached out to seize the edge of the rock to his right. Its surface was slick with saltwater and algae, but he managed to cling to, and with all his might, he pulled himself and the raft forward. Behind him, Dallion had lodged his own paddle between two rocks beneath the surface, and with a mighty heave, they sent the raft through the gap.

The power of the water on this side of the rocks was too much. As soon as the little raft was through the gap, a wave swelled up beneath it, and Journey's stomach dropped as the raft was swept upward. The back of the raft crashed against the rocks behind them, and shards of wood exploded in every direction. Journey was tossed like a ragdoll into the sea, and salty water forced itself into his mouth and down his throat. He flailed beneath the water as the next wave threaten to push him deeper under. His lower back crashed against a rock, knocking what little air he'd still had in his lungs out of them. Another wave turned him over twice, disorientating him, and the back of his head met another rock. For a few seconds, he flirted with unconsciousness, even as he tumbled over and over beneath the churning water.

His hand struck the ragged edge of a rock, and he seized it in his panic. He pulled himself in that direction, and by either luck or fate, his head suddenly broke the surface. He retched seawater and managed to draw half a breath before another wave washed over him, but this time, he was sent tumbling through the gap between the rocks. He scrambled with all his might to push himself through it, and when the wave had passed, he found his head above water once more. He slipped through the other side of the gap and into the calmer water on that side, still retching and struggling to fill his lungs with air.

He treaded water to keep his head above it as he turned toward the rocks again, his eyes straining to see through the saltwater running over them. He tried to call Dallion's name, but managed little more than a croak. His lungs were burning from the water that had gotten into them, and his head ached from the rap it had taken against the rocks. All the same, he started to swim toward the rocks once more, determined to search for Dallion. He'd nearly made it back to the gap when he spotted him. He was clinging to a sharp rock that was jutting out of the water a few yards away. The waves were rushing against his waist and legs, trying to pull him off of the rock, but he wasn't budging, for now. He was looking longingly out toward the open sea on the far side of the rocks.

"Dallion!" Journey called, and this time, he managed the whole word.

Dallion tore his gaze from their unreachable freedom to glance at him, but only for a moment. Then he looked back out to sea, and for a few seconds, Journey was terrified that he was going to try to swim for it, anyway. He called, "It's over, Dal! We need to get back to shore!"

"We could swim for it," he mused, as if doing so wouldn't be suicide. "We could get lucky and get picked up by a ship."

"The raft is smashed!" Journey scoffed. "There's nothing out there for us but death. We need to get back before they realize we're gone."

He continued to linger, and Journey had to fight the urge to wonder if he was right. They'd made this plan with the understanding that drowning or dying of thirst on the raft would be better than continuing to survive in this place, after all, and he wondered why he should feel differently, now. He thought of Mirelle, however, hugging her favorite doll close and asking him for another story at bedtime. If there was still a chance to make it back to her and her mother, no matter how small, he wouldn't throw it away in despair.

"Come on, Dal," he urged. "We'll try another way. I promise. We're not finished, yet."

It must have taken every ounce of willpower he had, but Dallion turned away from the open sea. He lowered himself down from the rock on the island side, and once he was back in the water, he started swimming for the shore. Journey went with him, and soon the sound of the crashing waves was far behind them. They didn't speak as they swam, but kept as swift a pace as they could, cutting quietly through the night-darkened waters.

When they reached the shore, they dragged themselves out of the water and collapsed on their backs in the sand. Journey stared up at the moonlit sky as he caught his breath and wondered over the fact that he'd survived the ordeal. His head was pounding, his back ached, and he must have cut his hand on the rocks, because his palm was burning. Every muscle in his body felt like it was thrumming.

Dallion, lying in the sand beside him, said quietly, "I'm sorry."

"We both knew it probably wasn't going to work."

"No, I mean I'm sorry for everything. You wouldn't be out here if I hadn't convinced you to leave Stonewell."

Journey heaved a sigh that only made his irritated lungs hurt some more. "I stopped blaming you for all of this months ago. I never should have left Saige like I did, but that's my fault, not yours. Right now, all that matters is figuring out how to get out of here. We can't give up."

"Maybe Jimmy was right," he muttered, and Journey hated to hear that. Jimmy Two-Tales had died two months ago. He'd simply stopped eating and drinking, and one day, he'd fallen over in the eastern sugarcane field, and he never got back up. The guards had told them it was dehydration and the heat that had killed him, but they both knew better than that; Jimmy had simply decided that death was better than continuing to toil away on this awful island.

As much as he disliked hearing Dallion talk like that, he didn't have it in him to argue against it. Instead, Journey forced himself onto his hands and knees, then onto his feet. He offered his hand down to Dallion, saying, "Let's get back to the bunkhouse."

Dallion seemed to consider not going back, but finally took his offered hand and let him help him up. They collected the shoes they'd stashed behind a large rock and then slipped between the nearby rows of sugarcane to start for the bunkhouse together, walking in defeated silence. They crept past the nearest guardhouse and used a key Dallion had pickpocketed off a guard to let themselves into the bunkhouse. The sound of their footsteps on the hard, dirt floor was concealed by a chorus of snores as they slunk down the rows of bunks. They reached their own bunk and Dallion climbed up onto the top bed, while Journey collapsed onto the bottom one.

He didn't sleep, but stared up into the darkness that was the bottom of Dallion's bed above him. He let his tired mind chase whatever thoughts it would. Unsurprisingly, they kept returning to his family. Eventually, the gentle light smuggling itself through the small gaps between the boards in the bunkhouse's wall told him that the night was behind them. As he waited for the bell to toll to announce that it was time for the prisoners to get up and start working for the day, he used the infant light to consider the thin gouges in the wooden slats above him. They were tally marks, and they had served as his only way of keeping track of the passing days and months since coming here. One hundred and eighty-six tally marks stared back at him. As the bell began to toll outside, he slipped a small, sharp stone out from beneath the edge of his mattress and placed it at the end of the line of marks. He pressed the stone into the wood and drew another one.

Chapter Thirty

KATRIA, Lucien, and Wee Bit stood on the cramped bow of the *Lady Swift* and watched as an island slowly came into view on the horizon. Two weeks had turned out to be all that it had taken them to get here from Stonewell, after all, and Katria was glad. She hadn't lied when she'd told Saige that she had a good feeling about the island that was now within sight. From her right, Wee Bit considered the distant swatch of land and asked, "What's the name of this place again?"

"Dove's Roost," Katria answered without looking away from it. The afternoon sun was shining brightly off of the water, making her eyes water, but she didn't look away. "I bribed a captain's mate back in Darry who used to sail for Whitefish. He was drunk, but he swore this would be the place."

Wee Bit gave her a doubtful look, but that wasn't surprising. It was how they'd gotten many of their leads, so far: gossip during card games, rumors over drinks in skeevy taverns, and company sailors-turned-pirates who were willing to talk for the right amount of money. All of the companies owned islands where they could stash criminals away and force them to work. Most of those places didn't show up on most maps, and those that did were labeled as regular sugarcane or rice plantations.

Over the last six months, however, Katria and Lucien had gotten very good at rooting out the truth.

Now, Lucien told them, "Wee Bit, you'll stay here with Pigeon and Brain. Make sure no one comes aboard, no matter what. Katria, Gabe, and I will go ashore and stick to the same story we always use. Make sure the *Lady* is ready to go in a flash, in case there's trouble."

Wee Bit gave him an exaggerated salute that had become something of a joke on the *Lady Swift* since Saige had made Lucien the captain, but Lucien was in no mood for jokes. He waited for Wee Bit to wander off to relay the orders to the others, and once he was gone, Lucien said to Katria, "Let me do the talking to start off. You always have a hard time with that."

"I will," she vowed, and willed the gap between the sloop and the distant island to shrink faster. She realized her fingertips had been unconsciously toying with the shark tooth on the necklace around her neck, but she didn't make them stop. It had been a habit she'd picked up while waiting for rescue on Tall Island, and it served as a comfort whenever she was anxious. That was certainly the case, now; Dallion may have been on the island just ahead, and her heart was racing in her chest.

As they reached the island, they found that it only had one harbor. It had a narrow opening that was guarded by two watchtowers on either side, and large, wooden signs posted on their walls prompted incoming ships to wait for permission to enter. Pigeon waited for a signal from one of the towers, and once it was given, he maneuvered the *Lady* into the harbor. There were several ships here, and they saw that all but one of them were cargo vessels that were dropping off or picking up loads of sugarcane that had been grown on the island. The last ship was a brigantine that had over a dozen swivel guns mounted along the edges of her deck. The name *Patroller* was painted in a fancy script on her sides, and Katria shuddered to think that a vessel like that wasn't meant to defend the island's inhabitants from outsiders; it was meant to keep them from leaving.

Pigeon brought the *Lady* right up to the only vacant dock, where they were tied off by a dockhand in a filthy hat. His shirt was tied around his waist in a battle against the heat, and as he secured the ropes, Katria spied a series of numbers on the back of his left shoulder. They appeared to have been branded into his flesh, judging by the look of the scar, and she shuddered again. She'd visited enough of these islands during her search to know that this was a common practice. Criminals or not, she hated the thought of people being treated like cattle.

Once they were docked, Lucien led Katria and Lil Gabe ashore. They were met by a man in a tan uniform that clearly designated him as a guard, and Katria had to focus on keeping her gaze off of the rifle slung over his shoulder. The guard eyed the flag hanging from the *Lady's* mast, and his frown told them that he didn't recognize the green background and white swan that graced its center – the logo for Travert Holdings and a design of Saige's own. He said sternly, "State your business on Dove's Roost."

Lucien took on his most professional-sounding tone and recited, "My name is Bill Wells. I'm a sheriff on an island out west. I need to talk to the man in charge of this place about a couple of escaped prisoners."

The man eyed Katria suspiciously, but she gave him a look that dared him to question her. Lucien pressed, "Where's your boss?"

He hesitated for a moment longer, but must have decided that it wasn't going to be worth his time to question them further. Instead, he motioned for them to follow him and started up a gravel road that stretched toward the center of the island, weaving its way between sprawling fields of sugarcane. Lucien ushered Katria and Lil Gabe after him, and they walked in silence as they made their way past prisoners who were working in the fields. They were all dressed in stained and tattered clothes that had been dyed an unremarkable brown. Katria scanned each of their faces as they passed them, searching for one she knew, but all she found were exhausted, hopeless strangers from all corners of Cruxes. Her heart threatened to break for each of them.

The road wound its way through a cluster of warehouses, before finally ending at a large building made of gray stone. A sign above the door declared that this was the warden's office. The guard stood beside the door and instructed, "Go inside and tell Phillis that you need to see Mr. Aims."

Stepping into the headquarters building was a relief from the heat of the glaring sun outside. They found themselves in a sort of sitting room, complete with a bookshelf and a pair of couches. There was another door in the far wall, and as Lucien and the others entered the sitting room, a young woman – assumably Phillis – poked her head out through it to see who had arrived. When she didn't recognize them, she came out to greet them. She was dressed in a neat blouse and long skirt. Her appearance and overall cheeriness said that she probably wasn't a prisoner here.

Katria fought the urge to hit her and demand to know just how long her soul had been poisoned.

Instead, she returned Phillis' smile and was glad when Lil Gabe did the same. Lucien did not – he rarely ever smiled, anyway – but when the young woman asked if she could help them, he answered pleasantly enough, saying, "We're here to see Mr. Aims. Someone told us we could find him here."

"Send them in, Phillis," a man's voice called from the next room, and Phillis simply stepped aside to let them through the doorway. That welcoming smile was still on her lips, and it took every bit of control that Katria had not to smack it off of her.

She and Lucien left Lil Gabe in the sitting room to head through the doorway. It gave way to a large office that was decorated with expensive oil paintings. A rug made of some type of large animal was stretched across the floor in front of a desk made of stained wood. Behind it sat a skinny man with very little hair left on his head. What remained was hardly more than a few gray wisps that stuck out at crazy angles. He stood politely as his guests entered, and he motioned to a set of wooden chairs on their side of his desk with a well-manicured hand.

"Come in," he invited. "I'm Merrick Aims. What can I do for you?"

"I'm Bill Wells," Lucien lied as he took a seat in one of the chairs. "I'm the sheriff for a string of islands out west. They're owned by a man named Gerald Tailor, and this is his wife, Kate. Mr. Tailor is partnered with the Whitefish Trading Company, and right now, he needs your help."

It was a rehearsed pitch that had started off numerous conversations like the one they were about to have with this man.

It worked well to transfer the conversational lead over to Katria, even though she was a young woman, and none of the prison wardens they'd used this on so far had objected. Aims was no different. He turned his attention to her, and although he offered a patronizing smile, he seemed ready to listen.

"Mr. Aims," she began, careful to keep her voice sweet, "Last year, three men beat and robbed my husband and his nephew outside our home on Quill Island. My husband may never fully recover, but I'm thankful he's still alive. His nephew wasn't so fortunate. The men got away with the money and jewelry they'd been wearing, but Mr. Wells tracked them down and arrested them in less than a week. They were put on trial and sentenced to hang for their crimes."

"I'm sorry for your family's loss, Mrs. Tailor," Aims said.

"Thank you. Unfortunately, the three men escaped from jail before their sentence could be carried out. They stole a sloop and disappeared in the middle of the night. My husband is determined not to let them get away with their crimes. He and Sheriff Wells have been following some leads, and we believe the men were arrested for other crimes and sentenced to hard labor on Dove's Roost."

Aims reached into a drawer in his desk, just as all of the wardens on the other islands had done, and took out a thick, leatherbound book. He set it before him on the desk and opened it somewhere near the middle. The pages were covered in carefully-printed names and strings of numbers. He wet his finger on his tongue and began to turn the pages, asking, "What are the names of the men you're looking for?"

"Dallion Romilly, Journey Travert, and James Williams. They would have arrived here six months ago."

Aims continued to flip through the pages. Katria held her breath as she watched him scan the names on each page. Out of the corner of her eye, she thought she could see Lucien doing the same. It took more patience than she'd known she had, but she managed to stay quiet as Aims searched. Finally, he closed the book with a decisive *thud* and said, "I'm sorry, Mrs. Tailor, but there aren't any men here by those names."

She forced that sweet smile back onto her face. "I'm not surprised, Mr. Aims. They may have given false names when they were arrested, so they could avoid being recognized as wanted murderers. Luckily, I witnessed their attack on my husband and his nephew. If I were to see them again, I'd recognize them."

Aims pushed back in his chair with a huff. This was the part where many of the other wardens had started to lose their desire to be helpful, and Katria had expected the same from this man. He asked, "What are you hoping to accomplish out here, Mrs. Tailor? Even if you go out into the fields and find these three men, what good will that do you or your husband? Everyone on Dove's Roost is serving a lifetime sentence. They'll be here until they die."

This was Lucien's cue, and he reached into his pocket to draw a folded piece of paper from it. He unfolded it before offering it across the desk, and as Aims took it from him, Lucien explained, "This is a letter from Oliver Morris, the vice-president of the Whitefish Trading Company. When Mr. Tailor wrote to Mr. Morris to tell him what was going on, he sent a letter back that said to show this paper to the warden in charge of the prison here on Dove's Roost. It says that the three men should be turned over to my custody and be taken back to Quill Island, where they'll finally hang for murder."

Katria found herself holding her breath again while Aims read the letter in his hands. Saige had paid good money for such a believable forgery, and no one had dared to question its authenticity so far, but that didn't mean Aims would buy it. Seconds ticked by on the clock behind Aims' desk, and her anxiousness got the better of her. She offered, "My husband is willing to pay good money for your troubles, Mr. Aims. I know it must be an inconvenience for us to take up your time like this."

Whether he'd had doubts before or not, that convinced him. He set the paper aside on his desk and told her, "I'll tell you what: you go out there and have a look around, and if you find the men you're looking for, I'll hand them over to your sheriff right away. Just check the back of their shoulders for their numbers, and I can look them up in my book that way, fake names or not. Your husband can send me whatever money he thinks is fair. Just address it directly to me. Got that?"

"I'm sure he'll be generous," she agreed, once again tempted toward violence. She stood to go, but before she could start for the door, Aims pointed a finger at Lucien.

"I can't guarantee her safety out there," he warned. "I won't be held responsible for anything that might happen to her while she's poking around in the fields."

Lucien stood from his chair and patted the pistol that he'd taken to carrying on his hip to better play his part in these lies.

"I'm not worried about unarmed prisoners," he replied, and Aims gave him a nod, satisfied.

They returned to Lil Gabe in the front room, and he followed them outside, where the heat from the afternoon sun struck them again. Katria shielded her eyes to look out over the cane fields. From here, she could spot more than a hundred people working among the crops. Gabe asked, "Now what?"

"Now, we go shopping," Lucien said, a sour look on his face. "If we don't find what we're looking for here…"

"Let's split up," Katria interjected, not wanting to hear whatever he had to say about giving up. "Gabe, go look in the two fields closest to the docks. I'll take the fields on the western side of the island. Lucien, go check out those warehouses we passed on the way here." She paused, remembering their technical ranks, and added, "Please."

"They'll have numbers on their shoulders," Lucien told his son. "We need those numbers. If you find them, don't make it obvious that we're all on friendly terms. We're supposed to be trying to haul them back as prisoners, remember."

Lil Gabe nodded, but started down the road in the direction of the docks again without further comment. Katria understood his lack of enthusiasm – how many times had they searched islands like this before, only to come up empty-handed? The odds that they were on the right island and that the men they were looking for weren't already dead…

Lucien must have seen the hopeless look on Katria's face, for his own expression softened, and he said, "They're resilient boys, Kat. Wherever they are, I'm sure they're still alive. And who knows? They might be here."

She looked up at him and offered him her best attempt at a confident smile. "I know. It's just…hard."

"Hard or easy, daylight's wasting. I'm going to go check the warehouses, but you should come with me. The warden wasn't wrong when he said it might be dangerous out here."

Katria seized the pistol in its holster without warning and pulled it from his hip. She tucked it into the back of her pants, where it nestled against the small of her back. Then she cocked her head to one side to silently ask if he was going to put up a fight about it. Lucien frowned, but turned and marched back down the gravel road, grumbling something about not coming to help her if she needed it. Katria watched him go and wondered just how much farther the man was willing to go for his lost comrades. He'd left his rather lucrative career as a pirate behind him for this, and although he didn't show it often, Katria didn't doubt that he was just as frustrated and disheartened as Lil Gabe. She needed them to keep going…but she knew that wasn't completely true. She would search until the end of her days without them, if she had to. She just hoped it wouldn't come to that.

Chapter Thirty-One

DALLION looped a red ribbon around a sugarcane stalk and tied it tight. The fields here on the western side of the island were nearly ready to be harvested, standing nearly twenty feet tall and stretching themselves toward the sun as they soaked up its rays. He and Journey had been given the task of measuring out and designating the rows that would be chopped down by tying ribbons around some of the stalks. It was dull, boring work, but it was far better than actually harvesting the cane would be. Soon, they would be back out here with dozens of other men, armed with cane knives and hacking the plants low to the ground. That work was backbreaking, and in the months they'd spent here, they'd already done plenty of it.

Dallion made his way to the next stalk he needed to mark, but he paused for a moment to wipe sweat from his brow. He looked west. The next field of cane had already been harvested, so he could see past it to the ocean beyond. The sun was getting closer and closer to the horizon, and the water there was already lit a beautiful golden color. A feeling of loss – quite common, now – stabbed at his heart. Somewhere out there, the *Jubilee* was free on the wind. They knew that Fleury hadn't found her when he'd gone looking in the shallow waters off of White Crest, because there would have been a battle while he and Journey had been aboard the *Huntress*. If he still hadn't found her yet, then Dallion hoped that she was somewhere safe. When he closed his eyes, he could almost hear the wind whipping at her sails and the waves slapping her hull. He missed that freedom almost as much as he missed Katria Laurent.

"The foremen are doing their rounds," Journey warned from his left, taking one of the last few ribbons from their basket on the ground to begin tying it to yet another sugarcane stalk.

Dallion ignored this, his gaze still on the sea. The *Cherub* was also still out there, cradling her treasures in the clear waters of her secret lagoon. Had Katria and Horus found it after Fleury had hauled them off? Had they managed to get off the island somehow? Was she thinking about him nearly as often as he thought about her, which was every damn day while he was stuck in this place? There was some sort of irony in the fact that he'd lost her again so soon after finding her. All those years of wishing he'd known where she was, just for him to get yanked away from her once more.

"We need more ribbons," Journey told him as he finished the one he'd been tying.

It was Dallion's turn to go get more from the foreman, but he found that he couldn't pull himself away from his thoughts. Instead, he mused aloud, "I'd give my right arm to be out on the water right now."

"I'd give more than that, but it's not going to help us. Go get more ribbons, Dal."

"Do you think Kat went back to her fiancé?"

Journey flapped a hand at him to signal he was giving up. He dumped the three remaining ribbons out of the basket and left them on the ground to head down the path between fields. Dallion heaved a heavy sigh and tore his gaze from the sea, at last. He collected the ribbons and tried to keep thoughts of Katria and the *Jubilee* out of his head as he tied one around the next stalk, but it was no use. He could still feel sea spray on his cheeks, feel the smooth wood of the helm beneath his palms, and hear Katria's melodic voice saying his name.

When she really did speak, he thought that his imagination had taken a leap to another level. It had been as if he'd actually heard it, and he wondered if it meant he was going insane. Did it matter? Losing his sanity at this point may have been a blessing.

She called his name again, and this time, it was accompanied by the sound of running feet. He turned slowly, as if in a dream, and understood that he had, in fact, gone crazy. That was the only way he could explain what his eyes were telling him: Katria was running up the path between this field and the next, her eyes brimming with tears. There was an undeniable mixture of joy and relief on her face. She'd cut her hair short since the last time he'd seen her, and it looked good on her. She was wearing pants that had been fitted for her, and they hugged her hips and thighs. Her blouse was simple and patterned with roses. It was an outfit that was fit for sailing in, and he supposed it made sense that his crazy mind had conjured her wearing something like this. After all, he often imagined her still sailing aboard the *Jubilee*, an all-out pirate with a gun on her hip and an arrogant grin on her lips.

He didn't realize that the vision was real until she was in his arms. She crashed into him with so much force that he stumbled and almost fell down. She smelled of the sea and some sort of sweet perfume. Her lips were pressed against his in an instant, even as she sobbed in relief, and he kissed her back, still struggling to accept that this was really happening. She clung to him like her life depended on it, and when Dallion broke their kiss to ask if she was real, she let out a weepy laugh that somehow convinced him.

He swept her quickly into the rows of sugarcane to get them out of sight of any other workers or foremen that might happen to wander by on the path. He was in such a hurry that their feet tangled together, and they both went to their knees on the hard ground between the stalks. Still, she clung to him, her arms around the back of his neck, and as he kissed her lips again, he realized that he was weeping now, too. This was too good to be true, and yet it somehow was. He'd never had much use for a belief in any deity, but he silently thanked them all now.

He pulled back again to get a look at her at her face. Her tears had streaked the little bit of makeup she'd been wearing, but her eyes had more happiness in them than he'd ever seen in anyone's. In his shock, the best he could manage to ask was, "What are you doing here?"

"What do you think?" she laughed, but kept her voice low, mindful of the patrolling foremen she'd passed during her search through previous fields. "We've been looking all over for you. I was so afraid that we wouldn't find you. We had no idea where Fleury had taken you."

He pulled her close again and squeezed her so tightly that it hurt. He confessed, "I didn't think anyone would come for us."

"Of course, I came," she whispered into his ear. "I love you, Dallion. Do you really think I'd give up on you that easily?"

Something within him broke – some calloused, painful lump of anguish that had encased his heart over the last few months. He supposed it had started to form long before Jimmy Two-Tales had died, but it had really hardened after that. For the first time in far too long, he felt a sliver of hope and true joy. He realized now that he'd nearly forgotten what those things felt like. He was smiling when he whispered, "You're crazy, Kat."

"I'm not the only one. Saige Travert has been funding the whole search. She's been spending all her money on it. I've been going to every prison island that we can find to look for you. Lucien and Lil Gabe are around here somewhere. I'm sorry it took us so long. You have no idea how worried I've been…"

He stopped her words with yet another kiss, but she didn't mind. They were still kissing when Journey's voice called his name from where he had returned on the path outside the rows. Dallion stood and pulled Katria by her hand to help her to her feet, and he called as loudly as he dared for Journey to come into the rows of cane. He did so, still carrying the basket of fresh ribbons, but as he pushed through the last of the stalks before them, his steps faltered and his jaw dropped. Katria left Dallion's side to throw her arms around Journey. She planted a hearty kiss on his cheek. The ribbons spilled out all around them as Journey let the basket fall to the ground. He hugged her with everything he had.

"Saige sends her love," she told him, and he squeezed her even tighter, until it was hard for her to breathe.

"The baby?" he whispered, his eyes squeezed shut against tears that threatened to fall.

"She's gorgeous. Saige named her Francine, after her adopted father."

He merely nodded, still struggling against tears. Katria kissed his cheek again before stepping back, and she told them both, "We have a plan, but it's going to take some good acting and playing along. My name is Kate, and Lucien is Sheriff Wells. I don't have time to explain it all, but I need to know the numbers that they put on your shoulders. That's the only way the warden is going to be able to find you in his book."

Dallion turned around and pulled the back of his shirt all the way up to his neck, revealing the brand he'd been given upon their arrival here. Katria winced at the sight of it, though it had healed into a scar by now. Four numbers had been seared over his left shoulder blade in a neat line. They were legible, but he recited them for her, all the same. "Three-one-nine-six. Journey's number is three-one-nine-seven."

She repeated the numbers to commit them to memory, then asked, "What about Jimmy Two-Tales? Do you know his number?"

The solemn looks on both their faces was enough to tell her what had happened. Journey said quietly, "Jimmy's gone. He died two months ago."

Dallion hated to see the expression of guilt that crossed Katria's face at that, as if she could have saved him if only she'd somehow found this island sooner. He put his arm around her to draw her closer to him again, and he whispered, "We didn't think anyone was going to find us, Kat. You've done more for us than we thought you could. Now, can you really get us off of this island?"

"You're less than an hour from freedom now," she vowed, and as impossible as that seemed, he believed her. That sliver of hope had overcome him, and he would have believed anything she told him, no matter how crazy it seemed. He hugged her tightly, but the nervous glances that Journey kept casting toward the path on the other side of the cane they were behind reminded him of the danger they were in. He didn't want to imagine what their punishment might be if they were to be found back here with her.

Katria must have been afraid for them, as well, because she said, "I need to get back to the warden's office and give him your numbers. I'll be back as soon as he says you can go. The ship is waiting for us down at the docks. We'll leave this place and never look back, alright? I swear it."

Letting her go was the last thing he wanted to do, but he braced himself for it and said with a composure he hadn't expected from himself, "We'll see you soon."

She placed one last kiss on his lips, gave Journey a reassuring smile, and slipped out of the cane and back onto the path. Dallion let out his held breath once she was gone, and Journey threw an arm around his shoulders in a celebratory hug. They were almost free.

Chapter Thirty-Two

"NO," Aims said, pushing the open record book toward the far edge of his desk. "I'm sorry, but no."

Katria and Lucien were once again seated in the chairs before the desk. They'd both been beaming, but now Katria's smile faded. She demanded, "What do you mean?"

Aims motioned toward the open book. "The prisoners you want can't leave. I'm sorry."

"That's not what you told us when we talked about it earlier," Lucien growled. "Keep your word. Name a price, if you have to."

"I wish I could. You see, the two men you want were brought here by Captain Bertrand Fleury, himself. He gave me clear instructions that they were never to leave Dove's Roost. I'm not sure what they did, but if it was bad enough that he had a personal interest in making sure they never stepped foot off this island again, I don't want to know. Those two boys are going to stay here for the rest of their lives."

Katria struggled between her desire to try to talk sense into this man and the urge to shove his record book down his throat. She managed to keep her anger in check enough to say, "Mr. Aims, we showed you the letter from Mr. Morris. Whitefish wants these men to be handed over to Sheriff Wells. They need to face justice on Quill Island. My husband is already going to be upset to find out that one of them has died here. The two who are left need to come with us."

"There's nothing I can do," he said, and the dismissiveness in his voice told her that he wasn't going to budge. "Three-one-nine-six and three-one-nine-seven are a special case. I gave Captain Fleury my word that they were never going to leave Dove's Roost alive. If you don't know who Captain Fleury is…"

"I know he's a piece of shit who's taken away people that he had no right to take away!" she cried, standing. Aims pushed back in his chair farther, alarmed by her fury. She planted both of her hands atop his desk and leaned over it to snarl, "I'm not leaving this place without them. If I have to write to Mr. Morris and tell him that you're refusing to turn these men over, I'll do that."

"That's a good idea," he said, unshaken. "In fact, I'm going to write a letter to Mr. Morris, too. I'll ask him to verify that the paperwork you brought with you is genuine, and that he really wants me to override Captain Fleury's wishes. Something tells me that Mr. Morris doesn't know the whole story."

"These men were never convicted of their crimes! You're hiding them away here without a trial. What you're doing is illegal!"

"That's something that you can take up with Captain Fleury," Aims growled. He pointed toward the door and told Lucien, "Get her out of here before I do it myself. If your ship isn't out of my harbor within the hour, I'll have my men set fire to it. You just try me if you don't believe me."

"You son of a bitch!" Katria roared, starting around the desk toward him, but then Lucien's hand gripped her arm, and he pulled her toward the door. She put up a fight, screaming that she was going to kill Aims, but Lucien wrapped his arms around her waist and hauled her out the door. Lil Gabe was waiting for them in the sitting room, and he gaped at the sight of Lucien carrying the furious woman out. Aims was shouting something about having her thrown in jail somewhere, but Lucien got Katria outside. Lil Gabe followed, and he slammed the door closed behind them to mute Aims' yelling.

Lucien let go of her, at last, and she whirled to face him. Before she could say anything, however, he raised a finger to his lips in a shushing gesture and nodded toward a group of men who were walking past the building on the dirt path that would take them to a set of buildings that may have been bunkhouses. Katria bit back her words until the men had passed, and once they were gone, she told Lucien, "I don't care if I have to strangle that crooked bastard with my bare hands. We're *not* leaving without Dallion and Journey."

"Where are they?" he asked her.

She pointed west. "They're on the far side of the field next to the stone well. I told them I'd be right back, Lucien. They think I'm going to come get them so we can all get out of here. We can't just leave them here…"

He shushed her again as another group of men walked past them. Somewhere near the bunkhouses, a bell began to ring as the prisoners were called in for dinner. Lucien pointed toward the docks and ordered, "Go back to the ship."

She gaped. "You expect me to leave them here? We've finally found them! They're right here!"

To Gabe, Lucien said, "Get her back to the *Lady*. Don't let her set foot on land again until I say so. I don't care if you have to tie her up."

Katria started to protest, but Lucien set a calming hand on her shoulder and bent lower to say into her ear, "I'll take care of this, Kat. You have to trust me."

A dozen arguments threatened to spill from her lips, but she somehow managed to bite them back. Instead, she looked him in the eyes and vowed, "I'll die before I leave either of them here to rot."

"It won't come to that," he assured her, and nodded toward Lil Gabe to get him going. Gabe placed a hand on Katria's arm, but she shook it off and began the long march back toward the docks on her own. Her hands were clenched in fists and her eyes were stinging with tears of frustration, but she kept her head high.

Chapter Thirty-Three

THE dinner bell had rung, but Journey and Dallion didn't dare to move, worried that Katria wouldn't be able to find them again if they left the place at the edge of the field. They continued tying ribbons on the stalks, working as slowly as they could so that the job wouldn't end and take away their excuse for still being out here. They were both grinning like fools. Any moment, now, Katria would reappear around the corner of the path, and they would be able to leave this terrible place once and for all. She would explain everything on their way to the waiting ship, and years from now, they would all laugh about everything that had happened to them.

But it wasn't Katria who appeared around the corner. They were surprised to see Lucien, instead, and they were both so excited about leaving that they abandoned their basket of ribbons and hurried to greet him. It was only once they'd reached him that they saw the apologetic look on his face. Even so, Dallion threw his arms around him in a rough hug, laughing, and announced, "It's about time!"

Lucien hugged him back for a moment, but then let him go and ushered him and Journey into the safety of the tall sugarcane. Once they were hidden from view from anyone else once more, Journey dared to ask him, "What's wrong?"

Lucien set a hand on his shoulder and gave it a squeeze in greeting. Instead of giving him an answer, he said, "I didn't let myself hope I'd see you two fools alive again. I couldn't bring myself to tell Katria and Saige, but I thought you were dead."

"Close, but not quite," Dallion said. "Where is she? Where's Kat?"

Lucien gave Journey's shoulder another squeeze, and they both felt their hearts sink. He confessed, "I sent her back to the ship. There's been a hitch in the plan."

"Aims won't let us go," Journey said, and it wasn't a question; it was the only thing that made sense.

Lucien nodded. "It's fine. We just have to figure something else out, instead."

Dallion cussed, scuffing his boot against the bottom of the nearest sugarcane stalk. Journey shared his frustration. After so long, they finally had a reason for hope…only for it to be dangled just out of reach. He saw that Lucien was watching Dallion closely, as if waiting for him to suggest a solution to the impossible task at hand. And why not? Hadn't he been the one to do exactly that throughout all their years together?

Dallion took a deep breath and held it as he looked up at the blue sky above them. Finally, he let his breath out, and he said with a casualness Journey couldn't believe, "We'll swim for it."

In another time and place, Journey would have assumed he was joking, but this wasn't it. He asked, "Have you forgotten what happened last time we tried to get through the barrier?"

"We'll use the harbor," he replied, as if the idea wasn't completely insane. "We'll wait until tonight, when it's dark. Lucien, you have the ship ready and waiting for us due south of the harbor. Get as close as you can without letting the towers spot you. Got it?"

Journey asked with real wonder, "How are we going to get down to the harbor in the middle of the night without getting caught?"

Dallion flashed him a grin that was as arrogant as it was clever. "I've got an idea for that, too. You just worry about being ready for a long swim. Everything's going to be fine."

As impossible as it should have been, Journey found himself believing him. It may have been out of desperation, but that hardly mattered. Lucien was waiting patiently for him to agree to the plan, so Journey gave him a nod. They had no other options. Either this was going to work, or they would die in the attempt. No matter what, this was the last evening they'd be spending on this forsaken island.

*　　　*　　　*

THEY parted ways with Lucien and got to the bunkhouses just in time to still get some dinner. Dallion ate every bit of his serving, but Journey found that he was too anxious about the escape to have much of an appetite. He let Dallion finish off his share. They both went to bed immediately after, and Journey stared up at the tally marks in the wood above him. More than a hundred marks ago, he'd started to believe that he'd never see Saige or Mirelle again. He'd thought he'd never meet his youngest child. Far away from here, the baby girl was waiting for him. Her name was Francine, according to Katria. If he had to swim thirty miles through the dark, he would do it. A hundred, even. Anything to finally hold her.

He listened to the usual commotion as the other prisoners embarked on their nightly game of dice. Someone must have won big, because a tremendous cheer erupted in the bunkhouse, but Journey ignored all of this and kept his gaze on those tallies. Finally, the guards announced that it was time for bed, and he listened as the other prisoners all settled into their bunks for the night. Darkness engulfed the place, and he lost sight of the tally marks, but he still continued to stare up at the place he knew they were. A chorus of snores soon filled the air, but Journey remained patient. Around what must have been midnight, Dallion whispered his name from the darkness on the top bunk. Journey didn't answer. It wasn't time. There were always a few foremen who stayed up later than everyone else, usually to drink rum or ale and play a card game near the bathhouse. He didn't hear them out there tonight, but he wasn't willing to take the chance of running into anyone. Not when they were this close to salvation.

Finally, around one o'clock, Dallion whispered his name again, and Journey got moving. He'd kept his boots on when he'd gone to bed, and now he sat up to place them quietly on the floor. The dimness of the moonlight stealing through the cracks in the walls meant that he could only see a short distance down the rows of bunks, but from what he could tell, everyone was sleeping peacefully. He stood and waited for Dallion to climb down from the top bunk. His feet were so light on the floorboards that he may have been a cat creeping across them. They used Dallion's stolen key to let themselves out the door, and cooler air embraced them as they stepped out into the night.

Dallion took the lead, and Journey followed. They made the shadows their home, slipping through them as silently as they could and hardly daring to breathe as they went. The moon above them was a sliver in the sky. In its meager light, they found that there were no foremen out and about, and the night watch that occasionally patrolled this area of the island was nowhere to be seen. They took the darkest paths to the western side of the island. Dallion paused at a wooden shed that was nestled between a warehouse and a field of ready-to-cut cane. He edged the shed's door open, then motioned to two small drums of liquid sitting in the corner. It was what they sometimes used to burn the leaves off of the cane stalks before harvesting. Journey hefted one of the drums onto his shoulder without question, and had no choice but to breathe in the pungent scent of the stuff inside. Dallion picked up a second drum, then headed back outside. They paused once more at the entrance to the warehouse, where Dallion took the small, brass lantern down from its hook near the door. Its warm glow was going to make them easier to spot, but Dallion started off with it in his hand, all the same. Journey followed him to the field they'd been measuring the cane in earlier that day. He had a good idea of what they were about to do, now, and he felt a great deal of satisfaction at the thought of destroying some of the crops they'd suffered so much for.

They made quick work of emptying the drums. Every rustling sound the breeze made in the sugarcane made Journey's heart skip a beat. He was so convinced that a guard's shout would sound at any moment that he thought he heard it happen twice, and he nearly dropped the metal drum both times. If they were caught out here, he wouldn't be surprised if it meant their deaths. He'd seen prisoners get shot by the guards for attempting a lot less than what he and Dallion were currently up to.

Once the drums were empty, they set them aside, and Dallion retrieved the lantern from where he'd left it on the ground nearby. Its little flame flickered hungrily as he held it out at his side. He paused before tossing it, however, to look at Journey. In the moon's low light and the gentle glow of the flame, Journey saw the grin on his face.

"Ready?"

"Do it," Journey urged him, his heart racing. After six long months, he didn't want to waste another minute.

Dallion lobbed the lantern into the nearest row of cane. For a terrifying second, Journey thought that the flame had gone out as it had traveled through the air, and a dozen thoughts about roaming the island to find another burning lantern raced through his head. Then he caught sight of a small, orange flicker between two sugarcane stalks, and his heart leapt. He held his breath as he waited, and after a few seconds, the flame doubled in height and width, then tripled. It began to spread so quickly that his eyes couldn't keep up with it. The flames raced across the accelerant-soaked bases of the sugarcane, and acrid smoke climbed into the air.

One glance at Dallion said that he was mesmerized by the sight. The growing flames painted him orange, and his eyes were shining with excitement in that light. Journey seized his arm and pulled him away from the fire, hissing, "We need to get moving!"

They took off at a run, cutting through another cane field on their way back toward the bunkhouses. The leaves on the plants slapped at their faces and necks, but Journey barely felt it. His heart was racing as his blood raced through his veins, and his boots pounded against the ground. He burst through the edge of the crops and into the clearing beside the bathhouse, Dallion on his heels. The dinner bell was a large, bronze thing that hung from a post beside the bathhouse, and Journey rang it with all his might. Its piercing *clang* split the silence of the night. As it rang, Dallion went to the bunkhouse and used his stolen key to unlock the door. He threw it open and shouted into the dark interior, "Fire in the western fields!"

Prisoners began to pour out of the bunkhouse, blinking away the last of their sleep and sharing looks of confusion. They all looked toward the western fields, where the island was illuminated in an orange glow. The first guards arrived at a run, and they hurried to organize the prisoners into fire brigades. Hundreds of feet thundered west as they all rushed to save the burning cane. In the commotion, Journey and Dallion slipped back into the shadows between the empty buildings. They watched from there as the others stampeded toward the fiery glow in the west. Despite the coolness of the night, they were both slick with sweat, and Journey had to wipe it from his eyes as he waited for the right moment to move again. His heart was still hammering in his chest, but when Dallion abandoned the safety of the shadows to start down the gravel road at a run, Journey followed without hesitation.

They could hear another bell as it began to clamor somewhere else on the island, and the smell of smoke reached their noses as they made their way down the road toward the docks. Three guards appeared on the road before them, coming at a run, and Journey grabbed Dallion's shoulder to shove him toward a tall stack of wooden barrels beside the road. They hurled themselves behind the barrels and laid on the ground, where they strained to hear the sound of the guards' approaching boots. The sound came and went as the guards ran past the barrels. As soon as they were gone, Dallion was on his feet again, and Journey sprang up after him. A cool breeze coming off of the water greeted them as they reached the docks, at last, and on it, Journey could taste freedom.

If there were men sleeping aboard any of the ships currently tied to the docks, none of them had woken yet. The peace here was in stark contrast to the chaos happening on the rest of the island, and Dallion and Journey allowed themselves to slow down to grant their hearts and lungs some reprieve. They headed for the dock that was closest to the harbor's entrance, and Journey had never been so glad to hear the sound of the nearby sea. The water was black in the night, and in just a few short seconds, he would be beneath its surface, swimming with everything he had toward the promise of the open ocean. Lucien and the others were somewhere out there, and the last thing he wanted to do was keep them waiting.

Just before they could reach the last dock, a voice called out for them to stop, and Journey fought a desperate urge to just keep going. Whoever it was, he'd outrun him…but it would ruin their chances of swimming out of the harbor unnoticed, and that would be the end of this entire escapade. He forced himself to come to a stop and was glad when Dallion did the same beside him. They turned slowly to find another dock guard, a lit lamp held out before him to dispel the night's darkness.

"What the hell's going on?" the guard growled, coming to join them at the edge of the water. "What's all the commotion?"

Journey had thought the sounds of shouts and ringing bells had faded behind them, but now that his heartbeat and ragged breaths had quieted a little, he realized that those noises were drifting over the fields and all the way down here. The guard was waiting for an answer, so Journey panted, "We came to get help. There's a fire in one of the western fields. The cane's burning. We need everyone to come help save as much as we can."

The guard's eyes widened with alarm, and he whirled to start down the row of docks. "I'll wake everyone on the ships! We have to hurry…"

That was as far as he got before Dallion was on him. He laced his hands together in one large fist and brought it down against the place where the man's neck met his shoulder. The guard grunted, going to his knees, and the lantern tumbled out of his hand to shatter on the dock. They were doused in darkness as the flame went out, but there was just enough moonlight for Journey to see both men by. The guard took in a breath, meaning to scream for help, and Dallion wrapped his arm around the man's neck from behind before he could get so much as a squeak out. The guard panicked and flailed. Dallion struggled to keep his arm around his throat tightly enough to keep him quiet. As the guard tried to stand, Dallion used a little too much force to keep him down, and they ended up in a heap on the dock. The guard bucked wildly, and Dallion's hold on him began to slip.

Journey stepped forward and brought the toe of one of his work boots against the side of the guard's head with as much force as he could muster. The man's struggles ceased as he went limp, either unconscious or dead. Dallion let him go to roll onto his back on the rough wood of the dock, panting hard. Journey offered him his hand, and Dallion let him help him up. Wordlessly, they each grabbed one of the guard's wrists and began dragging him toward the edge of the dock.

They lowered him as far as they could before letting him go, trying to minimize the size of the splash he'd make. Even if he was only unconscious, he would be dead soon, and Journey was alright with that. He'd killed plenty of men in the two years he'd served as a pirate aboard the *Jubilee*, after all, and he had no remorse for this one. Anyone willing to help keep this hellhole of an island running deserved a worse death than what this man had been dealt.

That done, he followed Dallion to the end of the farthest dock, where they stripped out of their boots and shirts. There were still lights burning in the two towers that guarded the entrance to the harbor, but the water between them was black in the night. With any luck, the attention of anyone still left in the towers would be on the orange glow of growing flames to the west. They tossed their clothes into the water, then took a round of fast, deep breaths to ready themselves for the dive. Between gasps, Dallion told him that they would take their time with the swim. They had a long distance to cover, after all, and the irony there would be in their drowning after all of this was too much to think about.

The black water swallowed Journey up as he dove into it, and he swam as far as he could beneath the surface before he had to come up for air. Dallion was right beside him, and they began paddling. The lights in the tower windows were like menacing eyes, winking in the nighttime, but they had no choice but to swim past them. They kept their pace slow to stay quiet as the towers loomed up above them. They could hear excited voices coming from one of them – the guards there were likely watching the fire's glow in the distance – and Journey silently willed them not to look down here. He'd seen from the dock just how dark this area of the water was, but now he felt terribly exposed, as if under a spotlight, instead of in the shadows. There was the sound of a door opening and closing above them, followed by more voices, but no one called out that they'd spotted two escapees, and no lights were aimed in their direction. Journey kept his gaze on the open sea before them, and after what felt like a very long time, the noises from the towers were fading behind them. Dallion matched his pace when he started swimming a little faster, and the wide-open ocean welcomed them on the other side.

Chapter Thirty-Four

THEY settled into a maintainable pace, but after a few hundred yards, they needed to stop to rest. Journey's muscles thrummed as he treaded water and caught his breath. He dared to look back toward the island, where the lights from the watchtowers were still twinkling, as if trying to entice him back to the safety of dry land. He recalled his near-death experience in the water only two weeks ago, as well as the time he'd nearly drowned between Stonewell and Sandhill several years before that. This was different. Lucien, Katria, and the others were waiting for them somewhere out there in the darkness, and the most dangerous part of the night was over. The ocean didn't feel like a threat, but more like a companion, and one that was going to help him get to safety. He turned onto his back and looked up at the starry sky as he floated on the calm water. Their light was much more welcoming than the lanterns in the watchtowers.

Dallion was floating on his back to Journey's left, and his voice was hardly louder than a whisper as he said, "We're going to make it."

"We are," Journey agreed, and couldn't help but grin.

"When I get on the ship, I'm going to find the closest bottle of rum and get drunk. And I'm going to dedicate my first cup to Jimmy Two-Tales."

It stung to think that Jimmy could have been out here with them, if he hadn't given up. Journey pushed that thought from his head, however. It wasn't the time for regrets, yet. He turned himself over in the water and turned his back to the island once more. As he began to swim again, he said to Dallion, "Let's go find you that bottle."

The *Lady Swift* was a dark silhouette on the black sea. Her lights were out in an attempt to keep from being noticed by the guard towers less than a mile away. Lucien, Pigeon, Katria, and Brain stood on the starboard side of the deck as they peered into the darkness that cloaked much of Dove's Roost. Lil Gabe and Wee Bit were keeping an eye out on the other side of the ship for any sign of approaching vessels, just in case one was due at the island tonight. So far, everything had been quiet. The warm glow of a fire had been visible until recently, and they could still smell the occasional wisp of smoke as it came skirting over the open water, but the people on the island must have been able to extinguish it. Katria could only hope that wasn't bad news for Dallion and Journey.

Brain startled them all when he spoke from where he was standing between Katria and Pigeon. "What if they're lost?"

Katria placed a comforting hand on Brain's shoulder, but didn't answer. There wasn't much of a chance that they had gotten lost, since Lucien had positioned the ship due south of the harbor's entrance, as Dallion had instructed. Both men were strong swimmers, so she wasn't all that concerned about them drowning, either. Her real fear was that they hadn't been able to get off the island in the first place. They could have been caught lighting the fire. Maybe they had been spotted on their way to the docks. Or even worse, they could have been seen by the men in the watchtowers and stopped at the mouth of the harbor, so close to the freedom that they would never find. And even if they did get through all of that unnoticed, this was the season for sharks in this area. They'd spotted two different sets of fins on their way out of the harbor earlier, and now Katria couldn't get the thought of them out of her head.

What felt like an hour passed, although it had likely only been a few minutes, before Pigeon pointed a finger to an area of the water that was as pitch black as any around it. Everyone else strained to see what he'd noticed, and he kept his finger pointed at it. After a few seconds, Katria urged him, "What is it?"

Before he could answer, she saw it, too: two figures were materializing out of the blackness. They were bobbing on the gentle waves. She held her breath, and after a few more seconds, it became clear that they were the heads and shoulders of two swimmers who were trying to be as quiet as they could. Katria clapped a hand over her mouth to stifle the cry of relief that threatened to escape from her lips. Lucien grinned as he leaned against the banister to drop one end of a rope over the side. As soon as they were close enough to hear him without having to raise his voice to yell, he called down to them, "I've never seen such ugly fish."

"Come on in, Lucien," Dallion panted, still just a silhouette in the water. "The water's fine."

"I'll pass," he replied, and as soon as he felt one of them on the end of the rope, he and Pigeon hauled up their catch. Wee Bit and Lil Gabe hurried over, as well, and when Dallion's hand gripped the ship's banister, they seized his arms and pulled him up and over. He collapsed onto his back on the deck, exhausted and half naked, but there was a smile on his face that not even the darkness of the night could conceal. Katria went to her knees beside him, and he laughed as she began planting dozens of kisses across his face.

Journey was helped over the side next, and Lucien had his arms around his shoulder in a joyful hug as soon as his feet were on the deck. When he let him go, Journey sat down with his back against the banister as he tried to catch his breath. Wee Bit, Pigeon, and Lil Gabe all gathered in close to greet both men with claps on their shoulders and welcoming words. Lucien waved them off and got them moving to get the *Lady* underway, and while they scurried to do that, Dallion sat up on the deck and demanded, "Where the hell is the *Jubilee*?"

Katria, still kneeling beside him, wouldn't meet his gaze at that, and that was enough to confirm his suspicions about what had happened. Lucien sighed, resting his lower back against the banister behind him, but before he could explain, Brain blurted, "Horus is the captain, now. He has the *Jubilee*."

Dallion gaped at Lucien, but the look on Lucien's face told him that he shouldn't have been so surprised. He explained, "There was a vote, and most of the crew decided not to search for you. The last we heard, Horus has been voted captain and he's out near Port Kelsey, hiding from the *Huntress*."

"Katria says they're all cowards," Brain told them matter-of-factly. "But we weren't afraid to come find you."

"Who's we?" Dallion asked, but he was relatively sure that he already knew the answer to that.

"Everybody you see here," Lucien confirmed, and swept one arm over the *Lady's* deck. "This ship belongs to Saige. We're all technically on the up-and-up and on her payroll."

Dallion's shoulders slumped, and Katria comforted, "We'll start over. It won't be like we'd hoped, since we never found the treasure, but we'll still be alright."

He was on his feet in an instant, his exhaustion forgotten, and he called, "Pigeon! Set course for Tall Island!"

"No," Journey and Lucien objected in unison. Lucien said, "The search is over. After all of this, nobody here is willing to waste any more time on that wild goose chase."

Dallion looked to Journey, grinning like a madman, and Journey told the others, "We found the *Cherub*. Right before Fleury showed up on the island, Dallion and I found her."

Katria, Lucien, and Brain gaped at him, but Journey's focus was on Dallion. He told him, "I'm not going to Tall Island, Dal. I'm going home. My wife hasn't known if I've been alive or dead for the past six months. Mirelle must be a mess about it, and I haven't even met my youngest daughter."

"But just imagine taking a share of that treasure home to them with you…"

He didn't bother hearing him out, but called to Pigeon, "We're going to Stonewell!"

"Don't do that, Pigeon!" Dallion objected.

Lucien held up one hand to settle it all and said, "In case you weren't listening, this is Saige's ship, and I'm the captain. Pigeon doesn't take orders from you, anymore, Dallion. My job is to take you back to Stonewell. We're not going to Tall Island…yet."

Dallion struggled to decide how to handle this sudden shift in power, but when he looked at Journey again, he saw only a desperate hope in his friend's eyes that he wouldn't argue this further. Dallion's pride left a bitter taste in his mouth as he swallowed it, and he told Journey, "Alright. Let's go meet your little girl."

Chapter Thirty-Five

LOW candlelight brought some warmth to the dining room, but it wasn't enough to dispel the gloom. The only sounds were the tinking of silverware against fine dishes as Saige, Francis, and Abigay ate their chicken and vegetables in silence. Mirelle was perched atop her wooden booster seat on the chair beside her grandfather's, but she hadn't eaten more than a few bites. Instead, she pushed a piece of baked carrot around the edge of her plate, her hazel eyes never looking up from the table. Saige had given up on urging the girl to eat. She could only hope that the broken heart that was keeping the child's appetite at bay would stop doing so soon.

Francis set his own fork aside and said with false cheeriness, "You'll never believe what I saw today. I was out in the garden, and I heard chirps coming from a bush. Would you believe that there's a nest of doves out there with two chicks inside? I saw the mother, and she's as white as a bride's gown. White doves are good luck, you know."

Saige didn't have it in her to tell him that they were beyond any help that luck could bring them. They were in grave need of some sort of miracle. Instead, she managed a pained smile and a passive, "That's nice."

"Mirelle," Abigay spoke up from across the table from her, "you'll starve to skin and bones if you don't eat something."

"I'm not hungry," she pouted, laying her fork down beside her plate. To her mother, she said, "I'm tired, mummy. I go bed?"

Saige nodded, and the girl climbed down from her seat. Abigay followed her to the door, promising to tell her a bedtime story to help her sleep. Mirelle's head hung low, however. Her brown curls bobbed as she walked. Saige worried about her. She'd had a physician come to the island to take a look at her, and he'd assured her that Mirelle was a healthy, young girl. She was mourning the absence of her father, but she was otherwise alright. He'd also told her that if Journey didn't return, Mirelle would likely begin to forget about him before long, and her sadness would be replaced by the happiness that should have been at home in a two-and-a-half-year-old. Saige wanted that happiness for her, but thinking that Mirelle might soon forget Journey was nearly painful enough to kill her.

Even worse was the guilt she felt for whatever had happened to him. Every night, she replayed their last conversation over in her head. She'd convinced him to go with Dallion on that damned adventure of his, and it had very likely cost Journey his life.

Saige realized that Francis had spoken her name from across the table, and she turned her attention back to him. He asked gently, "Are you alright?"

"I'm fine," she lied, but not very well. She'd only cleared about half of the food on her plate, but she had no desire to eat more of it. All she wanted right now was to crawl beneath the blankets on her bed and cry.

Before she could go do that, the sound of her youngest daughter's wails reached her ears. Hannah, the girl's caretaker, stepped into the dining room, cradling the crying baby in her arms. Hannah appeared frazzled, and as she curtsied to Saige, she explained, "I can't get her to stop crying, ma'am. She's dry and fed, but she won't calm down."

Saige left her chair and went to collect the baby. As soon as she was in her mother's arms, she began to quiet, and Hannah let out an audible breath of relief. Saige rocked her gently, and Francine peered up at her through teary eyes. Saige smiled at her, although what she really wanted to do was join the baby in her wailing. She told Hannah, "I'll take her to bed with me. Maybe we'll both be able to get some rest."

Hannah scurried off, not about to let this promise of freedom slip away. Francis wished her goodnight as Saige carried the baby out into the hall and toward the stairs. The paintings on the walls that depicted beautiful sunsets and calm seas did nothing to lighten her mood as she passed by them. Francine had fallen silent, and her eyes were drifting closed as she lost the battle against sleep. Saige envied her. It had been a long time since she'd slept so soundly.

Hannah's voice cried out in surprise from the other end of the hall behind her. Saige was going to ignore it, but then she heard hasty footsteps coming back into the hall from the foyer, and the young woman called, "Ma'am! Come quick!"

Saige couldn't tell if it was excitement or fear in Hannah's voice, and she dreaded finding out which. She'd been so close to laying her head on her pillow and letting her tears come. Now what? She turned and commanded her feet to start in the other direction down the hall. Hannah was standing at the end of it, and maybe that was excitement on her pretty, tan face, after all. There was a smile on her lips, at least, and Saige allowed herself to hope for some sort of good news. It was desperately needed around here.

Hannah stepped aside for her as she reached the foyer, and she saw that the mansion's front door was ajar. She couldn't see much through the small gap, but she could make out the voice of Samuel Brown, the butler. He sounded excited, as well, and with the way that Hannah was beaming…

The door opened the rest of the way, and Journey stepped inside. He looked ragged – his hair was far too long, there was a scruffy beard on his cheeks, and he was dressed in rough, dingy clothes. He'd lost nearly enough weight to be considered gaunt. The expression on his face was somehow both apologetic and joyful, however. Saige had come to a stop near the center of the room, the sleeping baby still held in her arms. She couldn't bring herself to believe that he was here, and long seconds dragged on as they stood in silence. When Saige finally spoke, there was composure in her voice that she hadn't expected.

"You're late," she said.

Journey closed the gap between them in a few long strides, and he took her into his arms, the baby between them. Saige didn't realize that she was crying until she felt her body jerk in his arms in silent sobs. Journey held her close, and by the waver in his voice when he spoke, he was crying, too.

"I'm so sorry, Saige," he told her, his face hidden in the untamed curls of her hair. "I'm so sorry."

"You're home," she breathed against his chest, finally grasping the truth. "You're alive and your home."

"I love you," he said, and tasted her salty tears as he kissed her painted lips. She kissed him back, shifting the baby to one arm so she could wrap the other around the back of his neck. He tasted of the sea, and it was hard to kiss him past the genuine smile that had finally found its way to her lips. His unkempt beard scratched at her chin. He nestled one hand in her hair as the other kept her close, and Saige wanted to scream in relief, slap him for making her fear the worst, beg him never to leave her again…instead, she stayed there in his arms, wondering if her heart would burst from the joy and relief that she now felt.

Francine squirmed between them, waking, and Journey pulled back enough to get his first good look at her. She peered up at him with his own hazel eyes. Saige whispered, "Francine, this is your father."

Francine merely offered a sleepy yawn and closed her eyes to go back to sleep. That was alright – Journey's heart was filled with enough love for both of them. Saige spotted Hannah standing in a corner that she'd retreated to in an attempt to stay out of their reunion, and she told her, "Go fetch Mirelle and Abigay, please."

Hannah hurried off to do so, and once they were alone, Saige asked her husband, "Dallion?"

"He's fine," he assured her. "Everything's fine, Saige. And everything's going to stay that way now."

She believed him. As their lips met once more, she wondered if she'd ever be able to bring herself to let this man out of her sight again. She doubted it.

*   *   *

A half a mile off the coast of Stonewell, the *Lady Swift* had wind in her sails once more. Dallion stood at the aft banister and watched as the island grew farther and farther away. Katria was at his side, and his arm was around her waist. The sun had set, and the last of its dying light was bleeding out of the world. They watched that little speck of land until they couldn't see it, anymore.

Lucien joined them, standing on the other side of Dallion, and warned, "This is the last time I'll remind you, but we don't have Saige's permission to take this ship anywhere now."

"I don't think she's going to care about it too much," Dallion grinned. "Besides, what else would she expect from us?"

"Alright, then where are we going?"

Dallion looked at Katria, and in her eyes, he found the same eagerness that was in his own. With a sly smile, he said, "Let's go get our treasure."

Acknowledgements

I'd like to thank everyone who has come along on this adventure over the seas so far. The best thing in the world is hearing that you're having fun with it. I'm also grateful to Line by Lion Publications for their continued faith in me. Last but not least, I would also like to thank a future author named Blake for reminding me how big dreams can be. Don't give them up.